Filthy PROFESSOR

NIQUEL

Editor: Mackenzie, Nice Girl, Naughty Edits,
https://www.nicegirlnaughtyedits.com

Interior Designer: niquelDesigns

Proofreader: Virginia Tesi Carey

Contents

This book is dedicated to the dreamers!
No matter how long it takes you to tell your story,
write it/create it because that magic within you deserves
to be shared with the world.

Synopsis

I HAD TWO RULES in life:

Never fall in love.

Never have sex with a student.

As a college preceptor, you're not supposed to fraternize with your pupils, but what happens when you get a taste of the forbidden before you know it isn't supposed to be yours?

That night at Brian's bachelor party was epic. We danced, I dominated, and she left. One night, no further contact, no regrets, just how I liked it—until she walked into my algebra class the next week, and I knew the two rules I had in place had to change.

Never fall in love.

Never *get caught* having sex with a student.

Chapter One

Caspian

"DUDE, I CAN'T BELIEVE you're getting married in a few days!" Carlos exclaimed as he slammed his mug of beer down on the bar, the foam spilling over the top and onto the wood. "Shit, I didn't mean to do that."

"I know, and I'm nervous as fuck," Brian replied. He wiped a bead of sweat from his brow and took a sip of his Corona.

"I don't know how you do it," I hissed.

"Do what?" Brian questioned.

"The whole 'till death do us part' thing. Don't get me wrong, Lex is a great chick, but I couldn't do it."

"I'd do anything for her. You're just jealous because you haven't found the one worth risking it all for yet."

"Jealous...right," I said, as I tipped the entire cup of whiskey up to my lips, the amber-colored liquid burning as it slid down my throat. I signaled the bartender for another.

"Don't worry, guys. He'll find one to trap him soon enough. He'll fall so hard his balls will be permanently attached to the ground." Carlos laughed.

"Enough about 'the one' bullshit. There are some smoking hot chicks in the cabana over there. We're in fucking Vegas; it's time to live a little!" I shouted.

Looking over at the group of girls, one in particular caught my eye. She was tall, curvy, with smooth cocoa brown skin and sexy legs that went on for days. Her lips, thick and full, would look great wrapped around my cock. I shot her a grin, and she waved me over.

"I don't know about you, dickholes, but I'm going to get laid tonight."

As I slung back my second shot of whiskey, I gave the guys a look, and we all went over to talk to the girls.

Her perfect body swayed from left to right as the bass thumped through the club. The sound echoed off the walls as I got lost in the music, letting myself move right along with her. She bent over in front of me, her firm, plump ass winding against my jeans as my cock twitched behind the zipper. *Fuck.*

I grasped hold of her hips, trying to get as close as I could, before running my fingers up the exposed part of her thigh. A shiver went down her body as she turned around. Looking up at me, her eyes, lust-filled slits with a flicker of hazel behind them, bore into me. "What's your name?" I asked.

"Taylin, you?" she shouted over the music.

"Cas. Why don't we take this back up to my room, or yours, if you prefer?" She sucked in her bottom lip, her teeth clenching down as she drew in a breath and smiled. *An effortless win, as usual.*

"Yours is fine."

Grabbing her hand, I yanked her toward me. The smell of vanilla faintly coated her skin. We rushed through the crowd, my adrenaline flowing as we reached the elevator. Once inside, she was all mine.

I pushed her up against the wall, her leg wrapping around my waist as my hands roamed up the soft blue material of the short dress she was wearing. I tilted her chin, licking and biting the delicate part of her neck as she let out a breathy moan. Her nipples pressed against her dress, and I wasted no time paying them attention, sliding the low-cut opening over and pulling out her breast, then circling it with my tongue before I heard the elevator door ding. Not giving a damn that someone had joined us, I continued flicking my tongue around her stiff nub.

Glancing back, I saw we were fast approaching the tenth floor, so I stopped, also noticing that our guest of the moment was burying his face in his cell phone as he rushed off on the floor below us. As soon as the doors reopened, I grabbed her hand, eliciting a giggle from her in my haste as I led her down the hall to my room, quickly pulling my room key out of my back pocket.

The shades to my windows were pulled back, and the moonlight cast a blue shadow around the room. I shoved Taylin onto the bed, and her gaze locked on mine as I unhooked the thin string behind her neck, which was all that held her dress together. Eagerly pushing my hands off her, she dropped down to her knees in front of me, releasing my length from my pants and running her tongue over the tip and up the shaft.

She slowly took me into her mouth, inch by inch, until I felt her saliva drip down to my balls, making me groan. I grabbed the back of her head and thrust into her mouth, and she accepted all of me without gagging once. *Fuck, this is my kind of girl.*

Whatever she was doing with her tongue felt too good, and I didn't want to finish like this. I lifted her to eye level before me, and her dress fell right to the floor. Wrapping my hand at the base of her skull, I pulled her head back as my tongue traced the contour of her neck. I kicked her legs apart and ran my hand over her mound, the sticky wetness coating my fingers as I slid them underneath the lace material. Kneeling in front of her, I followed an invisible line with my tongue over the tops of her thighs as I ripped her panties down her smooth skin. She fell to the bed with a whimper, and I continued my teasing until I landed between her folds.

She tasted sweet and mildly salty; I couldn't get enough of her essence in my mouth. With my tongue, I spread her lips apart, continuing to circle her clit, before entering two fingers into her channel. She panted, and her body trembled under my touch. "Come for me, baby. Don't be shy," I whispered in between her slit, flattening, and twirling my tongue to make her come undone.

I grabbed a condom out of my pants pocket and slid it on, all while her orgasm tore through her body. Pulses of pleasure beat on my tongue as I kissed her lips goodbye before wasting no time to pierce her with my cock. She was warm, tight, and soaking wet for me. I had to restrain myself as she slowly adjusted to my girth with a choked moan. "Nothing about this will be gentle," I growled.

"I didn't expect it to be," she moaned, as our hips connected.

My thrusts picked up in intensity as I pulled her legs around either side of my shoulders. *Fuck.*

Our bodies fused in a rhythmic motion, an unspoken bond forming between us as her pussy clenched my cock. She was made to be underneath me, taking it all like a pro, but I knew I couldn't fuck with her again after this. No woman, no matter how good her pussy was, would be exempt from my rules.

One and done. No further contact. No *can I stay the night.*

Get out.

"Wow," she breathed out, exasperated.

"What?" I turned my head slightly to look at her, where she was still lying next to me. Hopefully not for much longer.

"That was amazing. I've never had someone make my body feel like that before." Well, that's a shame.

"It's called an orgasm, sweetheart. If you've never had one, that means you've never been with a real man."

"I hadn't...until now." She gulped, a flash of embarrassment showing on her face.

"Please don't tell me you're a virgin." That was the last fucking thing I needed.

"Hell no. I've had sex, just not with a *real* man."

"Well, now you can cross that off your bucket list."

"I guess I can." She smiled. She had an alluring quality about her, and I knew it would get me into trouble if I allowed her to stay around any longer.

"So, are you gonna go and meet back up with your friends?"

"Eventually, but there's no rush to get back to them," she replied, her eyes filled with hope. And we can't have that happening.

"I see. Well, I have shit to do, and people to see so—" I paused, looking down at the watch on my wrist.

"I get it." She paused for a moment, her lips rolling inward as she sat up. "I should have known better. I'll go. You're one of those one and done guys."

"You already know me so well." I couldn't help but smirk.

It didn't take but a second after seeing my expression for her to jump off the bed. "I know that you're an asshole."

"You're right. Remember what happens in Vegas, stays in Vegas!" Getting more comfortable, I watched her search the floor for her shoes in the darkness of the room.

"Maybe, but I'll never forget someone like you," she responded, looking back at me with an emotion I couldn't place but that I felt in my chest.

"I get that a lot," I stated despondently, with a shrug of my shoulders, trying not to let the look on her face get under my skin.

She slid her dress back over her shoulders, grabbed her purse, then stormed out of my room without even putting her shoes back on.

My heart skipped in my chest as the sound of the door slammed behind her. *Fuck, you may regret this one, Cas.*

Chapter Two

Taylin

"AND WHERE DID YOU run off to, Ms. Taylin?" Anna asked as I rejoined our group at the club, her hands placed on her hips as she gave me *the eyes*.

"It doesn't matter, Anna." I saddled up next to her at the bar, looking around to see if Cas happened to make a reappearance. "Where are the girls?"

"Jalia and Liz are on the dance floor somewhere. But enough about them. What happened?"

"I finally meet a guy who knows what he's doing in bed, and he's a complete asshole." I threw my hands in the air—defeated.

"That's usually what happens. Especially, if he's good-looking."

"He's more than just good-looking. He's gorgeous. I didn't even get his number," I said, feeling like an idiot.

"Girl, we're in the city of sin. He's probably out here cheating on his wife or something. So, of course, he's not going to give you his number. Did you at least get his name?"

"Yeah, it was Cas," I replied, as the pretty blonde bartender placed four shots down in front of us.

"He sounds like an asshole. But anyway, you should take this shot of Fireball, and you'll forget all about Casper the friendly douchebag!" she yelled enthusiastically.

"I doubt it," I replied with a sigh, tossing the spicy liquid back. Anna was the closest to me, out of our tight-knit group of childhood friends. I knew I could trust her with things I could never tell the others, and she never judged me. We had all come out to celebrate our friend Elizabeth's last few nights of freedom. Quite frankly, I never saw this day coming, but she was very reserved and selective about who she dated, and her fiancé, Sydney, was a reformed party animal. They somehow made it work, and now she's found her happily ever after.

"You need to make the most of this night, girl. We have the rehearsal dinner tomorrow, then Saturday is the big day. So let loose; you never know. Maybe you'll find someone better!" I raised my shoulders in disagreement.

I doubt it.

"What did Mr. Asshole look like anyway?" she questioned.

A smile turned up at the corners of my lips. "Cas was pure perfection. He was tall, his body in immaculate condition. Chiseled abs, with light hair covering his chest. He had no tattoos from what I could see, but I didn't get a chance to examine everything being on my back with my legs beside my ears. His beard and mustache were neatly trimmed, and his eyes were like a greenish-hazel? Is that even a real color? And just about everything about his presence was everything I needed." *I wish I could be around him again.*

Her eyes widened at my description. "Wow, and he put it down like that?"

"Yep," I replied, popping the P in my state of letdown.

"You're fucked. I'm sorry, girl," she said, sliding over another shot.

Where the hell am I?

I awoke in a hotel room that I did not recognize. I looked around, and a man I didn't even recall meeting was next to me, snoring loud enough to wake the dead. He was cute, but nothing like Cas. *Shit, Taylin. You know Fireball is the devil's drink. You black out every time you have it.*

Peering under the covers, there was no bra or panties in sight. My body was naked and sore, but I didn't feel like it was from him. I slid from under the sheets quietly to search for my things. One of my shoes was underneath the bed, the other was on an armchair, but my dress was still missing in action.

As I went into the bathroom, there it was, lying on the floor beside the shower. I picked it up, and it was heavily soaked with water and dripping. *What the hell did I do last night?*

"Morning, beautiful. Where you off to so early?" the mystery man questioned from behind me, making me jump.

"I'm sorry, I don't remember anything from last night. Who are you?" I smiled tightly.

"Jackson. You were drunk. You jumped into the pool with your dress on."

"I did?" I questioned, my mouth agape.

"Yeah, it was pretty funny—until." He paused, staring at me.

"Until *what*?" My heart beat rapidly in my chest, trying to recall anything that happened.

"Until you stayed under the water a minute too long," he answered with a wince, and I could feel my eyes popping out of my head with mortification.

"Oh my God, and let me guess, you saved me?"

"No, actually, some other dude grabbed you out of the water, and when he made sure you were breathing, he left." My brow furrowed in confusion.

"Huh. That's weird. So...how did I end up here?"

"Well, you followed me up here. I'm guessing your room is nearby, but you didn't make it."

"Did we?" I asked, looking myself up and down.

"No, we didn't. I'm not the type of guy who takes advantage of drunk, almost dying girls. Now that you're awake, though, I wouldn't mind having an honest chance." *Not a chance in hell, buddy.*

"I'm sorry, but I have to go." I grabbed a robe I spotted hanging behind the door and slid it over my shoulders. Collecting the rest of my things, as my dress dripped water everywhere, I then hightailed it out of his room.

The room I shared with Anna was two doors down, and I felt like such an idiot. I figured my girls would have saved me from making a complete ass of myself. They all had some explaining to do.

Grabbing my keycard out of my purse, I let myself in. Anna was nowhere to be found. *Okay, what the fuck is going on?*

I sat down on the side of the bed and pulled out my phone. I had a shit ton of messages, Instagram tags, and voicemails. I listened to one and laughed. Anna was hammered when she left it. "Girl, I, no, where you go? Don't die, okay?"

As I sifted through the rest, Anna called me.

"Bitch, what happened?"

"Dude, I don't know. One minute, we were doing shots, then the next, you decided you would jump into the pool fully clothed. I don't remember much after that, but I know I couldn't find you again, and then I blacked out in some old dude's bathroom. I'm on my way to our room right now, so let me in."

There was a knock on the door just a second later, and I let her in. Her makeup was smeared down her cheeks, her dark hair a tangled mess twisting down her back. "Damn, girl."

"You don't look that great yourself, toots." She laughed.

I walked into the bathroom to see my reflection, and she was right. I certainly looked like a hot ass mess. My hair was no longer straight, my natural curls were tangled and unruly on my head, and my makeup was entirely gone, but I still didn't look half as bad as Anna did. Considering I'd almost died the night before.

"I need to hop in the shower."

"Hurry up, Taylin. I need to get in there too!"

Nodding, I shut the door and turned the faucet on, letting the room fill up with a light haze of steam. Then I twisted my hair up and clipped it off my neck, not needing the extra battle.

As the water cascaded down my back, I thought of Cas and how he made me feel the night before. My body ignited with renewed fire, and I slipped my hand in between my thighs, trying to recreate that feeling of euphoria. I made myself come harder than I ever had before, but it still didn't compare to the orgasm he'd given me. *You have to let him go, Taylin.* You'll never see him again, so this should be a walk in the park.

I hope.

Chapter Three

Caspian

A FEW DAYS HAD gone by, and Brian was no longer a free man. We were all on the plane heading back to Boston, and I had a horrible hangover. I couldn't get that girl, Taylin, off my mind. My dick was an uncooperative piece of shit and wouldn't stay up for the single drunk sluts at the wedding. It pissed me right the fuck off. I never had a problem getting it up, but erectile dysfunction decided to take over for some reason. My cock had finally betrayed me. *Son of a bitch.*

"So, Cas, what happened with that girl, Melissa?"

"Not a fucking thing," I grumbled.

"What? Caspian Wyatt The Great was unable to perform? I don't fucking believe it!" Carlos laughed, and I gave him the finger.

"Neither can I. Apparently, my dick and I weren't on the same page this weekend."

"Shit, you got attached. Who was it?"

"No one." It was a lie, and I knew he would call me out.

"Cas, this has only happened to you one other time, and that was with Melinda," he stated. Like I needed a reminder.

"I know, but this was just a one-night stand. Not four soul-crushing years of my life. Can we drop this?"

"Yeah. So you ready for school?" He quickly changed the subject.

"No, but guess I don't have much of a choice. The fall semester starts next week, and I don't even have my lesson plan mapped out. So, I'll be getting drunk and figuring that out this week."

As I pulled up to Warren University, I knew this year would be a challenge. This school was one of the lowest-ranked schools as it pertains to math. And I was not going to let that deter me from teaching to my potential.

I sat at my desk, trying to create an easy-to-follow syllabus. College-level algebra wasn't always everyone's top pick, but it was a requirement, and I loved to torture my students.

After several hours spent last week ruffling through paperwork and ideas, I finally had the perfect lesson plan mapped out for the entire fall semester. It would bring out the best of the best and make the others go home and cry to their mommies.

Every year, I had that one student who would try to cross boundaries with me, and that shit was not going down. I refused to fuck my students. I stayed away from bars around the area, and I didn't volunteer for shit because I didn't need them trying to yank my cock out in the bathroom at a fundraiser. I usually met women far away from Boston or online, but they didn't know shit about me even then. I trusted no one, and I was never breaking my number two rule. *Never fuck a student.*

Chapter Four

Taylin

THE PAST FEW DAYS had been Hell. No matter what I did, I couldn't stop thinking about him. That night in Vegas consumed me. I tried hooking up with a few other people to forget about him, but I couldn't go through with it. Cas had left an impression on me, and I hated it. The last time I'd gotten stuck on a guy like this, he turned out to be a major liar. I lost myself listening to him trying to make our relationship work when I knew it was over in my heart of hearts. I went against my intuition instead of focusing on what I wanted. You know, young love.

I'd wasted the entire summer trying to figure out what I was going to do with my life. I was twenty-one years old and had nothing to show for it. I tried the whole liberal arts community college thing a few years back, and it wasn't for me. I wasn't about that lifestyle. I felt pressured to go right out of high school by my parents, then fell apart once I got there. I couldn't handle the pressure of continuing school so soon. I wanted a break, and my mom realized it was too much, so she allowed me to drop out.

I still studied math and stayed current on the latest trends. I loved numbers and enjoyed solving complex mathematical equations, but I didn't know what to do with it.

"Tay, what are you going to do?" my brother, Constantine, questioned.

"About what?"

"Life. Are you going back to school? You're too smart to be sitting at home, crunching numbers and journaling in your notebooks. Get out there and do something!"

My older brother had his life together. He had a well-paying job as a paralegal, and although he had just bought his own house, he was always here and occasionally barked at me to get my shit together. Even when we were younger, he acted as more of a dad than a brother. He always told me that he was only being that way because he wanted what was best for me.

"Tine, I'm going to go back, okay? Stop hounding me about it."

"Good, but you do know that classes started yesterday, right?"

"Shit!"

Luckily, I had already pre-registered, but I totally spaced on the start date. *Why didn't I set an alert on my phone?* Oh yeah, because I was being forced to do this again. My stepdad and I made a bet, and I was going to crush it.

As I rushed to get dressed, I stopped to gaze at myself in the mirror, trying to amp myself up for the long day of classes. The first class of the day was MA001 college algebra, and if I hurried, I'd get there about ten minutes late.

I tossed on a tight floral dress, slipped into my flats, grabbed my backpack, then ran out to my car. My mom yelled something in passing, but I was too focused to stop and chat. *Let's do this.*

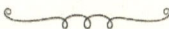

Warren University was such a huge college, I had to ask for directions to get to the admissions office. After I parked my car in the student parking, I went to the admissions office to grab my schedule and check-in. While I was there, I was given very confusing directions to my classroom. In passing, I saw a hot guy in the hall and asked him where the algebra class was, and he smiled, his eyes traveling the entire length of my body before he responded, "It's two doors that way."

Great, I'm going in the wrong direction.

After running around like a madwoman, I finally found Professor Wyatt's class. It was already in session and was surprisingly packed. *I wonder why. I didn't think this many college kids would be that interested in math like I was.*

I opened the door, and all eyes were on me. "Sorry, I'm late. New student," I stated with a shy smile, trying to eye the room for an empty seat.

I found a spot in the third row, and as I'd gotten settled, I noticed the teacher had stopped speaking. As I looked up to see where he was, I couldn't believe my eyes.

What are the odds?

"What is your name?" he asked. The serene tone of his voice almost made me forget where I was for a moment.

"Taylin Bradford."

"Nice to meet you, Ms. Bradford. Since you missed an entire lesson yesterday, I'll need you to stay after so I can get you up to speed."

A few girls giggled beside me, and I knew I was in big trouble.

"Yes, sir."

Shit.

Professor Wyatt made math make sense. Every equation he demonstrated how to solve was clear and concise. When he explained PEMDAS, it made the entire class laugh because instead of the standard Aunt Sally version most of us learned in grade school, he said, "Please excuse my ditzy ass sister."

He'd given us a worksheet of equations to solve with the newfound knowledge we received from him, but I had finished well before half the class. It seemed like most of the girls were in this class to give googly eyes to the professor, but I wanted to learn—well, try to, anyway.

After the bell rang, I tried to sneak out with the rest of my classmates, but he called me out before I could make it far. I stopped, and a short, blonde-haired girl smiled at me. "Try not to get into too much trouble." She punctuated her statement with a wink, and I knew instantly what she was insinuating.

"I won't. I'm not that type of girl." I shook my head with a shrug to brush it off.

"Sure, you're not. We're all that 'type of girl' when it comes to him. Why do you think we're all here?"

I rolled my eyes, then descended the stairs toward him, as the last student shut the door behind them.

"Listen, I'm sorry I missed yesterday. I—" I started, but he cut me off by putting his hand up.

"Save it. How did you find me?" There was an apparent bite to his tone, but his question confused me.

"What are you talking about?" I asked warily.

"How the fuck did you find me?" Then it clicked, and I knew what the cocky asshole was getting at.

"How could I have found you? All I knew was your first name. And shocking, I know, but I actually live in this state. So, sorry, not a stalker. I came here to get a college education, not follow some guy I fucked in Vegas. So, if that's all you have to say, give me the work I need to make up, and I'll have it back on your desk along with tonight's homework first thing tomorrow."

He reached into his desk and pulled out a small stack of papers. He could not be serious. "Here."

"You're joking, right?"

"I'm not. I can tell you're smart. You finished the assignment I'd given way ahead of your peers. This should be a piece of cake." A devilish grin spread across his face.

"Thanks," I snarled, turning my back toward him. I couldn't face him anymore. The more I gazed into his eyes, the more soaked my panties became. And that pissed me off even more than the ludicrous amount of homework I was now carrying.

"See you tomorrow," he taunted as I approached the door.

"That you will, Mr. Wyatt." Mr. *Cas* Wyatt.

It was hard focusing during my next class after encountering Cas. Thoughts had consumed me ever since Vegas, but I never in a million years thought he'd pop up as my fucking algebra teacher. *How am I going to get through this semester?*

The way his white button-up shirt clung to his well-sculpted torso flashed through my mind all day. When he paced back and forth while giving his lecture, I couldn't help but focus on his round ass in his slacks. The fire in between my legs needed to be put out, and I knew he'd be the only one who could do it, but it was going to be complicated. *Really complicated.*

"Hey, new girl, what's your name?" a voice boomed beside me, snapping me back to reality.

"Taylin, what's yours?"

"Trevor. Hey, listen, Friday we're throwing a party back at the hall near our dorm. Want to come?"

"How many people are going to be there?"

"Lots of people. Wild House throws the best parties."

"Okay, where is it?"

"Give me your number, and I'll text it to you."

Trevor was a cutie. He was tall, with brown skin and brown eyes. Athletic build, meaning he was most likely a football player, and I was always down to party. We exchanged numbers, and he held the door open as I walked out to my car.

"See you, Friday," he said, flashing me a flirty smile.

I walked to my car and sat inside the blazing hot Corolla. Pulling out my phone, I saw that I had a text from Anna.

I put the keys in the ignition and dialed her quickly before putting the car in drive.

"Girl, I'm coming to your apartment right now."

"What happened, T?"

"Cas happened," I deadpanned.

"What?" she screeched, causing me to pull the phone away from my ear.

"Exactly, be there in ten."

As I drove to her apartment, I remembered the way he commanded my body, the rasp of his voice as he claimed my entire being. The way our bodies synched together. I got so caught up in the fantasy that I almost rear-ended the car in front of me.

Get a grip, T.

"How the hell did this happen?" Anna asked as soon as she opened her front door for me.

"That's what I would like to know!" I stomped my way inside her apartment, throwing my hands into the air.

"Maybe it's a sign, T. Maybe he's the one." Of course, she would say that. I don't need to get my hopes up again. Ever.

"Yeah, right. There's no such thing as the one." I sighed as I sat on her couch covered in way too many throw pillows.

"Lies. My mom knew when she met my dad." She waves her fingers at me.

"I'm sure, but I don't buy into that *only one* fantasy. Do I believe you should settle down and have a family? Yes, but *the one*, no." I shook my head.

"You're so dense. Anyway, what are you going to do? There's no way you can wear panties in his class. They'll disintegrate every day." I would laugh if this wasn't as serious of a problem as it was. Because she's right...I already felt the effect on my panties all day.

"I know. He looks ever hotter than I remembered too, which sucks. And since I missed a class already, he's got a target on my back."

"Damn. Well...he's hot, you've already fucked him, and now you're on his shit list? Good luck, girl," she said nonchalantly, flipping her dark hair over her shoulders.

"You're no help, bitch."

"I know, but you should definitely try to fuck him again after-hours or something. That man's cock has you dickmatized—bad." Rolling my eyes, I lay back, trying to forget every line of his muscles playing through my head.

Chapter Five

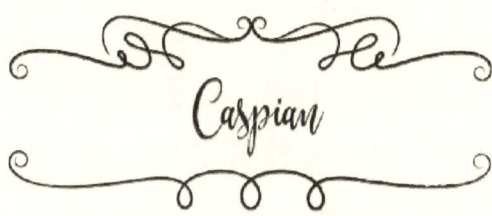

"CARLOS, I HAVE A goddamn emergency," I barked into my phone through Bluetooth while driving way over the speed limit.

"What is it?" he answered with a slight slur to his words.

"I'm coming over right now."

"Don't you have another class to teach?" *How fucked up is this dude? It's not even 9:00 p.m. yet.*

"No. Dude, do you even know what fucking time it is?"

"No." Well, this should be interesting.

"How much have you had to drink?"

"Not enough, Emilia left me." *Oh, shit.*

"Fuck. I'm on my way."

I couldn't wrap my head around her showing up in my class. I had no idea how she found me, and even if it were a coincidence, the universe was firmly kicking me in the balls—repeatedly.

I pulled up in front of Carlos's apartment, and he was sitting in the grass with a bottle of gin. "Dude, get a fucking grip. It's not the end of the world."

"She found out about Vegas."

"How the fuck did that happen?"

"Her sister's friend was an attending guest, and I had no fucking clue. She saw me with that girl, Julianna."

"You could have denied it."

"Emilia has always been able to see through my bullshit, man."

Fuck. How was I going to complain about my problems, and this man's whole fucking world just fell apart? Easy.

"We're going out tonight."

After partially sobering up my best friend, we decided to travel to a bar in Rhode Island. We both needed a fucking escape.

We fought our way through the crowd and found a spot with two seats at the end of the bar. The bartender came right over to us, and I ordered two beers to start things off.

"I can't believe she showed up in my fucking class."

"Dude, that shit's crazy. Are you going to fuck her again?" He laughed, placing his mug back down on the bar.

"I don't know. I mean, fuck, I want to, but you know my rule." And *wanting* to fuck her was an understatement. She was even hotter than I'd remembered. Her skin glowed as she walked into my classroom. I couldn't even speak when she came in because seeing those familiar brown eyes caught me off-guard. And the way that floral dress clung to her hips and ass as she approached my desk...it made my dick as hard as a rock. *I don't know how I'm going to make it through the semester seeing her like that.*

"But that doesn't really apply to this, does it? You already fucked her before she became your student."

"It still applies because she's my student now, you ass." But how I wish it didn't.

"I think you're looking into this way too much. Just fuck her again. Keep it discreet."

"Fuck you."

"It's going to happen. You're attached to that girl, and you don't even realize it." I rolled my eyes and took another sip of my beer.

"How so?"

"You've mentioned her to me every damn day up until yesterday. She has you pussy-whipped. That's why you jumped into the pool to save her that night, isn't it?" Have I really mentioned her *every* day?

And I'd forgotten all about that pool incident. Anyone could have saved her, but I saw the opportunity and jumped. I couldn't see something as sexy as her die in front of my eyes, even though I knew I'd never see her again. I guess you could say that I had a partial soft spot in my dark soul.

"I think you should call Emilia and beg for forgiveness." I decided a subject change was probably best, considering Carlos is the one who actually wants to be in a relationship.

"I've tried. Why do you think you found me on the lawn in my robe? She told me to go fuck myself."

"Well." I paused, looking around the bar. "There's plenty of ass here right now to make us both forget."

"That there is, my friend."

"Two shots of Fireball, please." I motioned for the bartender. She smiled at me and sent three shots down the bar, coming over only a moment later to down the third one with us.

"They're on the house."

"Thanks."

"Oh fuck, that feels so good!"

As I plowed my dick deep into her asshole, her moans were like music to my ears, and it made me forget for a bit. The bartender, Nancy, with the luscious tits, wasn't really my type, but now that I hadn't had to fight with my cock for an erection, I was going to fuck anything that moved to get Taylin out of my head.

Carlos had disappeared, and I hoped he found a rebound to fuck into oblivion as well.

As I felt my orgasm tingle from my balls up my shaft, I exploded into the condom, fisting Nancy's long blonde hair. I thrust as deep as I could into her tight hole until I had nothing left. The only place we could go to fuck was the bathroom, and it made no difference to me. I was down to fuck wherever. Hell, I would have done it on the dance floor if I could have.

"So, can I see you again?" she asked, her cheeks flushed, as she pulled her shirt back down over her breasts and adjusted her skirt.

"Nah. That won't be necessary. Thanks for the offer, though."

"You're a dick."

"So I've been told." She slammed her fist into my chest, storming out of the bathroom as I pulled my pants back up around my waist.

Another one bites the dust, Cas.

As I adjusted myself and washed my hands in the sink, I had to think long and hard about where to find Carlos. I walked out the door and heard faint crying down the hall. *Fucking Carlos.*

"What the fuck are you doing?" I pulled his drunk carcass off the floor. He was curled into a ball, lying on the nasty, sticky floor.

"Emilia," he cried out.

You've got to be shitting me.

"I told you to fuck someone and move past this!"

"I can't, Cas. I'm not the manwhore you are!" He wiped the tears from his face. His beard was matted, and his hair was an unruly mess.

"You don't have to be me; you have to be you. And this shit right here is not you!"

"Leave me here to die, in peace."

Fuck my life.

Chapter Six

AS I LOOKED THROUGH my bag for the stack of papers Cas had given me, I yelled when I pulled out the pages, and every one of them was blank. *What the hell?*

Why would he play this kind of sick and twisted joke on me? *Asshole.*

I stayed up half the night stressing for nothing.

I stormed into his class the next day and smiled, tossing the now stapled blank pages onto his desk. Before running to take my seat, I whispered, "There's a note on the last page for you."

I laughed to myself. "Now, class, who can solve this equation for me $-5 + (-2)$? Raise your hand."

Of course, no one was going to raise their hand. "I'll answer it," I said, trying to catch my breath.

"Come on down, Ms. Bradford."

I solved the equation and came up with the answer, which was negative seven. "Can you explain how you got that answer?" he asked, his eyes watching me much too intently for a math lesson.

"Well, if both parts of the equations have the same sign, you add. If one is a negative and one is positive, then you subtract. So, you would take five plus two and keep the same sign, and then you get negative seven."

"Good job. Class, I didn't even teach her that yet; all of you had better step up your game."

"Someone's going to be the teacher's pet," my classmate, Debbie, snarled as I returned to my seat. Debbie reminded me of an old lady trapped in a twenty-something body. Her blonde hair was cut into a long bob with red highlights through it, her glasses were a bit too large for her pointy nose, and she dressed in oversized sweaters. It was as if she was trying to hide her curves, which was a shame. She had the potential to look really cute.

"I'm good. Maybe if you were here to study instead of fuck the professor, you'd know the answer too."

I moved my attention back down at the board, and Cas was still staring at me. He gazed at me as if we were the only two in the room, and it rocked me to my core. I imagined him running up the steps, kissing me in front of everyone, and ripping my clothes off. His big, strong hands caressing my body, setting it ablaze as his tongue traced the contour of my neck. *Calm down, girl.*

"Who can solve this next equation? $-7 + 3$?"

His eyes met mine, but I quickly looked away. I knew I could solve it easily, but I kept my hand down for the moment. I didn't want to come off as the teacher's pet again to jealous Debbie, but I did scribble the answer down in my notebook. It was negative four, by the way. He wrote the entire equation out and explained how he had come up with the answer in great detail. I still didn't believe no one else understood it but me, and I found that kind of sad.

As the bell rang, everyone scurried out of the room except me. I needed answers. I needed to know what the hell those blank pages he gave me were about.

I marched toward him, slamming the worksheet from his last lesson down on his desk.

"Woah, what's this all about?" he asked, rearing back his head to look up at me.

"What was the deal with the blank pages you gave me? I was up half the night worried I had to do a stack of worksheets, and nothing was printed on them," I scoffed.

He smiled, a sly grin forming on his face. "It was a test."

"What kind of test?"

"The pissed-off test." He flipped through them and got to my note on the last page. Chuckling when he saw the words *fuck you, have a nice day* written on it. "Very nice. I figured you would have checked it before the end of the day and came back in here and cursed me out. I didn't expect you to take it so seriously and freak out until you got home. Although, the look on your face right now is priceless."

"You, sir, are a dick."

"So I've been told. Oh, and Ms. Bradford?"

"What?"

"Don't ever feel like you can't answer an equation. I can tell how many people are here to learn, and I can tell how many have attended just to catch a glimpse of the eye-candy professor. You don't have to dumb yourself down to fit in."

I leaned down beside him, my lips mere centimeters from his ear. "Don't flatter yourself," I said and walked off.

The nerve of this man. Yes, he's definitely eye-candy, but I would have never joined his class for those reasons. I'm not as shallow as the other ditzes in the class. I love numbers, and anyone who can help me retain the knowledge to continue loving numbers is a win-win in my book.

I had no idea how I would get through this semester if he kept calling me out. Every time he said my name, I nearly melted into a puddle, and I hated that he affected me. Perhaps if I hadn't already slept with him, I wouldn't feel this way. If I could have done it over, or if I had the knowledge I had now, I still wouldn't have changed a damn thing. I must try not to let him know he's getting to me, but how?

"Hey, Taylin. You got my text, right?" Trevor asked, pulling me out of my own head as I walked through the hallway.

"Yep. I'll be there! I promise!"

"I sure hope so," he replied, pulling his lip in between his teeth.

I know he doesn't think I'm going to sleep with him. I have a deal with one asshole per year, max, and Professor Wyatt had already filled that spot.

Chapter Seven

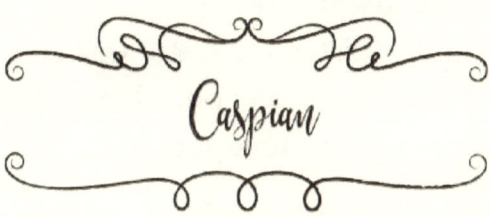

Caspian

I LAUGHED AS SHE stormed out of my classroom. Her tight shirt and oversized jacket she was wearing made it hard to admire her curves, but I knew they were there.

She was so easy to rile up that I knew I had to keep fucking with her. I loved how her nostrils flared as she slammed the papers down on my desk.

I had about an hour's break until the next class came in, so I created a new assignment for homework that weekend.

Carlos: Cas, I need to talk to you.

Me: About what? You haven't stopped crying over Emilia, and quite frankly, it's depressing as fuck.

Carlos: I know, but I need you.

Me: Meet me at my house in ten minutes. I'm just now leaving school.

Carlos: K.

Christ, what does he have to cry about this time?

As I got into my Mercedes SUV, I watched as a few hot female students walked by my car, glancing at me as I switched on my headlights. *Not today, Satan.*

I turned on my favorite rock station, and an oldie but goodie by Van Halen had come on. I jammed out all the way home and found Carlos's truck parked in front of my place. He was sitting on the porch, staring off into space as I pulled into my garage.

"What?" I asked as he followed me inside through the garage door.

"She's pregnant." My eyes widened as I shook my head, opening the door for him.

"Fuck. So, what does that mean?"

"Emilia told me she wanted to keep it, but she doesn't know if she can trust me." *I fucking hate the word trust.*

Classic hormonal woman bullshit.

"So, what are you going to do? Did you even want kids?" I asked, trying to decide if I wanted a beer or scotch.

"No! I don't know. I don't know what the fuck I want, except for her. She's it for me, man."

"Then why did you fuck it all up in Vegas?" I asked, sitting down on a stool in the kitchen.

"Because I was being a selfish asshole. We had got into a fight before I left," he replied, sitting down on the stool beside me.

"Okay, but how do you even know it's yours? Maybe she freaked out because she cheated on you. Did you ever think of that?" *Seems to be the common theme of my life.*

"No, but she's not that kind of girl, man. She's loyal."

"Sure, that's what they all say. Listen, I don't know what you expect me to say. I don't do babies. I don't do love, and I for damn sure don't do relationships." He knows this. I am probably the worst friend for him to talk to about this kind of thing.

"What does make you happy, Cas? Seriously. You're almost thirty, and there's more to life than just being a bachelor."

"Says who? Quit whining and grab me a beer, and if you must know, teaching makes me happy and pussy. Lots and lots of tight, wet pussy."

"Good luck with that man," he said, clinking his beer bottle against mine.

I hated to admit it, but he did have a point. I couldn't parade around like this for the rest of my life, but I wasn't looking for anything serious. I wouldn't become utterly oblivious if something slapped me in my face, but for right now. It's time to get drunk.

"Guess what, class?"

"What?" they responded enthusiastically.

"It's time to do my favorite thing in the entire world."

"What's that?" a random female in the front row asked.

"Fractions." The entire class groaned, and it was like sweet music to my ears. "Aw, c'mon, they're not that bad," I taunted, trying to make eye contact with someone from every row. I gazed at Taylin, and she was beaming.

"Here's an easy one." I walked over toward the board and wrote forty-two over twelve. "Who can solve this?"

"I can," a guy from the back answered.

"What's your name?"

"Johnson," he said, walking toward me. I handed him a dry erase marker.

"Explain your answer, please."

"Well, first, you have to find a number that both numbers can be divided by."

"What number is that?"

"They're both divisible by six."

"Continue."

"After dividing both by six, you're left with seven over two."

"Perfect. See, that wasn't so bad. Johnson, can you grab that stack of papers on my desk and hand them out to the class, please?"

"Sure, Mr. Wyatt."

"Class, you have thirty minutes to complete this assignment. If you fail, you'll have extra homework for the weekend, and I'm sure that sounds fun, right?"

"Hell no!" a jock from the back yelled out.

"Then if you expect to get drunk and fuck your way out of a plastic bag, I suggest you pass." The entire class erupted in laughter as I returned to my desk.

I had only given the class five fractions that they had to simplify and half of them failed on the spot. Some had a few answers right, and the only ones who ultimately passed were Taylin and Johnson. "This is a damn shame. I'm going to have to sign half of you up for fucking tutoring before the semester is over. Good job, Johnson and Taylin; you both have passed with flying colors and won't have any homework this weekend. The rest of you, come to my desk and grab a packet. And if it's not completed by Monday, well, let's try not to find out what happens then, okay?"

The bell rang after the last student grabbed a packet, and they all headed out the door except Taylin. "What now? Go home and enjoy your weekend."

"I will, I just..." She paused, looking me up and down.

"What?" She started to speak, and I zoned out while staring at her perky round breasts as she leaned over my desk. The skirt she had on fit her hips snugly, and I imagined ripping it off with my teeth as I bent her over my desk and plowed my cock deep inside of her as she screamed my name.

"Did you hear what I said, Mr. Wyatt?" Shit.

"What? Huh? No," I replied, sitting back in my chair, my hands falling into my lap, hiding my erection.

"I said, I'd like to get tutored." Tilting her head to the side, her gaze hardened.

"Why? You don't seem to need it."

"I know, but I want to stay sharp."

"Okay, well, when the time comes, we'll see."

"Thank you. I hope you enjoy your weekend," Taylin said, running her hand across the length of my desk.

I wished she ran it across the length of my cock.

I stayed after school later than I intended on that Friday night. Grading papers for four classes was a pain in the ass, but I wanted to enjoy my weekend and not have to think about this place again until I had to rise from the dead on Monday morning.

I gathered my belongings and shut my laptop before turning toward the whiteboard, spraying it down with cleaner and wiping it down. I stacked all my markers facing the same way and ensured my class was in order before walking out to the parking lot. Only one other teacher stayed late, Ms. Beau, the sexy-ass French teacher. She had a few students in her room, and I couldn't even be mad at them for staying after hours; her accent could bring any man to his knees.

I had overheard some students in the hall earlier talking about a party over at Wild House and decided to walk by and check it out. It was damn near ten o'clock at night, so it had to be well underway by then. I tossed my things in my SUV and removed my tie, popping my collar and rolling up my sleeves. I pulled out my phone and had a shit ton of texts from Carlos that I decided to ignore because I didn't feel like being his therapist tonight.

As I approached the block the party was on, I heard a girl screaming. I picked up the pace and listened to a guy yelling. "C'mon, baby. We always have sex with a freshman. I saw the way you looked at me when I invited you. Don't be a fucking prude!"

"Get your hands off me. I don't want to fuck you!"

"Mr. Hill, do we have a fucking problem here?"

"No, Mr. Wyatt. I just—" He paused, looking at Taylin, tears flowing down her cheeks, and I saw red when I noticed her blouse had been torn.

I grabbed Trevor by his collar, shoving him up against the hard brick of the building. The hard thump of his head bouncing off the wall gave me satisfaction. "Leave right now, and I'll pretend I never saw this. And if I ever catch you near Ms. Bradford again. Or if I even catch you thinking about her, I'm going to cut your tongue out and shove it up your anus, got it?"

"Yes, sir! Sorry, Taylin!"

He ran off, and I put my hand on her shoulder. "Are you alright?"

"No," she said, wiping her eyes.

"Want to get out of here?"

"Yes, please."

"Do you want me to bring you home?"

"No. I can't let my parents see me like this."

"Where do you want to go?"

"Somewhere far away from here, just for a bit." I pulled her in for a hug, her tears lightly soaking my shirt. *Shit. This isn't good. What are you doing, Cas?*

Chapter Eight

Taylin

THE PARTY HAD STARTED around eight, but I hadn't shown up until about nine. I could hear the music blaring from down the street and saw colorful strobe lights flashing through the door as I arrived. I wasn't sure what I should wear, so I tossed on a sexy, off-the-shoulder blouse and a pair of shorts. I was greeted at the door, and a guy stamped my right hand with a horse and gave me a green band to wrap around my wrist.

"You're over twenty-one, right?"

"Of course."

I walked through the doors, and the inside looked way bigger than I thought. Girls were already sloppy drunk inside. Dancing on tables, passed out in corners with a bunch of horny guys surrounding them. It was a disgusting sight to see. I decided to hurry up and look for Trevor, since he was the only familiar face I knew would be here. It sucked being the new girl on campus. I didn't know who to trust, but he seemed like he was trustworthy.

I asked a guy that had a similar varsity jacket like him, where he might be, and he pointed to another room. Making my way down the hall, I opened the door, and there were a bunch of guys and girls; the room was full of smoke and reeked of weed. "Hey, T, you made it!" he said, climbing off the table he was sitting on, staring in amazement.

"Yeah, I did. Can you get me a drink?" I replied, nervously.

"Sure, would you like a beer?"

"Yes. please." *Be careful, Tay. You don't know these people. Pace yourself.*

"Cool, follow me. There's a keg in the corner."

I followed behind him, and a few of the girls smiled and waved at me as I tailed him. I smiled politely, but they all seemed kind of fake. Trevor handed me a red plastic cup and pumped the keg, the cold, frothy beverage quickly filling it. I took a sip, and it was actually pretty good. I always preferred beer out of a keg; it seemed fresher.

"So, how do you like the beer?" he asked.

"It's pretty good."

"Good. We always get the best shit for our parties. The Diamond House tries to copy us, but wherever they get their shit from, it tastes like horse piss."

I laughed, taking another sip of the beer. "So, do you guys battle a lot?"

"Yeah. They knew we were throwing a party tonight, so they're going to have one tomorrow. If they did it tonight, they knew no one would have shown up, and it would have been a major embarrassment."

"I see. Do you normally charge for these?"

"For the first party of the year, no. But after, yes. Don't worry; you'll never have to pay. Just let them know you're with me, and you won't have any problems." As he faced me, his eyes became hooded slits, and he grabbed my hand. "Let me introduce you to some friends of mine."

We went into another small room that was much less crowded. There were a few guys with jackets that matched his, along with a few girls. "This is Taylin," he introduced me to everyone.

"Hey," they all greeted me. They seemed more friendly than the other people I'd seen earlier.

"So, what sport do you play?"

"Football and soccer."

"Is this a football jacket?"

"Yes, it is. You should come to a game sometime. It'd be nice to have a girl as beautiful as you cheer me on from the sidelines." He flashed me a dimpled smile.

"I'll think about it," I replied, sucking down the rest of my beer. He brought me to refill my cup and asked me to dance.

Dancing with him wasn't as synchronized as when I danced with Cas. Trevor and I didn't seem to vibe well, and I started to second-guess being there.

"Hey, wanna go outside for a bit?"

"Sure." *Thank goodness. It's a shame he's cute but has no rhythm.*

He grabbed my hand, and I held onto my beer tightly as we went through a side door I hadn't even noticed was there when I first entered the room. He stopped and leaned against the wall, and I did the same. Then he stood in front of me, placing his hands on either side of my body.

"What are you doing?" My nerves kicked into gear at what he was about to do. I needed to get out of here. *Now.*

"I mean, I figured you wanted this," he said, closing the remaining gap in between us. The heat from his breath and the stench of alcohol on my neck made me feel sick.

"No, I don't. You can back up now." I started to move away, but his arms and closeness kept me firmly planted in front of him.

"Now, why would I do something as stupid as that?" He ran his hand down my cheek, and I reacted, splashing my beer in his face. He jerked back, raising his fist.

"I told you to stop!" I screamed, my heart pounding in my chest.

"You stupid bitch." He flew toward me again before I could get away, ripping at my shirt and firmly pressing his body against mine, trying to force his hands into my shorts.

"Stop!" I yelled, trying to shove him off me. The music was so loud inside that I knew no one would come to my rescue, but I wasn't going down without a fight.

"C'mon, baby; we always have sex with a freshman. I saw the way you looked at me when I invited you. Don't be a fucking prude!"

"I don't want to fuck you!"

"Mr. Hill, do we have a fucking problem here?"

I couldn't believe of all people, Mr. Wyatt had come to my rescue. I was thankful, but it was unexpected. He grabbed Trevor and slammed him against the bricks, making him apologize to me before he ran off like a punk.

Everything happened so fast that I couldn't quit crying and followed Cas away from the party. I climbed into his SUV, still in a state of shock. It was nice and expensive looking. Everything inside was chrome, and he had custom lighting. The features kept me momentarily distracted from what had just occurred. He asked me a few questions, and all I knew was that I needed to get as far away from that place as possible.

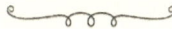

We drove around for what felt like an eternity, and at some point, I'd dozed off.

"Where are we going?"

"To a place I rent out in New Hampshire."

"Why New Hampshire?"

"Why not New Hampshire? It's beautiful, serene, and it gets you away from horny pigs. Well, most of them."

We pulled into a long driveway with tall trees beside it as we approached a huge cottage. There were no other houses within walking distance, but it didn't bother me. However, it should have because no one would know if Cas were to murder me out here.

He turned off the ignition and climbed out, rounding the front of the car to open my door. Then he grabbed my hand as I stepped out, placing his arm around my shoulders and shutting the door behind us.

We walked up a cobblestone path and underneath the porch to a side door with a single brass light fixture above it. He opened it up, and the lights automatically turned on inside. "Is this the basement?"

"Yeah."

"Wow, this is bigger than my parents' living room." The laminated floor was smooth, and there were several blue recliners spread out and a pool table in the middle of the room. Looking to the corner, I noticed a built-in bar with a mountain of liquors fully stocked behind it. "I could really use a drink."

"That I can do. Have a seat," he said, guiding me to one of the recliners.

I plopped down, hitting the button on the side to release the footrest, and sunk deep into the plush fabric. It felt as if I were being swallowed by a cloud. Cas slid behind the bar and grabbed a few glasses, and I watched on as he navigated around the space flawlessly. I had no idea how many times he'd been there, but he didn't miss a beat.

He returned with two glasses full of ice, blackberries, and red liquid inside, handing one to me. "What is this?"

"Try it."

I took a sip, and it tasted amazing. The bubbles from the tonic water tickled my tongue, and it all went down smoothly. I gulped it so fast, I hardly had time to think before I was devouring the leftover fruit inside.

"Guess I'll go make myself another one." He laughed as he handed me his drink, making me smile.

"Thank you."

I twirled the plastic stick around the ice cubes, until another drink came over my shoulder. The second one went down just as fast, and my whole body felt at ease. Cas sat down on the recliner beside me and locked eyes with me as he took a sip from his drink.

"What?"

"Nothing. I didn't realize how much of a lush you were."

"I'm not a lush! I just needed to feel good."

"Don't we all."

Looking over at the enormous flatscreen mounted to the wall, I asked, "Can you put something on the TV?" I tried not to let him being this close get to me.

He fumbled through the channels and stopped on a WWE pay-per-view. "Sorry, you're probably not into this, huh?" he questioned, searching my eyes for rejection.

"Oh my God, are you kidding me? Me and my older brother used to love watching wrestling," I exclaimed. I was so excited to see a show for the first time in years.

"Who's your favorite old-school wrestler?" He pursed his lips and squinted his eyes, trying to get a read on me.

"Kevin Nash, I had the biggest crush on him growing up. Him and Shawn Michaels. What about you?"

"Sting was always the man and Mr. Perfect. I have to be honest, Tay. I didn't peg you as a fan."

"I'm sure there will be more things that'll shock you about me." I giggled.

"I can only imagine," he said, placing his hand on my leg, and I put mine on top of his. I leaned in closer, and he pulled away.

"Let me go make us some more drinks and grab a menu. I'm starving." He hopped off the couch nervously. *Shit.*

After having a few more drinks and demolishing some chicken wings we'd ordered, we made our way upstairs. I was pretty tipsy, and my body rocked from left to right as I ascended the stairs. "I think I need some air."

He placed his hand on the small of my back and led me outside a sliding door onto a large porch. There were lounge chairs, umbrellas with a grill, and small tables. It was dark, but the glow of the moon over the water was beautiful. The bright white ripples crashing ashore were mesmerizing. The smell of the freshwater hit my nose, and I wanted to run and jump inside, but I knew it probably wasn't a good idea.

I placed my elbows on the railing and looked up at the stars. I'd never seen them as clearly as I had that night. Back in the city, they always felt like they were so far away, but here, they felt like I could almost reach out and touch them. "It's so beautiful out here," I said, turning to face him.

"It sure is," he said with a smile.

I placed my hand on his cheek, and he grabbed it, putting it back down at my side. "Taylin, don't. We can't do this."

"Why not?" I pouted, poking out my bottom lip.

"Because you're my student." His gaze went cold.

"But what you did tonight—"

"It was only a distraction to keep your mind off what happened," he interrupted.

The tears pooling in my eyes made me feel weak and vulnerable, and I could tell he sensed it. "Hey, it's getting late. I'm going to head in and go to bed. There are three bedrooms here, so feel free to pick whichever you want."

Hearing him say that hit me like a ton of bricks. I don't know what I had expected from him. I was disappointed that he didn't just grab me and make me come to bed with him, but I guess that wasn't a good idea, seeing as what transpired prior to us coming here. However, I wouldn't have fought him off at all.

"Can you show them to me?" I asked, turning around to look at him.

"Sure."

We briefly walked through the living room and up the stairs, where there were two rooms side by side. The first room he showed me had wood paneling with an aquamarine color on the walls. The bedding was a little dated, but the mountain of pillows on top sold me. "I pick this room," I said, running and plopping down on the king-sized bed.

"It's all yours. Have a good night, Taylin."

The way he annunciated my name sent heat straight to my core. It was almost as if he were telling me that he wanted to ravish me without saying it. He walked out of the room, and I gazed at his firm ass as he disappeared into the hallway.

I awoke to the scent of maple syrup and bacon in the air. I descended the steps and into the living room. The high, vaulted ceilings were lovely, and so much natural light came in through the large A-frame windows. The lake was a beautiful shade of blue, and I definitely wanted to go for a swim.

The wooden floor was smooth, and the space was decorated with a red love seat, a recliner, and a blue and white checkered throw rug. The floor plan was open, and the living space went right into the dining space. Cas was in front of the stove with no shirt on. His back muscles tightened and released as he flipped a pancake into the air and then onto a plate.

"That's pretty impressive, Mr. Wyatt."

"Thank you. Now have a seat." He motioned, his back still facing me.

I found a comfortable spot on the love seat and sat with my legs crossed underneath me. Moments later, he walked over with a tray of food and a sexy smile plastered on his face. He handed me the tray of pancakes, bacon, eggs, a mug of coffee, a beautiful red and orange flower in a vase, and some orange juice.

"Wow, I had no idea you could cook."

"There are a lot of things you don't know about me, Taylin."

There are a lot of things I want to know about you.

I took the tray and immediately grabbed the fork, then stabbed the eggs. I didn't trust everyone's eggs, so if he nailed them, I just might have to stop myself from falling in love with this man.

The first bite of the fluffy pieces of heaven melted on my tongue. The faint hint of cheese brought out an explosion of flavors I'd never tasted before. I cut up the pancakes, and he brought over a bottle of syrup and sat down beside me with a plate of his own. His dish was twice as full as mine, and I had no idea where he put it all, but I loved a man that could eat.

The bacon was crispy and fell apart in my mouth, and I couldn't stop eating until my plate was cleaned. I nearly finished before him. Once I did, I uncrossed my legs and went to put my dishes away when he stopped me—firmly placing his hand on my arm. "I got it. Why don't you see if there are any clothes your size in the closet so you can change?" I could feel my cheeks heat and tried to keep my composure. This simple gesture sent chills through my body.

"So are you trying to say you don't think it's sexy that I'm still wearing the same outfit from the day before?" I teased, pointing to the torn blouse.

"You could wear a potato sack and still be sexy, but I'm pretty sure you'd like to wash the buffalo sauce stains off."

I looked down at myself, embarrassed. I couldn't help but laugh. I was such a messy eater, and there was no denying it.

"You got me. Where's the washing machine?"

"Downstairs. I have to wash a few things too, so just toss everything in the basket in the hall, and I'll handle it."

"Okay."

"Cas, can I ask you a question?" I asked, following him into the kitchen.

His eyes darted toward me as he placed the dishes on the counter. "Sure."

"What was your favorite Disney movie growing up?" His eyes lit up as he stroked his chin. "*Dumbo.*"

"Why *Dumbo?*"

"Because I thought it was cute that an elephant wanted to fly. I used to love elephants when I was younger. I also wanted to run away with the circus. What about you?"

I dismissed the circus thing because I felt like he was joking. "*Beauty and the Beast.*"

"Of course. A damsel kidnapped by a beast and locked away in his fancy castle. Let me guess; you loved the library?" He laughed.

"Shut up!" I sassed, hitting him on the shoulder. He wasn't wrong, though. "You're partially right, but I had a thing for singing inanimate objects."

We both broke out into a fit of laughter, momentarily stopping to catch our breath. Our eyes never broke contact, and I knew I had to go.

"Okay, well, I'll see you in a bit," I said, nervously placing some distance between us. I could feel the heat from his body, and it made my lady parts ache.

I had no idea why this man wasn't snatched off the market yet. He was funny, attractive, apparently a great cook, and he has his own place—I assume. A fancy car, too, and he was smart as hell. As I watched him wash the dishes and then wipe the counters down, I ran up the stairs. If I stared at that man any longer, I'd do something I'd possibly regret.

Vegas was a one time thing, Taylin. Get over it. Nothing is going to happen between the two of you again.

Chapter Nine

Caspian

AFTER BREAKFAST, I RUSHED to clean up. Being so close to her made every wrong thought in my mind almost happen, and I knew I couldn't go down that road, not right then. The sounds she made while she ate made my cock as hard as a rock, and when she ran upstairs, I was thankful as fuck because there was no hiding my erection.

I walked into the guest bathroom and turned on the shower, jumping in and letting the hot water roll down my body as I used it as lube to stroke my cock. I ran my hand up and down my shaft, pumping as fast as I could to release the pent-up aggression I was feeling inside. *She's your fucking student! She's your student, Cas.*

I chanted that over and over in my head as I visualized her curvy waist, beautiful eyes, and luscious tits, bouncing up and down as she rode my cock. Bringing her there was a fucking mistake, and I knew it. There was no way I was going an entire weekend without having her on her knees.

"Fuck!" I shouted as I felt the heat from my taint creep up, and the cum shot out of the head, ricocheting off the tile.

After my very intense shower, I tossed on a pair of shorts and threw the rest of my clothes in the basket, and then I went down the hall to grab Taylin's things. Her door was opened, and as I peeked in, she was standing in front of the mirror in a two-piece bikini that molded her body beautifully. She fluffed her curly hair, and she turned around with a smile, our eyes-catching. I couldn't even look away.

"I really need to feel the water on my skin."

I really need to feel your skin as you ride my cock.

"Cool. I'll go and toss this in the wash and meet you outside on the cock. I mean dock."

"Sounds good." She laughed, running her hands up and down the sides of her body.

I felt the blood rush right to my junk and held the basket in front of my waist, trying to hide the erection I knew I'd never get rid of this weekend.

After tossing everything in the wash, I grabbed a few towels and met Taylin down on the dock. She was sitting on the edge, her legs and feet dangling over the water. The sun enhanced her skin and gave her hair a hint of honey. I threw the towels down and ran, grabbing my knees in midair and crashing into the water.

"Hey! That's not fair. I waited for you, and you jumped in without me, you jerk!"

"Hey, sometimes you just gotta go for it."

Jumping right to her feet, she ran to the start of the dock. She gained momentum and copied the same movement as me, her body sinking into the water and barely making a splash.

She emerged from the bottom of the lake, and I swear it seemed like she was moving in slow motion. She flung her hair back, and everything was just like the fucking movies. When she looked at me, the water ran down her face, and I swam over to her and grabbed the back of her neck—pressing my lips against hers without even thinking. And once I felt the softness of her lips again, I knew I wouldn't be able to stop.

She broke the hold and looked me dead in the eyes. "I've been waiting for you to do that since breakfast."

"This is so fucked up, Taylin."

"So? You saved me from that asshole, and I owe you one. You didn't have to do that. You could have let my screams fall on deaf ears, but you didn't. That means that deep down, your inner asshole can be suppressed."

Our lips crashed together, and I couldn't get enough. I ran my hand over her breasts, fondling them, never breaking our kiss. My dick hardened in my shorts, and I knew I couldn't fuck around anymore. I wanted to pull her up onto the dock and fuck her until I saw only the whites of her eyes.

Chapter Ten

OUR BODIES MESHED UNTIL we reached the shallow end of the water, and he wrapped his arms around my waist and placed me on the edge of the dock.

I looked down at him and admired how good he looked with his dark hair slicked back. The beads of water trickled down his face and his chest as he looked up at me with his lust-filled eyes and spread my legs apart.

"Stay still," he commanded as he slid the fabric of my bikini bottom over, exposing my bare clit, and flicked his tongue over it.

His mouth was warm and comforting, and it was more complicated than I thought to keep still when all I wanted to do was let loose and release all over his face.

His grip tightened on my legs as he swirled around my bud faster with more force behind it. He slipped a finger in, adding to the intensity of the pleasure. "Don't hold back, baby. You can let it go; I can feel you tens—"

Before he could finish his sentence, I relaxed, and a gush of fluid came out of me. A tingling sensation flowed through my body, and the sun in the sky seemed to shine a bit brighter. The birds felt like they were singing a song just for me, and I was delighted.

He walked out of the water and climbed on the dock beside me. As soon as I readjusted my bikini and stood up to face him, he flung my body over his shoulders, my legs suspended in the air.

"Oh my God, Cas, put me down!"

"Not until I have you in my bed." Exactly what I was hoping for.

He carried me back to the cottage, caveman style, and brought me upstairs to his room. He tossed me onto his bed and reached into the dresser, retrieving a gold condom. His shorts fell to the floor, and his erection sprung free; everything about this man was perfect—well, everything except his attitude.

His body was sculpted to perfection, his cock was thick and long, and when he smiled, a hint of a dimple showed as he stalked toward me. My bottoms were soaked, and it wasn't from the lake.

"Taylin, if we do this, I need to know you're not going to get attached."

"Why are you saying this to me?" *It seemed like he needed to say it aloud to reassure himself.* "I know what this is, don't you?"

I fell to my knees before he could keep talking, taking the entire length of him into my mouth. I grabbed its base and licked and sucked, twirling my tongue around the tip and underneath. He grabbed my head and thrust in so forcefully, I gagged. "No gagging. You take all of it."

He ripped his cock out of my mouth and remained silent as he climbed onto the bed, his eyes telling me a secret that his lips wouldn't spill.

I sat up on my knees and unhooked the top and sides of my bikini, the orange material coating the bed. He swiped it to the floor and gazed at me, reaching behind my neck to pull me in for a kiss. Deep, passionate, our tongues danced, twirling around each other, not missing a beat. He pulled my bottom lip in, and I pulled in his top, alternating as his hands caressed the arch of my back, and my hands roamed through his hair. He pushed me back onto the bed, the pads of his fingers running down the middle of my chest and over my stomach. The sensation sent tingles down my spine. Quickly, he grabbed my hips and dragged me to the edge of the bed, settling himself on the floor in between my thighs. His tongue traced my outer lips, then he took me in his mouth and devoured me, leaving no spot untouched.

This man had the power to make me come undone within minutes, and I enjoyed every fucking moment.

"Cas, you're gonna make me come." He did this thing with his mouth, sucking my clit while flicking his tongue, and I lost it. He wiped his mouth and looked at me, sucking his lip in between his teeth, and I knew he was going to destroy me.

Pulling out a blindfold, he placed it over my eyes. "I like it better this way. It would be best if you feel me, not see me." I heard him take something else out of the drawer, and the next thing I knew, I heard him grab the condom from beside me and roll it down his shaft, stroking his cock. He rubbed the tip against my entrance, alternating between my clit and opening, the sensitivity making me pant in anticipation. Then, finally, he pushed in slowly, and my walls stretched to accommodate him. He made me feel so full as his fingers ran over my breasts, twisting each nipple in between until he was entirely inside of me. Something was placed around my wrists, preventing me from using my hands, and he plowed into me with deep, controlled movements. He rolled his hips from side to side and made me feel something I'd never felt before.

Love? No. Complete and utter satisfaction? Yes.

After sex, Cas went into the bathroom, and I grabbed my clothes and ran out of his room. I didn't want things to get weird. I needed to shower, but I didn't think it was a good idea to shower with him. Seeing as this was purely sex and nothing else. At least, that's what I tried to make myself believe. There was no way I wouldn't get attached to him with the way he made my body feel. Besides, he saved me from ending up as another freshman catastrophe.

I ran into the bathroom, and it was beautiful. The walls were painted a sky blue, and the tile patterns and backsplash were a nice cream color. I turned the nozzle and waited for the room to fill with a light haze before stepping inside. The water ran down my body and in between my legs, reminding me of what Cas and I had just done. I slid my hands in between, trying to recreate that feeling, and came hard. I pleased myself several times, trying to keep the sensation of euphoria going.

The last time I came so hard, I moaned out loud. I pressed my body against the glass, trying to catch my breath.

"I guess I didn't give you enough," a voice said, making me spin around. Cas was standing in my bathroom, naked and staring at me like a lion staring at his prey.

He opened the door and came inside. "Cas, wait."

His hand clasped around my throat, and he pushed me back against the tile, the door closing behind him. "Maybe I need to teach you a lesson," he said gruffly, spinning me around and slapping my ass hard. "If I didn't please you enough, you should have told me." He growled in my ear. I felt something slip into my ass, and it made me yelp. "That's a good girl. How does it feel?" I was at a loss for words.

He slapped my ass again. "I asked you a question, Ms. Bradford."

"It feels good," I whimpered as he slid it in and out slowly. I'd never experienced anything like this in my life.

He left the toy inside of me and spun me around, then lifted me up. Using the water from the shower, he slid back inside of me. My clit was so sensitive, I almost came again. I wrapped my legs around his waist as he placed a hand on either side of me, bracing himself on the tile as he thrust up into me. I rubbed myself against him as he pumped and cried out in ecstasy. Tears poured from my eyes, and he didn't slow down; he couldn't get enough of me, and I couldn't get enough of him.

He thrust and pumped until a loud, throaty groan escaped his mouth. "Fuck, Taylin. Come all over this cock."

My legs felt like Jell-O as they hit the floor, and he kissed me on my forehead before stepping out of the shower. I sunk to my butt and let the water run over my body, unable to get up. Tears sprung out of my eyes again, but this time, it wasn't the good kind.

After my soul and tear duct cleansing in the shower, I decided it was best that I bury my emotions. Someone like me could never tame a man like Cas.

Besides, I never asked for this. This was supposed to be a one time ordeal. I was never supposed to see this man again, yet I'm in his weekend getaway cottage.

Fuck my life.

Chapter Eleven

Caspian

JEREMIAH: WHERE THE FUCK are you, man?

Me: New Hampshire.

I knew as soon as I told him where I was, my phone would ring, and here it was, as if right on cue.

"Yes, Jerm?"

"Do I even want to know why the hell you're up there?"

"I had to get away."

"Who's the lucky lady?"

"Taylin."

"Wait, the chick from Vegas? How?"

"If Carlos hasn't already ratted me out, then I'm not saying shit. Just know none of this shit happened on purpose, but —"

"But, what?"

"I don't regret one fucking minute."

"You didn't forget about watching the game at B's tomorrow, right?"

"Shit, I'll be there. I'll just have to cut this short."

"Alright, see you then!"

After I hung up the phone with J, Taylin walked down the stairs and dropped her purse on the steps behind her. Her eyes were all puffy and red.

"Are you okay?"

"Can you take me home?"

"Now?"

"Yes."

"Why?"

"Being here hurts."

"Why?"

"It's giving me the false illusion of us."

"'Us'?" I repeated, dumbfounded.

"Yes. The way you look at me. The way you please me from head to toe and not just *fuck* me. Being out here is like being in my own personal Hell, because I know I can't have you. Thanks for getting me away from Trevor, but I can't be here with you anymore."

She grabbed her bag from the stairs, and since I had to meet up with the guys early the next day anyway, it was perfect.

"Okay, well, let me get changed." As I stood to my feet, she scoffed. Her eyes shot sparks. "What?"

"That's it? Are you just going to pretend like none of this happened? Like you didn't just hear what I said?" Her arms crossed over her chest. *She was pissed.*

"What do you want me to do? Take you and whisk you off into the sunset for our happily ever after? Sorry, sweets, but I'm not Prince Charming, and I don't do relationships or continuously save damsels in distress, although I've saved you twice now, so I'd say we're even."

"Even? How? I didn't ask you to 'save' me either time," she said, tears pooling in her eyes.

"So next time, I'll let you drown and let you become the new freshman groupie. Got it."

"What do you mean?" She paused for a moment. I could see the wheels turning by her facial expression. "You're the one who saved me in Vegas?"

"Yes, that was me. I never expected to see you again, but I couldn't let you die either. You were being so stupid and careless that night. You kept teetering by the edge of the pool before you jumped in like a crazy woman," I said, raking my hands through my hair. "So, as I stated, we're even now."

"Fuck you, Cas. Take me home right now!" She picked up a pillow off the couch and launched it at my head.

Shit.

The ride back to Boston was slow and torturous. Traffic coming into the city on the weekend was a fucking mess and a horrible decision, but she was pissed, and there was no way I could keep her there one more hour without her wanting to kill me.

She sat in the seat behind me and wouldn't say as much as two words to me. I tried to brush it off and figured that everything would go back to normal once we got back to campus. *Right?*

As we neared the campus, I tried to get her attention. I didn't know where she wanted me to drop her off. I figured pulling into the school parking lot on a Saturday night with a student wouldn't be a good look for either of us.

"Where are you going? We're getting close to the college, so you might want to cut the shit and let me know where the hell I'm dropping you off, Taylin." She flipped me off, and I parked the car in the middle of the road.

"Here is just fine. Fuck you very much." She unlocked the door and climbed out, running across the street. I put the car in drive and never looked back.

Fuck this shit.

As I walked from my car to Brian's front door the next day, I had to put my game face on with two twelve-packs in each arm. I knew at some point the guys would ride me about the weekend with Taylin, and I had to prep for it.

The night before, I tossed and turned, sleep eluding me. I thought about Taylin and if she'd gotten home safely. Granted, I'd know for sure on Monday if she hadn't, but as of right now, it seemed so far away.

"Cas, my man! Glad you could make it!" Brian said before I could make it up the steps.

"Damn, you weren't waiting for me or something, were you?" I laughed.

"Dude, you always bring the best beer," he replied, reaching for one of the cases, and I followed him through the foyer and placed the single case on the bar in his living room.

There was no doubt about that. I refused to drink the orange-tinted water these assholes usually brought.

"The lady's man is in the building!" Carlos said, the room erupting in laughter.

"I'm starving. Where the fuck is the food, and what time does the game start?"

"The pizza and wings will be here any minute, your majesty!" Brian replied.

"After this commercial break, the New England Rebels will be taking on the New York Cougars," the announcer on the TV said.

Good.

New England stomped a mudhole in New York's ass, and the guys had to pay up. They always doubted the Rebels, but 9x out of 10, they always came out on top.

"Pay up, dicks," I said, making my way around the couch with my hand out, collecting their hundred-dollar bills.

I placed them near my face and inhaled the scent. "You smell that, gentlemen? That's the smell of victory."

"Piss off, Cas," Jeremiah grumbled.

"It's been fun, but I have got to get out of here. I have to finalize my lesson plan for the week."

"Enjoy, and Cas?"

"Yeah?"

"Good luck tomorrow," Carlos said, getting up from his seat.

"Why do you say that?"

"I can see it in your face that this weekend didn't go well," he said, following me out to my car.

"It didn't."

"Wanna talk about it?"

"Not really. Everything good with you and Emilia?"

"No, now that she's pregnant, she's hormonal *and* hates my guts."

"Damn, well, maybe we can get together on Thursday. We can drink until we forget."

"Sounds like a plan," he agreed, putting his hand up for our signature handshake.

As I climbed into my SUV, I smacked my hand against the steering wheel.

Snap out of it, Cas. No girl's worth knocking you off your game.

I stayed up half the night drinking Jameson on the rocks and planning. I needed to challenge the class. I needed to challenge *her*, and this would be the best way with linear equations.

Chapter Twelve

Taylin

I NEVER THOUGHT IN a million years that I'd feel this way again. Lost, drained, *useless*. I had decided I would take a walk. Wander around to clear my head and watch on as his SUV disappeared into the abundance of streetlights. He never even bothered to stop or look back. Just as I had expected. There was no fight in him. I was nothing more than another young notch on his belt.

As I walked the empty streets near campus, I heard the faint thump of music off in the distance. I decided to live a little and check it out. Sometimes a girl deserves to be a little reckless.

I took a path and followed the sound until I ended up at a frat house I'd never seen before. Bright lights were flashing underneath the door and there was a crowd of people I hadn't recognized.

I tightened my bag around my body and rocked my hips left to right, grabbing the attention of the two jocks guarding the door.

"Hey there, beautiful. I've never seen you around here before."

"That's too bad. I can be a lot of fun," I replied with a wink.

"I hope to find out," he said, stamping a black flower on the top of my hand. "Enjoy, and if anyone fucks with you, tell them that you're with big Mel."

"Got it, handsome."

I walked inside, and "Shots" by LMFAO was blaring on the speakers. I found the nearest booze table and tossed a few shots back; the liquor was sweet and calm going down.

Shit, this is bad.

I always turned into a version of myself that I would not be proud of in the morning when I drank something sweet.

As the night progressed, I'd forgotten about everything. I danced with guys, girls, made out with guys, girls, and now I was on my way to have sex with some guy named Fernando.

After we made it inside, the first thing I noticed were the littered red plastic cups and empty pizza boxes all over his living space, but it was surprisingly clean once we reached his room. He shut the door behind us, and I found a spot on his twin-sized bed, glancing at him as he started removing his clothing.

He was tall, with smooth, deep bronzed skin and hazel eyes, and his body looked even better without his clothes on. His legs were cut and lean, and all I wanted to do was run my tongue up and down them. The imprint of his cock in his boxers sent an ache straight to my core. He reached on top of his dresser for a condom.

No. What is this feeling? My body heated up and not in a good way. As he neared me, I felt a pain in my gut, and before I could move, bile rose in my throat, and puke came spewing out of my mouth. All over myself, on Fernando's feet, and the floor.

"Shit, I'm so—" Before I could continue, Fernando laughed.

"You could have let me know I grossed you out without puking all over me." He left the room and re-entered with a shampooer and towels. He handed me one, and I tried to clean myself off as best as I could.

"You don't gross me out. Not in any way. I'm sorry."

"Don't worry about it. The bathroom is down the hall. Clean yourself up, and I'll loan you a pair of my sweats and a shirt."

"Really?"

"Yeah," he replied, starting the shampooer as I walked out the door right into a stack of pizza boxes and tripped onto the floor.

Get it together, Taylin. Christ.

I sat inside Fernando's bathroom, counting the tiles on the ceiling as I waited for him to bring me a change of clothes. I was so embarrassed. If he never wanted to see me again, I wouldn't blame him one bit. A subtle knock on the door grabbed my attention.

"Hey, I have the clothes. I'm going to open the door to give them to you."

"Okay," I said, squeezing the towel firmly against my body.

He walked in and had the most sympathetic look on his face. I had no idea why he was so nice to me after desecrating his room in vomit, but I was thankful.

"Here." He smiled, handing me a pair of gray sweats and a white tank.

"Thank you."

He ran out of the room and shut the door as I started to get dressed. I tossed the towel in the hamper and made my way back down toward his room. He had the bed stripped, and the floor was still a bit damp from being shampooed, but it smelled like nothing had even happened.

"I'm so sorry."

"It's okay, really. What's your name?"

"Which one would you prefer? Barf girl? Or Pukezilla?"

He laughed at me again. "I'd prefer the name your parents gave you."

"Taylin." I couldn't help but smile.

He extended his arm out toward mine, and I put my hand in his for a light shake. "Nice to meet you, Taylin."

Fernando had the personality of a saint. Most guys would have kicked my ass out, covered in puke or not.

"Why are you being so nice to me?"

"Because my mother taught me not to be a dick to a pretty girl. No matter the circumstances."

"Your mom sounds awesome."

"She was."

"Was?"

"Yeah, she got sick and died a few years ago."

"Wow, I'm sorry to hear that."

"It's okay. Well, I brought our stuff down to the laundry room; your clothes should be done soon. You're more than welcome to stay, or I can bring them to you. What year are you?" he said, standing directly in front of me, his hands in a relaxed position by his sides.

"A freshman," I replied, twirling a loose curl around my finger.

"I'm a sophomore. What's your first class tomorrow?"

"Algebra," I sighed, bitterness filling my mouth.

"With Mrs. Connors or Mr. Wyatt?"

When he mentioned his name, a chill went down my spine, and I was sure he saw how I reacted.

"It's Mr. Wyatt, isn't it?" he replied, stroking his chin.

"How could you tell?"

"Lucky guess."

"Would you mind bringing them to me? I don't want to ruin anything else in your apartment." Embarrassment flooded my cheeks.

"Okay, I'll see you around."

"Thank you. See ya!"

I grabbed my purse and slipped into my shoes, then walked out of his apartment without a clue of where I was going. I had parked my car somewhere on campus but couldn't remember where.

This shall be fun.

Chapter Thirteen

Caspian

I SAT AT MY desk anxiously waiting for my class to show up. Anxiously waiting for *Taylin* to show up was more like it. After the clusterfuck of a weekend we had, I wasn't even sure if she'd attend my class anymore. Not that it really should have fucking mattered, because I shouldn't have been fucking around with one of my students in the first place. *Idiot.*

As the bell rang, the door flew open, and the students poured in. The seats quickly filled up—all but one. I had a rule, excluding the first few days of school. The last student had five minutes to make it after the second bell rang before the door was locked.

I impatiently watched my clock, and three minutes in, I decided to say fuck it and get things going. I walked toward the door and paused when I saw Taylin in the hallway—talking to a former student of mine—Fernando.

"You have one minute to get in here, Ms. Bradford, before I lock the door."

She turned, startled, and grabbed a bag from his hands, then handed him one in exchange.

What the fuck was that all about?

Her eyes cut toward me like daggers as she stormed by me, shoving me back by the force of her march. I laughed as I shut the door behind us, and she took her seat. Slamming the bag on the floor beside her, she slammed her notebook and pencil down on the desk for extra emphasis.

She's affronted—got it.

As I took to the board to start my lesson, someone loudly cleared their throat. I turned around, and Taylin's arm was raised. The short skirt she was wearing made it hard to keep my cock under control. She purposely opened and crossed her legs, letting me see that she hadn't had on any panties.

"Yes, Ms. Bradford?" I asked, stepping behind the desk to hide my erection.

"Please don't bore us to death. Make it something challenging. I'm ready to take you on."

"Shut up, Taylin! Just because you're super smart doesn't mean you should piss him off and ruin it for the rest of us," Debbie retorted.

I smiled and turned toward the board to start the linear equations, and heard grumbles from every angle behind me.

"Keep it up, and you'll all stay after school for an extra assignment."

After class was over, everyone came down to turn in their worksheet. Well, everyone but *her*. It was just her and I left in the classroom, and you could cut the tension between us with a knife.

"What's your problem?" she asked, flashing me once more.

"What do you mean? And it's not nice to tease me like that."

"I can do what I want. And you didn't even stop or come back to check on me. What if some asshole tried to kidnap me or something?"

"You're a big girl. You can handle it, right? You don't need me to save you—again."

"You know what, Cas, fuck you."

"That's Mr. Wyatt to you. Turn in your assignment, Ms. Bradford, and kindly get the hell out of my classroom."

"Why are you so rude?"

"You're the one that said, 'fuck you,' now, please get out. Better?"

"You're unbelievable," she scoffed. Storming down the aisle and placing her worksheet on top of the stack of papers, she stormed off. Her ass looked glorious, and if I could have had it my way, she would have been bent over my desk getting dicked hard.

"Quit looking at my ass, Mr. Wyatt." I heard as she continued down the hall.

All eyes were on me, and I laughed as I turned around and went back into the room to prepare for my next class.

The rest of the day had passed by in a blur. Nothing of importance happened, but I couldn't get the one thing off my mind that I needed to keep my distance from. I was getting ready to leave for the day and walked out of my classroom.

"Hey, Mr. Wyatt, you have someone in your office," the secretary Gina said over the loudspeaker in my class.

"Be right there."

I made my way down the empty hallway to my office, and when I saw the silhouette of the person in my office, I almost kept going. But I didn't.

"What the fuck do you want?" I barked out just as I threw the door open.

"Cas, listen, we need to talk." *Like hell we did.*

"About what, Melinda?" I asked with a bite, slamming my briefcase down on the desk. She was the last person I expected to show up here. "I told you to stay the fuck away from me."

"I know, but I miss you. I reached out to Brian." She bowed her head in shame.

"For what?" I interrupted. "I'm fine, and even if I weren't, you're the last person I need help from."

"Cas, I know what I did to you was wrong, but I'm sorry. I've changed," she pleaded, reaching for my hand.

"Oh, so you learned to stop being a whore. What took you so long?" I snapped, pulling away. Tears formed in her green eyes.

"That's not fair, Caspian. I never meant to hurt you."

"You say you never meant to hurt me, but you did. Whatever, what do you want?"

She paused, raking her hands through her curly brown hair. She wore a skirt that hugged her hips and a fitted blouse with the top few buttons open to expose her breasts.

"I wanted to see if maybe we could go out to Jillian's and hang out. You know, reconnect and see if there's anything still there between us."

A deep throaty laugh erupted from me, and she looked mortified. "This has got to be a joke. Are we on an episode of Punk'd? I would never take you back. Now get the fuck out of my office." *She never fucking listens to me.*

This was the day. I was going to ask Melinda to be my wife. I had the guys help me decorate our apartment with flowers and candles. I had her favorite bottle of Moscato chilling, and I had my sharpest suit on. I was on my way to pick her up from her sister's house and felt like I was going to fucking puke. We'd been together for four years, and I knew she was it for me.

I pulled up in front of Julie's place and saw a Jeep that I'd never seen before. Julie was into guys with money, so I figured it was her new billionaire flavor of the month.

I grabbed a small bouquet out of the backseat and made my way to the front door. I heard loud banging and opened the front door, rushing in to see something I never expected to see in my fucking life.

Melinda's legs were in the air, and a guy I thought was only her best friend was pounding the fuck out of her.

"Melinda, what the fuck?"

"Oh shit, Cas, I can explain."

"Fuck you, Chauncy," I shouted, lunging toward him and connecting my fist with his jaw.

His tall frame fell back onto the floor, and I looked down at Melinda, trying to cover herself with a blanket from the back of the couch.

"No need to cover up now."

"Cas, I don't know what to say." She was panting and had the audacity to look sad.

"There's nothing to say. Here I was, getting ready to pledge my life to a whore. Guess I dodged a bullet there."

"Wait, what?"

"Bye, Melinda, maybe you can spend forever with the asshole I socked in the face." I punched him once more for good measure before heading back to the car.

Never again will I let anyone in. Just sex, no strings, no attachments.

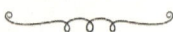

"You need me, Cas."

"I don't need anyone, so fuck off!"

She looked at me with her sad puppy dog eyes and turned on her heel to leave.

"You'll regret turning me away," she snarked over her shoulder.

"I doubt it."

As she slammed the door shut behind her, I swiped everything off my desk and onto the floor.

Fuck.

"Is everything okay, Mr. Wyatt?" Gina asked.

"No, but I'll be alright. Next time you see or hear from this woman, give me a heads up, okay?

"Okay."

"Have a good night, Gina."

Chapter Fourteen

"HEY, PUKEZILLA!" THE NICKNAME stopped me in my tracks, and my cheeks heated with embarrassment.

"That's my name, don't wear it out," I said as I turned around, nearly crashing head-on into Fernando's chest.

"Well, hello," he greeted with a smile.

"Hi," I replied, looking up into his eyes, quickly taking a step back.

"So, what are you up to tonight?" he asked.

"I don't know, studying probably. Why what's up?"

"Well, I thought maybe we could hang out."

"Really? I figured you'd never want to see me again."

"Why not?"

"Because—I barfed all over you and your room, need I say more?" I questioned, my voice barely an inaudible whisper.

"Hence why I want to get to know the real you. Yes, I could judge you based on one bad night, but where's the fun in that?"

Fernando was proving himself to be a diamond in the rough. He showed genuine interest in me, although I thoroughly embarrassed myself in front of him. He had every reason not to be seen with me, yet he wanted to give it another shot, which made me quite a bit nervous. But at least the awkward stage had already passed, so what did I have to lose?

"Okay, take my number and tell me when, where, and what time, and I'll be there."

"Sounds good. It's a date!"

After exchanging numbers with him, I heard a roar of commotion coming from the opposite direction as I continued down the hall. As I followed the sound closely, I quickly figured out it was coming from Mr. Wyatt's office.

No way, I am not getting involved in that.

I saw a nicely dressed woman with curly hair and heels hightailing it from his office, and I immediately felt something in the pit of my stomach, and I was not too fond of it. *Let it go, Tay. It's not worth getting your heart broken over.*

I took one last look at myself in the mirror, admiring the long dark, flowy dress I had on. I twisted the back of my hair up and pinned it, letting the curls flow from the top of my head. Fernando texted me the details, and I was on my way to some place called The Lodge. The parking lot was packed, and live music was blaring in the air. I luckily found a spot close to the front of the building and made my way up the stone steps to the front door. As I walked inside, I caught a glimpse of Fernando as he waited for me. He was sporting a nice collared shirt with a relaxed pair of jeans.

"You look beautiful," he said, handing me a single rose I hadn't even noticed he was holding.

"Thank you; you clean up nice." I smiled up at him.

"Thank you."

The hostess seated us at a small table near the bar, and as we took our seats, I noticed a beautiful, tattooed singer on the stage belting her heart out. Her long dark hair flowed over her shoulders, and the black and white portraits and flowers on her arms were a beautiful reflection of her soul. She had an edgy, rebellious look, with her septum pierced, and I loved it. She sang something along the lines of "Is there such a thing as happily ever after?"

I don't know why that line hit me so hard. Maybe because I never thought I could find someone to give me that happily ever after.

"Tay, are you okay?"

"Yeah, why?"

"You're zoning out. Do you like this song?"

"Yeah, something like that. Anyway, let's order. I'm starving!" I said, trying to change the subject while listening to the lyrics.

Let's get lost in this world
Thoughts that I feel out of control
I'm feeling alone and so cold
An emotional block is so bold

The heat of the night
Your arms around me so tight
I can't explain how I feel
Is there a chance for our bond to be real?
Are you ready for it?
My heart is open, and I'm ready for you
Our chapter of love to be so honest, so true
It's time for a happily ever after
To have our happily ever after

After a quick bite, Fernando and I decided to go out onto the patio. It was a chilly fall night, but not too cold to enjoy the view. I learned a lot about him over dinner, and I couldn't wrap my head around the reason he was single. There had to be a flaw somewhere. He appeared to be too damn perfect, and I knew men like this were too good to be true.

"So, tell me something you dislike, Fernando."

"I dislike it when people are dishonest with me. It's a real pet peeve of mine, and I can't seem to let it go," he replied.

"Give me an example."

"Well, for instance, if I'm trying to get to know a girl. I like to know upfront if they're with someone or interested in someone."

"Why?"

"Well, because it determines how hard I should try. I know that sounds messed up, but it's true. If your heart is elsewhere, I know I need to protect mine," he said, gazing deeply into my eyes. That feeling of despair crept up my spine. "What about you?

My shoulders tensed, and I drew in a sharp breath. "I dislike it when people play with your emotions. I dislike it when they get your hopes up, make you feel wanted and appreciated, all to turn around and treat you like a piece of shit despite the bond that had formed between the two of you." My words were so rushed and cold, it wouldn't take a genius to know I had already experienced all of this. And *currently* was.

"Ouch, sounds like someone hurt you," he replied, extending his hand out for mine.

"Yes, I've been hurt on many occasions, but they're all a learning experience, you know?"

"Yes, I've gone through my fair share of heartache." He bowed his head, releasing my hand.

"Tell me about one," I asked out of curiosity. He was so kind, I couldn't fathom how someone could ever hurt him.

"Well, when I was seventeen, there was this girl who was my high school sweetheart at the time. I thought she was going to be my forever girl. We had been inseparable since freshman year, and I thought she was the one. I was on my way to her parents' place to ask her to be my date for our senior prom, and when I got there, the front door was wide open. There were clothes sprinkled all over the house leading up to her room. I walk upstairs to find her sleeping with my best friend, Ryan. At the time, I realized he was never really my friend; he was a pig. But he always got all the girls. Well, I thought I had the off-limits one, but in the end, he took her too."

"I'm so sorry." I could feel the pain in his voice as he told the story. Like he was reliving it all over again.

"It's okay, lesson learned. What about you?"

"Well, I dated my ex, Emmett, just shy of three years. I was head-over-heels in love with him. It wasn't about his looks because we clicked and bonded over so many different things, but he became physically abusive as the years went on. I learned from his mother that he had been flirting with and kissing other girls at work, and one day I finally got the nerve to leave him. He had been lying to me saying he was working late, and lo and behold; he was over another girl's house. He was acting as if he wasn't even with me. So I called him and told him that I wanted to meet up and talk. He went all the way home, and I never showed and broke up with him on the phone instead. I couldn't bring myself to face him because I knew I wouldn't have been as strong as I should of that day. I almost gave him my virginity, but I was glad I waited."

"Wow, you are so strong, Tay. I'm proud of you, and we hardly know each other." Affection glowed in his eyes. "That took a lot of courage to get away. If you don't mind me asking, how did your friends and family take this?"

"I hid most of it from my family because I'm sure they would have tried to kill him. My best friend, Anna, knew, and she would help me with makeup to cover up the bruises. He never hit me in my face or anything, but it still sucked."

"Well, if I ever see him, I will gladly teach him a lesson on your behalf, of course." He flashed me a comforting smile.

"Thank you. I appreciate that. You seem strong and well-rounded yourself."

"So, what do you want to do now?"

As much as I wanted to hang out with him more because I felt something shift between the two of us, I knew I had to go. I didn't want to start getting attached. And being around all these lovebirds made me feel a certain type of way.

"Honestly, I think we should get going. I need to study, and we both have classes tomorrow." I took a look around the patio, and a few couples were talking and eating, and they were sitting at glass tables with giant umbrellas overhead. A beautiful stone pattern made up the ground, and the foliage in the background tied it all together. It was beautiful out there.

As we made our way inside, I stopped to find out that the live singer's name was Dauphinee. I was going to look her up and listen to more of her music. She had a lively, soulful voice, and the rasp tied it all together. I could hear her sing for hours. Her lyrics rocked me to my core, and I needed more of it.

Fernando walked me to my car and gave me a friendly hug. I knew I had to take things slow with him because I was damaged goods. He seemed to have it all together, and I felt that I was only pretending that I did.

Get it together, Tay. You can do this!

A few days passed, and I kept my contact with Cas minimal. Occasionally, I wore something that made him stare, but I knew the further I distanced myself, the less he'd affect me. Fernando and I started to bond more. I had spent the night at his place the night before and met his roommate, Kyle, and his girlfriend, Marie. They were both a lovely, cute blond couple. They finished each other's sentences and shit. Yes, they were *that* couple. The kind that makes you sick if you're around them too long.

Fernando met me in the campus parking lot and brought me breakfast. I told him most days, I didn't eat before school because I always woke up late, and I was not a morning person by any means. He'd told me about some bakery near his dorm and told me I hadn't lived unless I had their confetti donut and French vanilla swirl coffee.

"Thank you so much," I said as I pulled the glazed donut with sprinkles out of the bag. I took a bite, and it practically melted in my mouth. "Oh my God, that's delicious." I quickly devoured it.

"You weren't hungry or anything, were you?" he teased.

"What made you think that?" I smiled, wiping my mouth with the back of my hand.

"Oh, nothing." He laughed. "Do you want the coffee?"

"Of course. I promise I won't devour the cup." I giggled.

He handed me the large cup, and I smiled as I made my way up the path to the side door. "Thank you!" I yelled to him as he split off in another direction. He gave me a one-sided grin, and I continued inside.

"Aw, did your new boyfriend buy you that?"

"He sure did. Why do you care? Don't you have some students to harass? Or better yet, a curly-haired woman to worry about?"

A stern look formed on his face after I mentioned the woman. "I'll see you in class, Ms. Bradford."

I was not too fond of the way he said my name. He had this gravelly rasp, and it sent chills right through me.

I was on time for school for once and sat in the student lounge. The week was almost over, and I needed to get out and relieve some stress.

Me: I need to go out tonight. Girls' night?

Anna: Sure, I found this spot in RI. It's usually pretty packed, and the drinks are top-notch.

Me: Great, who's our DD?

Anna: Jalia!

Me: Perfect. See you later!

Jalia and Anna were outside my parents' place, beeping the horn like a bunch of impatient psychos. I don't know why they just didn't come inside and say *hi* to my parents. They loved them. I guessed they were both dressed like sluts and didn't want my brother to see them like that. Being Mr. Conservative and whatnot.

I gave myself a once-over in the mirror and grabbed my long peacoat. I didn't need to hear it on the way out the door either.

"Where are you off to?" my mom asked.

"Going out with the girls."

"On a school night?" *Here we go.*

"Yes, Mom! See you later! I'll be home in the morning."

"Be careful, please, Tay."

"I will."

I ran out the door and down the sidewalk to Jalia's Camry.

"Sup bitches!" I said as I opened the door and slid into the backseat.

"Finally! We were about to leave without you," Jalia said.

"I know. My mom caught me on the way out."

"Oh no. Well, at least it wasn't Tine. You'd still be in there." Anna laughed.

"No shit. So what's the name of this club?"

"Diamond Lounge."

"Love it!"

It took a little under an hour to get there, and the line had already wrapped around the corner.

"How the hell are we going to get in?" I questioned.

"Bitch, do you not know me? There will never be lines for us," Anna retorted.

"You're right, my bad."

Jalia parked the car, and we all got out, heels clicking together in unison on the pavement. We sashayed by the line, and there were two bouncers in the front. Anna approached the biggest one. He had a name badge with the word Lamont scribbled across, and he didn't say a word. He lifted the rope, looked at her ass, and let us all in. Grumbles came from the front and back of the line, and I laughed as we disappeared into the bright lights and heavy fog.

We all dropped our jackets off at the coat check counter and continued inside. The club was beautiful. There were purple couches off to the side and a massive pool in the middle of the floor, and I'd never seen anything like that before. Two girls were dancing in elevated cages above the water, and around the bend was a huge dance floor. I *wanna try that.*

"DJ Lance Dub will be on in ten minutes, so ladies, get your drinks in now because you need to be on the dance floor shaking your beautiful asses!" a guy announced over the mic.

We sat down at the bar, and the bartender was sexy as hell. His hair was slicked back, and he was tall with a nice tight white shirt on, the indent of his rippling muscles flexing as he shook a martini shaker.

"What can I get you ladies?" He flashed us a dimpled smile.

"Three Bahama Mamas," I said with a smile.

"Tay, are you crazy? You know what happens when you drink sweet stuff," Anna said.

"So? maybe I need to forget for a little while."

"This is my only drink, and don't push it, or we'll be spending the night here!" Jalia shouted.

The lights dimmed as we got our drinks, and the water in the middle started glowing different fluorescent colors as the girls danced harder. DJ Lance Dub came on stage with this yellow tracksuit and big thick frameless glasses. "Y'all ready to get turnt the fuck up?"

"Hell yes!" the crowd replied.

I downed my drink and made my way to the middle of the dance floor. He dropped a real dope beat, and I lost myself in the sea of sounds echoing through the speakers.

A pair of hands wrapped around my waist, and I relaxed, allowing my body to continue to go with the flow. Whoever was behind me was keeping up with me, and it was refreshing. Usually, I'm stuck with a guy who has no rhythm, but they did try.

"What are you drinking tonight?" he whispered in my ear.

"Bahama Mama."

"I'll make sure they keep coming if you continue to dance with me."

"We'll see. You may not be able to keep up with me all night."

"Guess, we'll have to make a bet and see," he said. He spun me around and grabbed me close, his dark eyes connecting with mine. He flashed a devious smile, and I nearly melted into a puddle.

"What's your name?" I asked as the beat slowed down.

"Harry, yours?"

"Taylin."

"You're beautiful, Taylin."

"Thank you."

"Work" by Ciara came on, and it was like I had lost control of my body. My hair flipped from side to side as I rolled my hips around in a circle. Harry found the rhythm and stayed with me until our bodies nearly touched the floor.

The drinks kept flowing, and I had lost count of how many I had. I danced so much that the DJ called me out and told me to join another girl on stage.

"Now, ladies, I've been watching you dance since I've got on these turntables, and you both have been killing it. Am I right, fellas?"

The crowd erupted in cheers. I looked over and saw my girls beaming from ear to ear.

"Now, ladies, it's amateur night, and although neither of you are amateurs, we want to invite you to dance in the cages. Don't worry; you'll both be compensated if you can handle it."

"Shit, I'm game!" I yelled. The other girl agreed. Two guys helped us off the stage, and the cages lowered. A small platform cascaded over the water, and the previous girls exited. So *that's how they got in.*

I was going to be trapped in a metal contraption suspended over a pool of water. I climbed in one side, and the other girl rose in the other. Security bars were inside, and the metal chains pulled us up as the platform disappeared. It was scary, yet invigorating at the same time.

The liquid courage flowing through my veins and the beats vibing around the club made me feel alive. I danced as hard and as sexy as I could, and I was drunk and feeling divine.

After my stint in the cage, they let us down and gave us a couple of hundred dollars each. I slid the bills into my purse and found my friends back at the bar.

"You rocked it, Tay!" Jalia cheered.

"I did, right? That was scary as hell, but exhilarating at the same time."

"You couldn't tell. You looked like a damn natural up there," Anna said, bouncing in place with excitement.

"Yes, she did," a deep voice said behind me. "Bartender, can I get a few more rounds for these beautiful ladies?"

I was so drunk I couldn't even make out the guy's face. It was dark, and the lights were still swirling; the haze was robust and thicker.

"I'll have a water, but you can get these two as drunk as you please," Jalia said.

"Will do."

Chapter Fifteen

"DUDE, HURRY THE FUCK up!" I yelled, blaring on the horn.

Carlos emerged from his apartment, slow as hell—but he did look nice for once. "Sorry, I couldn't decide what to wear. Emilia agreed to start talking to me again, but then she cussed me out when I didn't accept her offer right away."

Oy vey.

Carlos made us way later than I wanted to be. They suspended new girls over the water when we got to the club. Both of them could move their hips, capturing the attention of many, but one in particular, I couldn't take my eyes off of. Her curly hair bounced side to side as she shook her ass, my cock throbbing in anticipation as I watched on. She was up there dancing like she'd been training to do this her entire life. And as soon as she was free, I was going to buy her a drink and make her mine.

Carlos and I tossed back Patron shots, and I felt pretty buzzed. The girls descended from the cages, and I watched as the girl I wanted made her way back to her friends at the bar. I moved quickly in their direction as Carlos continued to dance with a rhythmless skank.

I bought her and her friends a round of drinks. "Would you like to try those moves out on me?" I whispered against the nape of her neck, inhaling the familiar scent of vanilla.

She paused and shook her head. "Think you can handle it, Mr. Wyatt?"

"How did you know my name?"

She turned around, and after I got a good look at her, I realized why I was so attracted to her. I'd already had her. *Fuck.*

I'd come out here to avoid my students and run into one anyway. *What the fuck is going on this year?*

"Cat got your tongue? Or are you afraid I'll break you?" she taunted, sliding a cherry into her mouth and removing it from the stem with her tongue.

I grabbed her by her arm and yanked her back onto the dance floor. A song by J-Lo and Pitbull came on, and she pressed her ass against me, her hips circling as we danced as one. My dick didn't stand a chance. *This isn't going to end well.*

When the slow part came on, she broke our hold and spun around, looking me in my eyes. Her arms ran down her own body as she moved to the beat. This girl was intoxicating as fuck.

I pulled her back to me and turned her around, switching roles. I could roll my hips too.

"Taylin."

"Cas."

"We need to stop this," I said, my fingers tracing an invisible line down her arms.

"Why? You know you want it," she whispered against my skin, placing her lips on my neck. "No strings, no attachments."

"Yes, but you're drunk out of your fucking mind right now, and that wouldn't be fair of me to take advantage of you like that, would it?" I retorted.

"So, it never stopped you before?" she said, her tongue traveling up the side of my neck.

"Stop. I didn't come all the way out here for this. You were not supposed to be here, and this is not going to fucking happen. So, enjoy the dance. Enjoy the free drinks, and fuck off," I bit out, pushing her away.

"What the fuck is your problem? Am I not good enough for you? Is that it? Is it because I'm not that bitch I saw coming from your office the other day?" She spoke with her hands, as she stomped in place.

"You don't know her or what you're even saying right now," I roared. "You'd better stop before you royally piss me off."

"Fuck you!" she yelled, pushing me back.

"Calm the fuck down, Taylin!" Other people were starting to stop and stare at all the commotion.

"Or what?" Her nostrils flared as her arms crossed her chest.

"Or I'll have to punish you."

"Whatever," she spat, her eyes rolling.

"Girls, take your friend home before we both do something we regret."

"Like what, Mr. Wyatt? You already fucked me; what else could we possibly regret at this point?" She was right, but this couldn't go on any longer.

She stood in front of me and grabbed my dick in front of everyone. "I already know what it feels like, so give it to me."

I placed my hand around her throat and told her no. "You're my fucking student!" I yelled as her friend linked her arm with her. "Let's go, Taylin. You're causing a scene."

"That's just a fucking excuse at this point!" she yelled, backing through the crowd. Her friend whispered something in her ear. "Fuck him," she replied, her eyes boring a hole into mine.

"What the fuck!" Carlos placed his hand on my shoulder to calm me down.

"Dude, I don't think I've ever seen you turn anyone down like that before. Especially someone as hot as her," Carlos said.

"Yeah, but I can't keep breaking my fucking rules because I can't keep my dick in my pants. She will learn that you can't always get what you want, and that's final! Now take the keys to my SUV. You're driving!"

"Aye aye, captain!"

As soon as my head hit the pillow, my mind wouldn't stop racing. All I could see was Taylin's body. The curves of her hips winding slowly. The way her long wavy hair moved in slow motion. The way my cock twitched behind my zipper as we danced, and the way she stood up to me in front of everyone. *Fuck.*

I pulled my cock out of my boxers and ran my hand up and down the shaft, pleasuring myself to the replay of dancing with Taylin. Her tits were immaculate in the low-cut dress she had on. And the vanilla scent she wore always hit me in ways it shouldn't have—like an aphrodisiac. Her skin was glowing, almost as if she had added golden sparkles all over herself. I came hard as I imagined her bent over on my bed, her ass splayed in the air, her pussy dripping just for me.

I couldn't sleep for shit, and I felt like a dick, but I had to stand my ground with her because we couldn't keep going like that, and it wasn't right. I could lose my fucking job if anyone from the school ever caught wind that we were both at the club that night.

"Excuse my French, but you look like shit, Cas," Ronaldo, the history teacher, said as I refilled my mug with black coffee.

There were so many smart-ass remarks that I could have said, but I chose to ignore him instead.

"Rough night?"

"Nope. Fantastic night," I answered sarcastically. *Guess he can't take a fucking hint.*

"Well, I'd hate to see you on a bad night."

"You won't. Bye, Ronaldo."

I picked up my briefcase and slugged my way down the hall, trying to make it into my classroom without falling asleep on the lockers.

The bell rang as soon as I sat down, and I wanted to tear it off the fucking wall. The students marched in looking all peppy and cheery for a Friday morning, and it made me want to vomit.

"Sit down, shut up, and listen up!" I roared, and they all scrambled to find their seats.

"Who pissed in your Cheerios?" some random asshole questioned.

"Your mother, after I pounded the fuck out of her and left this morning."

The secondary bell rang, and she walked in. She had a scarf covering her head, a pair of dark shades that rested on her face, and baggy sweatpants that still showed off her curves, as she walked a little slower than usual.

She barely looked in my direction, and I knew I had fucked up. *And so, it begins.*

Chapter Sixteen

Taylin

WHAT THE FUCK WERE *you thinking, Tay?*

That sentence swirled around in my brain from when we left the club until the sun came up. I couldn't sleep. He rejected me. He actually fucking rejected me. I thought for sure we would have ended the night together. I couldn't stop thinking about the way he touched me as we danced. And the way his eyes darkened as he ran his fingers down my arms, sending chills throughout my entire body.

I tried to put myself out there, and I failed. I'm glad I was able to stand up for myself, though. I didn't care how much of a scene I caused. I wasn't gonna be treated like some deep dark secret, especially if we weren't anywhere near the school.

I fought with myself all morning about going to school. Anna called me, but I hit ignore because I didn't want to talk about any of this. I usually attempt to look decent when I go to school, but today was a *fuck it* kind of day.

As I entered the classroom, he looked just as bad as I had, and it brought a smile to my face, knowing he was probably up half the night too. Most likely regretting his decision. Maybe he had done me a favor by not sleeping with me. Deep down, I knew this couldn't continue because I would fall for him. My heart couldn't decipher the difference between love and infatuation, especially when I got my socks blown off.

Although he looked like shit, he was surprisingly easier on everyone that day. He didn't yell much except when we all first came into the room. He put on movies and kept his head down on the desk, as did I. Occasionally, I looked at him to see if he was looking at me. Most times, he was, and the way he looked at me now was different, and I couldn't quite put my finger on it.

When the bell rang, he waved everyone out, but of course, I went down to talk to him. A *glutton for punishment, I know.*

"Didn't sleep much?" I asked.

"Why does it matter?" He leaned back in his chair with a huff.

"Because you look like pure shit right now."

"It's because of you, Taylin. Because of last night. I don't know what the fuck is happening, but you need to leave!"

he said, slamming his hands down on the desk.

"Cas don't be like that," I replied softly, reaching for one of his hands.

"It's Mr. Wyatt. Please leave, Ms. Bradford."

Ugh, this man was so hot and cold. I know he felt what I was feeling, and I've had it since we met in Vegas. There's this shitty pull from the universe that keeps bringing me into this man's orbit, and I wish I had the power to break free from his forcefield.

"Fine," I seethed, slamming my fist down on his desk and walked out.

As I made my way down the hall, I felt everyone's eyes on me, but I ignored them. I just wanted to slip through the cracks of the worn laminate and disappear forever.

"Taylin?"

I heard a familiar voice and tried to walk faster. I couldn't face him, not now. Not like this.

"Taylin, please wait up!"

I stopped, drawing in a long breath before exhaling. "What is it, Fernando?"

"I was worried about you. You were texting me some weird things last night." His shoulders dropped.

"I was? I was so drunk last night, I don't even remember using my phone if we're being honest."

"I see. Well, I just wanted to make sure you were okay," he said, removing my sunglasses so he could gaze into my eyes.

"Please put them back on; the light hurts."

"Sorry, I just wanted to see your eyes. The eyes always tell the truth, even if the lips are spewing lies." *Why does he even care?*

"I see. Can I go now? I promise we'll talk later." *Although I rather not.*

"I hope so. I need you to be honest with me when we do."

Shit, what did I text him?

I walked into my art elective and sat in the back, trying to fish my phone out of my pocket.

I looked through the texts I'd sent him, and my heart sank in my chest.

What have you done, Taylin?

After my last class, I decided to meet Fernando at the bakery near his dorm to clear the air and get some food. I'd barely eaten, and the hangover was draining the life out of me.

He was standing in front of Edward's Bakery, slouching against the bricks. I felt like complete shit.

"Hey," he said as I stood in front of him.

"Hey."

"Let's grab some food. I'm starving," he said before I could think to start the conversation I knew we were about to have.

"Sounds like a good idea."

He opened the front door and held it for me to go inside. We found a booth in the back by the window and sat across from one another.

"Fernando," I started.

"What may I get for y'all today?" the waitress interrupted.

Rude.

"Two of the greasiest things you have on the menu, with fries and a Coke," Fernando replied.

The sparkle he usually had in his hazel eyes had dulled, and I knew his feelings were hurt. *This was not my intention.*

"So what's the deal, Taylin? I told you I need honesty. If you're interested in or sleeping with someone, even if it's just casual sex, I don't want us to waste each other's time." *When did I sign up for a relationship with this guy? I thought we were just getting to know each other.*

"Things are complicated right now, Fernando. I like you. You're the kind of guy I need to have in my life, but I always attract the pompous assholes that I have no business with. Before school started, something happened, one night that was supposed to remain one night. That night haunted me for some fucked up reason, and the guy and I found each other again. None of it was planned."

"So, are you going to pursue things with him? Because, by your texts, you seemed pretty pissed that he wasn't gonna fuck you and that no one would ever be able to pleasure you the way he had." He sniffed, his eyes tearing up.

Oh my fucking God. What did I get myself into?

"I'm sorry, I don't know why I even sent that to you." Tears rolled down my cheeks, and I lifted my shades to wipe them away with a napkin from the table. "I can't lie to you and tell you that I don't want to pursue anything with him, but the problem isn't about wanting; it's that—"

"What?" He leaned over the table, as if to try to hear me better through my tear-filled confession.

"It's that I shouldn't *want* him, and I shouldn't *want* to pursue anything with him. He's no good for me; our relationship would be seen as forbidden. But deep down, I know I want him."

"Okay, and what about us?"

I didn't know how to answer that. I knew him just as much as I knew Cas, if we were being honest. I enjoyed spending time with Fernando, and he was kind-hearted and so nice. He was gorgeous, and I was sure he could become a complete douche if he wanted to, and girls would still flock to him.

"Here are two Philly cheesesteaks with the works and my special hangover cure drink and two Cokes," the waitress said as she and another waitress placed our food and drinks down in front of us.

"Thank you so much," I replied.

"You're welcome, and here are your fries," she said as another person from the back came out and handed her a large basket of steak fries.

Fernando smiled at the waitress, and his eyes locked with mine. The feeling of despair settled in the pit of my stomach, and I knew I couldn't continue with this. I wanted to, but I didn't want to hurt anyone. And I knew if I tried to be with him, Cas would be in the back of my mind, and I wouldn't be able to fight the chance to have him if I could.

I popped a fry in my mouth and tried to choke back my thoughts before saying something I regretted.

"Do I have to make a decision right now?"

"No, but I expect to know something by Monday." I could do that...I think.

"Deal."

"I'm gonna hurt him, Anna. I can feel it deep in my core. I can't be with someone like him," I said as I sat down on Anna's bed. She asked me to come over after I had left the diner with Fernando.

"And why not? He's hot, and he's smart. He cleans! I mean, you told me he cleaned up your puke and washed your clothes, and I'd marry him on the spot if I were in your shoes."

"I know, but—"

"Cas has fucked your brains out, and you're conflicted," she said, with sarcasm in her tone.

"Yep."

"Let's be honest here for a minute. The last time you went based on sex and not instincts, you got hurt—badly. That man destroyed you, and you weren't even together that long."

"Are you talking about Miles?"

"Yes, Miles." Miles was a quick fling after Xavier and I broke up. I tried to listen to Anna's advice about finding a rebound to get over him and got myself into trouble. Miles was toxic as fuck, with toxic dick. Sex with him was so good, but I lost all concept of common sense. I knew he had other women, but I couldn't leave him alone for a while. I did smarten up after two months and blocked him on all social media.

"And now you want to get with someone with similar characteristics. This one is actually worse, and he can't even be seen in person with you without risking everything. I love you, girl, but I don't think it's worth it. Maybe you should leave them both alone and focus on school."

"That sounds good, but I don't know if I can do that. One of them, I see five days a week, and the other, I'll occasionally pass by in the halls. Either way, I'm fucked, and in the end, someone is going to get hurt."

"Sucks to be you right now, dude. I mean, if you want, I can take Fernando off your hands."

"Shut up, bitch!" I laughed, whacking her on the shoulder.

I decided to stay home the entire weekend and really think about my options. *Do I go with responsible Fernando, or careless Cas?*

That decision was more brutal than figuring out what to get my mother on Mother's Day.

The girls had begged me to go out, but I was still feeling like shit from my girls' gone wild night. I would be up for it any other time, but my body had yet to recover, which was so weird. I felt achy all over. My mom noticed I was moving slower than usual and yelled at me to soak in some Epsom salt, and I should have listened.

"Honey, are you okay?" she asked, her tone soft.

"I don't know anymore, Mom." I shook my head, my shoulders starting to slump with the weight I felt on them.

"What's going on? I feel like you don't tell me anything anymore."

She was right. My mom and I were pretty close up until this point. I had no way to tell her the truth about the situation, but I guess I could give her another scenario-sans teacher.

"I know, and I'm sorry. Things have gotten pretty complicated in the love department."

"How so?" she asked, sitting down on my bed beside me.

"Well, you know I went to Vegas for Liz's wedding?"

"Yes."

"Well, I met someone there. It was more of a hookup, and I didn't expect it to have such an impact on me. We didn't exchange information, and I didn't see him again after that. He was a jerk, to be honest, but he left an impression on me."

"I see. He gave you his magic stick, and now you don't know how to act." She giggled.

"Mom! That's not funny, but it is kind of true. Anyway, so I never expected to see him again, come to find out he lives here, and he goes to my school."

"Oh, so this is like a second-chance love affair?" Her lashes fluttered.

"I wouldn't quite call it that." I pursed my lips.

"Did he remember you at least?" She gave me a puppy dog look, placing her hand on my shoulder.

"He did, and he was shocked to see me."

"So? What's the problem?" She shrugged with narrowed eyes, like this shouldn't even be an issue.

"It's complicated. We shouldn't be together."

"I'm afraid to ask, but I feel like you won't tell me." A glint of sadness showed in her eyes.

She was right. "No, I can't, but then I met someone else."

"And?" Her ears perked up.

"He's amazing. Smart, handsome, funny."

"He's too nice, and you're not into him." She giggled.

"You know me so well."

"So, what's the problem?"

"I don't know what to do."

"I say, take a break from both situations. Focus on school, your friends, and whatever other academics you have to do, and worry about boys later. Whoever is meant for you will be with you. Somehow, someway, it'll all work out. I promise." She pulled me into a hug, and it opened up the floodgates. She was right, but I couldn't stop crying. It was almost as if I had a major release that I didn't realize I needed.

Chapter Seventeen

Caspian

BANG.

Bang.

"Cas, are you alive in there? I haven't heard from you all weekend!" Carlos yelled from somewhere outside my house.

I pulled the blankets from over my face and looked at the clock. *What the fuck is he talking about? It's only Saturday, isn't it?*

I slid my carcass out of bed and dragged my feet until I reached the door, and I unlocked it and turned back to head to bed.

"Dude, put some clothes on!" he yelled, covering his eyes.

"You came to my place. Feast your eyes on my glorious ass or perish," I deadpanned.

"Do you know what day it is?" *Does it fucking matter?*

"Saturday," I said, sliding my robe over my shoulders to shut him up.

"Incorrect. It's Sunday. Have you been asleep that entire time?"

"I guess I have, shit."

"Are you alright?"

"Yeah, why?" *Can't a man sleep the weekend away without something being wrong?*

"You never just fall off the grid like that. Something's got you distracted, bro."

"I partied a little too hard that night at the club."

"Maybe, but I think you're drunk on something else."

"What do you mean?"

"I don't know, Cas. The last time you were like this was after Melinda."

"Fuck Melinda. She came to my job the other day, by the way."

"Are you serious? Why?"

"She said that I needed her." *I didn't need shit.*

"She's the last person you need right now."

"No shit," I replied, sliding a pod into my coffee machine.

"Anything new happen between you and that girl, Taylin?" His brow raised.

Hearing him say her name made my blood boil. No other man had the right to annunciate her name in my presence, not even my best friend. When he saw the seething look on my face, his eyes widened, and his jaw went slack.

"Shit, I mean, the one that shall not be named." *That's right, correct yourself.*

"Well, as you know, she was at the club that night, and I turned her down. I thought about her all night, dropped loads of nuts visualizing her, then I dismissed her like trash when I saw her in class the next day."

"Damn, that's cold, even for you." *Is it really, though?*

"I know. It's just, I could lose my job for consorting with her. Even though the first time I didn't know. I should have known better the second time, but I still did it anyway. I couldn't let it continue a third time. It was a fucked up situation, man."

"So. You don't have to be with her. And both times you fucked, you weren't even in Massachusetts, so technically, I don't see what's wrong. Keep your sex life away from your home life, and everything will be fine."

"Carlos, your logic and reasoning suck." Although, he could have been on to something.

"I know, but I can tell you want her, man. You need to fix this before you damage her or yourself beyond repair."

"I know."

The problem is that I wish I knew how.

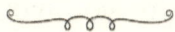

"You look much better today, Cas. Horrible night?"

"Shut up, Ronaldo."

It was time to get back on track and torture my class again. They had a nice fun break last week, and now it was time to make their brains hurt.

I walked down the hall toward my class with a bit of extra pep in my step that day. Before I reached the door, I felt a chill in the air.

"Cas?"

I froze in place. My palms sweated as my throat went dry. "What are you doing back here?"

"We really need to talk." *Un-fucking-believable.*

"Melinda, I have a class to teach in five fucking minutes."

"Please, just hear me out." Sorrow closed up her throat. *I wish you would hear me out when I told you to fuck off.*

I clenched my teeth and turned to head to my office. She followed behind and shut the door on her way in.

"Don't bother sitting. Say whatever the fuck it is you have to say and leave." I slammed my briefcase on the desk. *This is such a waste of my time.*

She hesitated before speaking, and I knew this wouldn't be good. "I attempted to kill myself multiple times after you broke up with me." Her voice was breaking.

"And why do I need to know this?" Heat seethed through my body.

"I was pregnant, Cas."

"So you tried to kill yourself while pregnant?" *I don't even know why I asked.*

"I tried to kill myself after you wouldn't talk to me. I didn't know I was pregnant at first."

I scratched my head. "So let me get this straight; you just fucking said you tried to kill yourself multiple times, but you didn't know you were pregnant at first?"

"Cas, I don't know how to answer this, okay? When I found out I was pregnant I tried to reach out." Tears pooled in her eyes, and she could hardly move.

Pregnant or not, I still didn't believe it was mine. She must have seen the thought flash across my face.

"It was yours."

"You're a fucking liar." My throat tightened in disbelief.

"I'm not, Cas. We were expecting—"

I couldn't listen to anymore of the shit spewing from her lips before a wave of nausea hit me. "Shut up. Shut up right now. Why, after all this time, would you tell me that? It's not like this was yesterday; it was two years ago. Seeing you fucking Chauncy fucked me up. And now you come in here with this bullshit? Do you think if I knew you were pregnant, things would have changed? I wanted to marry you, hell I had everything ready to bear my heart and soul to you, but you decided to spread your thighs apart for another man. Hell, how would I even know it was mine? It could have been his. I don't know how long you were sneaking around behind my fucking back."

"I couldn't handle the guilt, and I know for a fact it wasn't his. That was the only time I slept with him, and we didn't even finish."

"Don't give a fuck," I interrupted. *Glad to know the day I was going to propose was the day you decided to become a whore.* '

"I lost the baby, Cas. It really fucked me up. When I came to your place, I wanted to tell you, but you wouldn't listen. Then the drama with your sister didn't help. And afterward, you wouldn't see me or take any of my calls." *And rightfully fucking so.*

I knew I should have had sympathy for her in her state of weakness, but my blood had run cold. It took me a long time to get over this, and the trust between us had been broken.

"If it were that important, you could have sent a letter. You know my entire family and all of my best friends. You didn't want me to know, and you wanted to hold on to it and throw it in my face because you think I'm vulnerable now. Well, fuck you very much." I tossed a stapler across the room, and it shattered against the wall.

Tears fell from her eyes, and she stood there raking her hands through her hair. Her body twitched as the bell rang.

"Anything else? I'm late."

"I still love you."

"Get out. Get the fuck out." *Am I in the goddamn Twilight Zone?*

"Guess what class? Today we're going to discuss the topic of bullshit."

All eyes locked on me, and their ears perked up. Confusion spread across the faces of many.

"If you like a girl or a boy. Do not, and I repeat, do not ruin their fucking lives and try to come back years later with a bullshit sob story. Own your fuck up and move on. Got it?"

"Yes, but where is this coming from?" a student asked.

"Don't worry about it, but since I'm in such a giving mood tonight, let's solve some linear absolute value equations!"

"Ugh!" they all grumbled in unison.

Chapter Eighteen

Taylin

SOMEONE HAD CLEARLY PISSED off Mr. Wyatt. He came into the room looking messy, and entirely off his game. I wanted to pull him to the side and find out what happened, but I knew I was probably the last person he wanted to confide in. Seeing as the relationship or whatever the hell is going on between us was off.

As the bell rang, everyone practically ran out of the room to avoid the wrath of Cas. I was heading out the door too, but then something made me stay. I walked over to the door and closed it, making my way back over to his desk as he repeatedly slammed his fist atop of it.

"What's going on? You seem off."

"Of course, I'm off, but why do you care?" He quivered with indignation.

"I don't know, maybe because I have a soft spot in my heart for assholes."

His eyes locked with mine, and I felt the heat radiating through my body from the way he looked at me. He looked hurt, but his eyes were lust-filled slits.

"I'm sorry, Taylin. You don't deserve this, and it's not your fault. I don't want to talk about this. Not here. Here's my number. Call or text me later if you want. Or you can burn this piece of paper. Either way, I won't be hurt. There's a hollowed hole where my heart should lie." His mood plummeted, and the way he spoke to me was different. There wasn't any asshole to be found.

It broke my heart to see him like this. By day he was my teacher, but he was something else by night. I could tell by how he acted that someone caused him to react like this. And it sucks, especially when you're not expecting it; it had the power to break down all of your walls.

Ring.

Ring.

"Where are you right now, Taylin?"

"Walking around my neighborhood. Wait, how did you know it was me?"

"Lucky guess. Text me a safe place to pick you up."

There was a corner store two blocks away from my parents' house, and I texted him the address and waited for him there.

I practically had to fight guys off with a stick until he showed up. Once I saw that familiar SUV, I was thankful. I nearly ran into the middle of the street to get away from the thirsting scoundrels.

"Thank fuck you got here when you did," I breathed out as I swung the passenger door open.

"Do I need to kill someone?" he replied. His voice was low and husky. Almost as if he'd been crying or something.

"No, that's not necessary. Are you okay?" He'd shown up in a pair of gray sweatpants and a hoodie draped over his head. *This isn't good.*

"No," he responded short, the SUV picking up speed.

"Where are we going?" I questioned, clutching onto my seat belt.

"Back to my place."

"Okay." *Please let us get there safe.*

Although I was frightened by how fast he was driving, I wasn't questioning or fighting it. I wanted to go back to his place. I felt like I *needed* to be there.

He led me through the garage, and without saying a word, he pulled me close to him, the hint of vanilla spice on his tongue as he slid it into my mouth. He pushed me against the frame of the door, and his strong hands roamed freely up and down my body as our tongues continued to tango in each other's mouths.

"Cas, wait," I said, breaking our connection.

"What is the problem? Don't you want this?" His eyes searched mine.

"Yes, but at the club, you embarrassed me and made me feel like shit. I can never tell if you actually want me or just like to fuck with me."

He raked his hand through his hair and over his beard in frustration. "I want you, I just—"

"You just what?"

"I don't know what to do. There's no protocol about this, and no rules, no manual."

"There doesn't have to be. Who's gonna know? There is no way someone from school could find out. We don't show any hints of anything there. We have never been seen together except for when I stay a moment after class sometimes, but I always leave right away."

"I know. I'm being paranoid."

He closed the space between us and teased and taunted my nipples with his fingers. He bit the soft part of my neck before placing a kiss on my lips and running his nose back down my neck, leaving trails of kisses that sent chills down my entire body. His tongue flicked against the bottom of my ear, and he let out a low growl. He snatched my jacket off my shoulders and ran his tongue back down the side of my neck. I wanted to fight, but I gave in. I fumbled with his pants, feeling the imprint of his cock on his thigh as I slid my hands in. Then I grasped his girth in my hand.

"No, don't," he whispered against my neck.

He removed my hand and pinned it above my head. Grabbing my other, he locked it in place as well. "As much as I want to do this, I can't."

"Why?" I asked.

"Because I feel like I'm spiraling out of control." Sadness laced his eyes, and he excused himself, stepping out of the room.

Being around this man was so confusing. My body was on fire, craving his touch, but he was right. In a way, I felt like I was also spiraling out of control. Any other time, I could keep my sexual needs and wants under control, but with him, basically anything goes whenever he wants.

"Can we go to bed? I don't want to feel anything right now, but your skin against mine," he returned, climbing into bed beside me.

"Okay," I replied. His arm wrapped around my waist, pulling me close, and I had to control my urges. The heat from his body was comforting, and I melted against him. Needing to feel as much as I could. *I guess cuddling is better than nothing.*

Me: I almost did a bad thing last night.

Anna: What did you do?

Me: I almost slept with Cas.

Anna: And how is that bad, again?

Me: Because he was a total ass at the club that night.

Anna: Oh yeah.

Me: I can feel myself falling in love with him, though.

Anna: Shit. Where are you now?

Me: At his place.

Anna: Do you need me to come and pick you up?

Me: I don't know.

Anna: Text me the code number, and I'll track you down if need be.

My girls and I all had apps installed on our phones to track each other down. I know it sounded crazy, but people are weird nowadays. We hear about girls partying and disappearing all the time, so we would rather be safe than sorry.

"Good morning, beautiful." Words I hadn't expected to hear. He was such a different person that day, and I felt like he was a modern-day version of Jekyll and Hyde. One minute he was sweet and calm, then he transformed into this emotionless monster at the drop of a hat.

"Morning," I said, sliding my phone back underneath the covers.

"Are you hungry?" he asked, his spark returning.

"Always."

"Good. I'll go and fix us something to eat. Feel free to take a shower or whatever you need to do," he said, placing a kiss on my forehead.

"Thank you." The smile on my face couldn't be helped by his tenderness.

As he left the room in a pair of low-hanging shorts, I slid out from underneath the covers to head into the bathroom.

Wow. I wish I could get used to this.

His shower was very masculine, but updated and techy. The walls inside were a large tile with a gray-colored brushed metal look. The entire thing was surrounded by glass paneling, and there was a small wooden bench inside. A frosted window was inside with a textured rock strip stretched from the floor to the ceiling. I closed the door behind me and turned the nozzle, and warm water came pouring from overhead, feeling amazing. It was like the shower sensed precisely how I liked my water temperature.

As the water cascaded down my body, I felt an overwhelming sense of sadness wash over me. Tears came pouring out of my eyes, and I found myself sitting down on the bench as the water washed pieces of my soul down the drain.

I knew I couldn't keep up this charade, and we couldn't continue this because now it was interfering with school. There was no way we'd be able to show up together that day without anyone saying something.

"How are we going to pull this off, Cas?"

"You leave it to me."

As we neared the school campus, he pulled over beside a few girls that most likely went to our school. "Do you ladies need a lift? I'm in a giving mood today. See, I already picked up one, so don't feel like I'm going to kidnap you or something."

The girls smiled and melted like putty in his hands. "Thanks for the lift," one said as she and her friend climbed into the backseat.

I guess no one would suspect anything this way.

Chapter Nineteen

Caspian

IT TOOK A LOT for me not to fuck that girl last night.

I prided myself on not being vulnerable around people, especially ones I've already been inside of, but I fucked it all up.

It pissed me off to no end that Melinda could get a reaction out of me. She didn't deserve to be in my fucking presence, let alone be in my head. That night I was a mess, and I was surprised Taylin was so willing to be with me. It was as if she felt like she owed me something when she didn't owe me shit. I'm the one that treated her like an ass.

I heard Taylin have a meltdown in my shower when I'd come in to bring her breakfast. It was six in the morning, and I was sure she was freaking out about getting back to school without people being suspicious, but I was good in a pinch, and I knew I'd figure out something.

I dropped the group of girls off by the front office and made my way around back to the teacher-assigned parking. I skipped going into the office and headed straight for the classroom. I didn't feel the need to talk to anyone, and I had a lot of shit I needed to figure out and not much time to do so.

I needed to get on Brian's ass about talking to Melinda and not telling me in the fucking first place. No one needed her.

I didn't *need* anyone.

I didn't *need* this bullshit.

But I *wanted* Taylin. She gave me something I never had in any of my old relationships—comfort and understanding. I didn't have to try with her. I never did too much or too little to please her. She accepted me as I am.

Fuck, this is hard.

"Mr. Wyatt?"

"What?"

"This note was left outside your office," Gina said. *I bet I know who it's from.*

Cas,

I know it may be hard to believe me, but I truly am sorry for what I did to you. There hasn't been a single day that has gone by that I haven't been filled with regret and sorrow. I knew you were the man I was supposed to marry. You were supposed to be the father of my unborn child. The day you caught me with Chauncy was a moment of weakness. I have no other excuse. At the time, I hadn't realized what I had with you was so special, and I haven't found it since. You still mean the world to me, but I kept my distance all this time because I didn't want to cause you to spiral out of control, as I had. I can't even express to you how bad things got, but maybe we can meet and talk when things cool down, please? I'll never give up trying.

-xoxo Melinda

I wish she would just leave me the fuck alone. I kicked my desk out of frustration.

"Slow down, Cas. You don't need to murder your liver in one night," Carlos exclaimed, trying to pry the shot glass out of my hand.

"I tried to forget that she told me she was pregnant with my fucking kid!"

"Who?"

"Melinda."

"What? When?"

"Supposedly, after she cheated on me with Chauncy. She found out she was pregnant and miscarried, and I believe she mentioned something about suicide or some other bullshit."

"Fuck, I'm sorry, dude. Why would she choose now to fuck with you like this?"

"Because of Brian, and next time I see him, I'm going to murder him."

"Well, you'll have your chance because he's over there."

When I saw Brian's face, all I saw was red. I had never been so fucking angry. I slammed my glass down so hard on the bar that it cracked in half.

"You piece of shit!" I shouted, charging straight for his neck.

"Woah, chill, man!" he screamed as I knocked him on the ground, my hands tightly clasped around his throat.

"Alright, alright! That's enough, man, you're going to kill him!" Carlos yelled, breaking my hold by wrapping his arm around my neck.

"What the fuck did I do?" Brian gasped in between coughs, trying to regain his breath.

"Let me spell it for you, M.e.l.i.n.d.a."

"Oh shit, let me explain, man!"

"You have sixty seconds."

"She tracked me down after the wedding; she's still friends with Lex. She was crying and telling me how she knew she fucked up with you and all this sob story shit. I didn't believe her at first, but then she showed me an ultrasound picture and—"

"And?"

"I felt bad. I knew how much she meant to you, and the fact that she may have been carrying your child at some point, I knew you had to know. I didn't feel right telling you, so I thought she should."

"She told me you reached out."

"No, well, not originally. She had to contact me a few times, and I didn't believe her initially until she showed me that."

I couldn't take it anymore. I stormed out of the bar and jumped into my car, ignoring everyone's pleas not to leave. *Fuck all of you.*

It took me years to get over what she did to me. And now she's come back fucking with me again. When we were together, I wanted it all. The wife, the house, the family, and since then I've pretty much isolated myself from my own. My sister and I haven't talked in years, and the relationship with my parents is an entire clusterfuck.

When Melinda and I were together, things were good—at least I thought so. I was a much different version of myself than I am now. I had a heart back then. I wore my heart on my sleeve and did more for others than I did for myself, but I quickly learned to put myself first after that day. I couldn't be tied down. I didn't think about the future anymore. I'm nearly thirty, and all I have to show for it is a nice car, a nice place, but nothing else. I loved what I did, but something else was missing in my life—but it wasn't Melinda.

I need to disappear for a while.

Chapter Twenty

Taylin

"YOU HAD TO HAVE been on another planet if you hadn't heard what happened in Mr. Wyatt's classroom earlier." I heard a girl whisper to her friend as I went to my locker.

"What happened?" I asked.

"He lost his entire shit. His secretary went in and came out, then all people heard was loud yelling and things flying across his classroom."

Oh no. That is not good.

"Did anything else happen?"

"I have no idea, but whatever happened in there, I wouldn't want to be anywhere near him."

Exactly, but I would.

Me: Are you okay? I heard about your meltdown in school earlier.

I had zero faith that he would reply to me, but I wanted to reach out and let him know I was here if he needed me to be.

"Hey!" a voice called out, bringing my attention away from my phone.

"Hey, Fernando." I greeted him with a tight smile, much too distracted to want to talk to him right now.

"Can we hang out tonight? I feel like we haven't seen each other much lately."

As much as I wanted to say no, I needed the distraction for a bit. I knew Cas was probably out on a rampage at some bar, doing God knows what with some random women, and I needed something to keep my mind off of it. I knew it was a long shot that he would reach out to me anyway, but I wanted him to know I was thinking of him.

"Sure. Meet at your place?"

"That's cool. The couple went away for a few days, so we don't have to be repulsed by them."

"Good. I'm in no mood." I giggled.

I had no specific intentions or plans for tonight with Fernando, and I just wanted to chill, eat pizza, and take a nap if possible. Sex or any form of intimacy was the furthest thing from my mind. Besides, after being with Cas, I know no other man could compare.

"You look beautiful tonight, Tay," he said with a smirk on his face.

"Thank you, and you look beautiful yourself," I teased.

Honestly, Fernando looked handsome that night. He had grown his dark facial hair out, lightly covering his cheeks and around his lips. His tank top molded to his body, and the bulge in his sweatpants revealed all of his truths. He was huge. And as much as I knew he liked me, I felt like I couldn't appreciate it. He deserved a girl way better than me—one that was focused solely on him and no one else. I was so conflicted. I knew I had no business with Cas, but I couldn't just stop my feelings. I was in too deep, and after the connection we'd made that night, he was all I could think about sometimes.

We sat on his bed, and he popped on a silly rom-com on Netflix. He had set up a table with all of my favorite snacks; Sweet Tarts, Smarties, movie theater popcorn, and a massive box of cheese pizza.

"Taylin, wake up."

"Shit, sorry. I didn't know I fell asleep."

"Your phone has been buzzing for quite some time."

I grabbed my phone and had a shit ton of missed texts and a call. Cas.

CW: Taylin, I NEED YOU NOW!

CW: Quite irngorng meeee.

Oh no, he had to have been drunk. As I continued to read the other texts, he called.

"I'll be right back," I said, hurrying out of the room and into the bathroom down the hall.

"Cas? What's the matter with you!"

"I just die I want. Nothing matters." I could hear the despair in his voice.

"Woah, what happened? Where are you?"

"House."

"I'm coming over there right now."

"How you get?"

"Don't worry about it."

I walked back to Fernando's room, ready to lie right to his face. I took a minute to text Anna to come and get me before going back to him. *Why am I like this?*

"Listen, I have to go. My girl is in major crisis mode right now and needs me. Can we reschedule?"

"Sure, I hope everything is okay."

Anna pulled up in her gray Honda Accord with a confused look on her face.

"Don't ask any questions. I can see the thoughts forming over your head," I scoffed.

"But, Tay. You're ditching Fernando to run to Cas, and you need to be honest with him and tell him things aren't gonna move forward. You can introduce him to me, and I'll take real good care of him," she joked.

"Honestly, Anna, he's too good for either of us. He deserves a good partner—a great one. I love you, but I'm not gonna give him more problems. You're still not quite over Ro-"

"Don't say his name! He'll show up in the shadows somewhere like The Boogie Man," she interrupted. Her ex,

Rob, was definitely a monster, and it took her years to get over him.

"My bad, but I mean it, Anna—hands-off."

"Fine, but either way, you need to be honest, because this isn't a good look. Of course, I'll always bail you out if I'm able, but you shouldn't play with his emotions like this. And you need to figure out where the fuck you stand with Cas too. You're not just some plaything to run over at his beck and call in the middle of the night."

I hated when she went into an overprotective mode, but she was right. How could I live with myself stringing people on for a man I shouldn't even be with? I knew I should set better boundaries with Cas, but I didn't want to. *Sigh.*

"Wow, he bought this on a teacher's salary?" Anna questioned as we pulled up to Cas's condo. The outside was very modern, and black trim surrounded most of the foundation, with two floors and double-hung windows. He didn't have much of a yard, but he had a nice-sized garage attached to the side of it, with a small paved driveway.

"Honestly, I highly doubt it, but I never asked. I've only been here once, and we never talked about it."

"Be careful in there. If you need me, text me. I'll try not to fall asleep, but I do have a geology paper due—you know how much I love my Earth science."

"It's cool. I'll Uber if I have to. Thank you for the ride and don't tell the others about this. I don't need their judgment either."

"I won't, pinky promise."

As I shut the car door and made my way to the front door, it was slightly ajar, and I cautiously walked inside.

"Cas?" I yelled. I heard a slight movement down the hall, followed by a grumbled noise.

I ran down to his bedroom and found him on the floor with a bottle of McCallan in his hand.

"What's going on with you? I heard you broke down at school earlier today." I crouched down to get closer to him.

"More like mid-life crisis," he growled, closing his eyes.

"What do you mean? What exactly happened? He looked up at me with the saddest look in his eyes. It tore at my heartstrings, and I felt my heart thundering in my chest.

"Melinda," he heavily sighed. Tears started falling out of his eyes as he took another swig of scotch.

"Whoa, whoa, give me that!" I yelled, prying the bottle out of his hands. I walked to the other dresser and slammed it down on the top of it. "Melinda, who is she?"

"Someone I never wanna hear from or see ever again." He launched his phone across the room, and it thumped on the floor, but it didn't crack or break from what I could see.

"What did she do?"

"She cheated on me, then tells me a few days ago that she was preg—" he couldn't even finish the word.

I felt hot liquid creep up my stomach and into my mouth. I ran out of his room into the bathroom and puked in the toilet. A whirlwind of emotions hit me as I spewed my soul into the bowl. *Pregnant? What?* Is this the woman that damaged him? Turning him into this? I bet he used to be such a different person before this.

"Tay." I heard faintly from the doorway.

"I'm fine. I had greasy food, and sometimes my IBS acts up."

"Okay," he said, sliding his back against the wall and falling to the floor. His hands were falling to his sides. His eyes were bloodshot, and his hair a chaotic mess. Melinda did a number on him. *Poor guy.*

I cleaned myself up and swished my mouth out with a cap of Listerine I found on the sink. I was joining him on the floor in the hallway after. "Wanna talk about it? I'm here for you, and you're safe. No judgment—ever."

He turned his head and looked me in the eyes, the start of a half-smile turning upon his lips. "I don't feel safe with anyone, Taylin—but."

"But?"

"I guess I can semi trust you. Melinda is my ex. We were together four years." He paused, swallowing hard. "She was it for me, or so I thought. I was twenty-seven, but I wanted it all with her. The house, the kids, the commitment," he said sternly. "But she ruined it. The day I was going to propose, I caught her fucking her so-called best friend, Chauncy, at her sister's place. And I cut her off. That's all I feel like saying right now. Can we go lay down?" he said, partially sobering up.

Well, there it was. The reason why he wouldn't let me in. *Bitch.*

It was hard to see him in such a pitiful state—broken, a shell of the man he was days ago. Heartbreak fucking sucks and I should know I've had my fair share.

I awoke to Cas quietly wrapped around me. He was so silent that I thought he was dead until I turned around to see his face, which jarred him wide awake.

"Fuck! I haven't had a headache like this in a shit ton of years," he yelled.

He got up and grabbed the scotch, taking another shot.

"Uh, do you think that's such a good idea?"

"I'll be fine. This usually does the trick. Let's order in today. I don't feel like cooking, and I'm sure you have nowhere else you need to be," he said, searching my eyes for confirmation. *What the hell is going on here?*

"I don't know, Cas. I did have plans."

"Well, cancel them! You're mine for the rest of the evening," he demanded.

Usually when he was demanding like this, it would turn me on, but this was just weird. I rubbed my forearms when I was nervous, and he watched as I did. I hated being put on the spot like this, but I knew I had to say something. Although, I wasn't entirely happy about being put in this predicament.

"This is a tough decision, but I guess," I said, sucking in a breath. "But you have to tell me the rest of the story about Melinda."

He glared at me, his gaze piercing my soul. "Fine, now what do you want for breakfast?" he asked, handing me a menu.

I quickly scanned the menu for my go-to foods, and he typed my order in an app on his iPad.

We sat in silence, staring off into space until his iPad went off, and he told the driver to leave the food on the front steps. He got out of bed butt naked, grabbed a black robe from behind the door, and disappeared into the hallway.

Anna: You alright, bitch?

Me: Yeah, he just ordered breakfast. I'll text you later, but everything is okay so far.

Anna: Okay, keep me posted.

As soon as he came back, he had a tray under his arm and placed it over my lap, handing me the bag with my food in it, then disappeared again. Returning with another tray, he sat down with it, placing his food on top, but he didn't touch it right away as I did.

"Not hungry?" I questioned, popping a hash brown into my mouth.

"Starving, but I'm so fucking disgusted right now."

"You ready to tell me the rest?"

After he filled me in about her showing up, the baby, and everything, my heart ached even more for him. That's a lot, and to have that person come back after two years and drop that kind of bomb? That was messed up. I remember vaguely seeing her at school that day by his office. Honestly, she looked like trouble.

Chapter Twenty-One

Caspian

Two years ago

"CAS? WHERE ARE YOU?" *a voice pulled me back to reality.*

"*Fuck off, Jerm. How the fuck did you get in here?*"

"*I'm a locksmith, remember?*" *he said, flashing his tool belt.*

"*That's nice, but get the fuck out!*"

"*No, I won't. Dude, we've been friends since elementary school. I don't know what the fuck you were thinking, but I'm not going anywhere. It's been six months since anyone has seen you.*"

"*So? Let me wallow in my bullshit, for fuck's sake.*"

"*Nah, man, you are too good for this. You are Caspian Elliot Wyatt, for crying out loud. You can have anybody you want, yet you're isolating yourself from all human contact over a* whore. She cheated, not you. So go clean yourself up. I have food and beer in the truck. Then we can get the boys together and have a guys' night out. We need you to get back into the game—please shower asap, though. You smell like open ass on a summer's eve."

Jeremiah was always the more levelheaded of the two of us. He was more like a brother to me than anything else, and he always set my shit straight.

I cleaned myself up and trimmed my beard. I needed to look my best to leave the house, although my heart ached for that façade of a relationship I thought I had. That woman was everything, and I vow in this fucking moment to never let that happen again.

I created my first of two rules that day. Number one, never fall in love. I started my new job as a college-level algebra teacher in a few days, and I had to get my shit together.

Jeremiah brought me to a club in Rhode Island called The Temptation Lounge. Brian and Carlos were waiting by the entrance as we walked up. You could feel the bass bumping on the ground in front of the door. There were half-naked girls everywhere, and I could feel my cock come back to life with every step I took. I ran my hands through my hair as a few of them gave me the fuck me eyes, and I knew this was going to be a night to remember.

As we rounded the bar and ordered our drinks, my heart started racing in my chest. Why the fuck am I feeling like this? It was almost as if some force beyond my means made me turn around and that's when I saw her. You've got to be kidding me—Melinda.

"What's wrong, Cas? You look like you've just seen a ghost," Carlos questioned.

"Look," I said, pointing. She turned around at that exact moment and dropped her drink on the ground. She was chatting it up with some young punk, and I saw red.

"Cas, there are plenty of other women in here, so go find one—fuck her," Jeremiah egged me on, slapping me on the back.

I turned around and tossed back two shots of Fireball and took a deep breath. This bitch isn't going to ruin my first night out in fucking forever.

I scanned the crowd and saw two young girls dancing with each other: both hot, one redhead with thick hips and a huge ass. Our eyes connected, and she smiled at me, and I decided to insert myself in between them.

"Mind if I cut in?"

"No—not at all," the redhead hesitated, her eyes traveling straight to my pants.

Her friend tapped me on the shoulder, a brunette with big tits. She wrapped her arms around my neck, and I grabbed the back of her head, shoving my tongue down her throat. My cock throbbed in my pants. The redhead wrapped her arms around my waist, and we all danced in sync with one another.

"Would you like a drink?" I asked them both.

"No, thank you, but we do want to get out of here," the redhead said.

Now you're speaking my language.

I grabbed both of their hands, gave the guys a nod, and felt the heat from Melinda behind me.

As we exited the club, I realized I didn't have a car. "How did you girls get here?"

"She drove," the brunette said.

Thank fuck.

She drove a blue car with a bunch of decals on the back, and I knew this was going to be a night to remember.

We drove to a motel not too far away from the club, and of course, I paid for the room. It wasn't a 5-star place, but it was in decent condition, and I didn't see any bugs or mice running around. The guy behind the counter handed me the key and told us that the room was on the second floor.

As soon as we entered the room, a large king-sized bed, a TV, and two chairs were to the left. Not that we needed anything else, but the bed and a shower to clean ourselves up after. The bathroom was decently sized, and there was room in the shower for three.

Both girls climbed onto the bed and started making out with one another. They fondled each other's breasts as I stood and watched. Clearly, they were very comfortable with each other. I joined them, and the redhead started pulling my shirt over my head as the brunette began unbuckling my pants, quickly freeing my length and wrapping her lips around it. The redhead lifted the brunette's skirt and started going to town on her pussy. The brunette moaned as she swallowed more and more of me down her throat. Shit.

The brunette stopped and locked eyes with me. "My name is Kayla, and this is Kailey."

"Cas, now no one told you to stop."

"I know, but I have a surprise for you." She turned around and pushed Kailey onto her back, kissing the inside of her thighs as she rubbed her wet pussy against me. I pulled out a condom and plowed into her without hesitation. I watched as Kailey's eyes rolled into the back of her head from the pleasure Kayla was giving her, as Kayla started screaming my name. I released my belt from my pants, placed it around Kayla's throat, and felt my dick harden even more inside her. "Fuck, that's hot," Kailey said.

I couldn't get enough of these girls, and I used their bras to tie both of their hands to the post side-by-side on the bed. I slipped my cock back into Kayla as I fingered Kailey, feeling her squirt all over my fingers. Then I switched and fucked Kailey, but this time I placed my hand around Kayla's throat as I instructed her to play with herself until she came.

I awoke to both girls sound asleep on either side of me. I reached over the redhead to grab my phone and see what time it was—seeing my inbox had exploded.

Carlos: So how was last night?

I sent him a selfie of the three of us; both girls sleeping beside me.

Carlos: Damn, he's back!

Melinda sent so many messages as I scanned through the rest, and I immediately deleted and blocked her. I wasn't going to keep entertaining her bullshit.

Fuck you; you won't have access to me anymore.

I put the phone back down on the nightstand and licked my middle and ring fingers on each hand, running them down their stomachs and right to their clits, rubbing until they woke up. "Good morning," they moaned.

"Let's take this into the bathroom, shall we?" I suggested.

Kayla went in first and started the water. I slid my fingers inside of her as she bent over the bathtub. Kailey dropped to her knees in front of me, taking me in as I pleasured her friend. I grabbed the back of her head and thrust in deeply while Kayla bounced back on my fingers. Once the water was ready, we all stepped inside together. The girls kissed each other, then one after the other, swapping kisses with me. I sat on the side of the bathtub with a condom on as Kailey sat on my cock, grinding against me as Kayla licked her pussy. So fucking hot.

Kailey and I switched places as Kayla lapped her folds. I slid in from the back and grabbed Kayla's hips as she moaned from my strokes. My cock was hard as a rock fucking these two girls. They both felt so good, I never wanted this to end.

As my release built inside Kayla's perfect cunt, both girls climaxed together. I pulled out to stop mine, and both girls grabbed wash cloths and started lathering each other's bodies up with soap. I couldn't help but stare as the soap landed between their breasts, dripping down their tight bodies. I ripped the condom off and tossed it in the trash. They both surrounded me and lathered me up too. I rinsed myself off and pushed them both to their knees. Their tongues swirled around me in different places, Kayla on my balls and Kailey up and down my shaft. It was so intense having them both please me simultaneously, and I felt my orgasm coming faster than it should.

"Will we see you again?" they asked after I came all over their faces.

Something inside of me changed that day. It was invigorating tapping both of these beautiful women's asses, but I knew nothing more could come of this. I didn't want anything else to come of this. I didn't owe these girls a fucking thing. "No, but this was fun," I replied, walking out of the bathroom.

"Wow, what a dick!" I heard as I searched for my clothes and quickly got dressed. I ordered an Uber on the way out the door. No strings. No attachments. Gotta love it.

A few days later, I started my new job as a college professor at Warren University. I pulled into the parking lot and searched for the teacher-assigned parking the Dean told me about. I never liked being late, but I was running a few minutes behind due to not sleeping at all last night and dying five minutes before my alarm clock went off.

"Hello, Professor Wyatt. Welcome to Warren University. On the right is your office, and you have your own personal assistant secretary, Gina. She will help you with things you need, from coffee to office supplies and more.

"Nice to meet you, Gina." She was cute, bright-eyed, and eager to please, I could tell. She wasn't bad on the eyes either —not my type, but I wouldn't say no to having her on her back in bed. She smiled as the Dean tapped me on the shoulder.

"Let's go and check out your new classroom. It's on this level, right down the hall."

"Thanks."

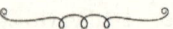

As the bell rang and my class started filing in, I adjusted my tie and could feel my heart pounding in my throat. It was a good mix of guys and girls, but one in particular—a cute brunette with quite the rack on her kept giving me the eyes, and I knew I needed to add rule number two to my list. Never have sex with a student.

Chapter Twenty-Two

Caspian

BABY. MY FUCKING BABY. I felt like a fucking trainwreck. Back then, I would have been over the moon to know I was having her baby, but she lost it, and I knew nothing— fucking *nothing*.

I grabbed my bottle of Jameson and attempted to guzzle half of the bottle, feeling very lightheaded but good. I went into my workout room and started annihilating the punching bag. Punching and striking as it bounced back close to the ground and back up at me. *I swear to God, every time my life gets back on fucking track, shit hits the fan— always.*

Why can't shit go right? Punch.

Why can't I stop breaking my fucking rules? Punch, kick.

I've been in love twice in my life, and I was cheated on both times. I used to love with everything in my heart and give my partner my all: affection, a shoulder to cry on—everything. I never wanted to be like this—a monster.

Taylin was different. I could feel it, but I couldn't get too close. Not again. I buried all capability to feel until—her, and now my fucking world feels like the walls are closing in on me. I can't risk fucking up my life anymore.

I chugged back the other half of the bottle, tossed it against the wall, and it exploded into millions of tiny pieces. *Fuck.*

Taylin scared the shit out of me, and I awoke out of a dead sleep with my arms around her, vaguely remembering what happened or why she was here, but I never let her go. It felt good to wrap my arms around her body.

My head hurt like a motherfucker. I took another drink and ordered us breakfast and other food all day long. It was like a lazy Sunday; only it was Saturday.

After dinner, she cleaned up everything and crawled back into bed with me. I grabbed her chin and tilted her lips toward mine, devouring her.

I ran my hand across her breasts, and her nipples hardened under my touch. Then I pulled her shirt up and over her head, breaking our kiss to trace my tongue down her neck and settling my mouth over her nipples—one after the other. A soft moan escaped her lips as I ran my nose down her stomach, leaving a trail of kisses behind.

As my lips touched the top of her pussy, I looked up at her and saw Melinda's face. I launched myself off the bed and demanded her to get out.

"How the fuck did you get in here? I thought I told you to leave me the fuck alone. Why do you have to keep torturing me?"

"Cas, what are you talking about?"

"Melinda, go to hell and get out!"

"I'm not—"

I shoved her out of the bedroom door and threw all of her shit out with her. I was not letting her get the chance to get dressed. "Get out. I don't know how you got in here, but never come back—ever."

How does this woman keep interfering with my life?

I sat on the floor beside the front door, and the tears began to fall. I slammed the back of my head on the doorframe, unable to feel anything.

Chapter Twenty-Three

WHAT THE ENTIRE FUCK *just happened? I come over to comfort him, and this is what I get?*

I left and blew off Fernando for what? To be Caspian Wyatt's fucking idiot puppy. As soon as he calls, I come running whenever he wants, but God forbid I need him—fucking crickets.

"It was as if he was not even seeing me. I swear he called me Melinda and everything," I said to Liz.

"Wow, Tay, I had no idea you had even run into this man again—and he's your teacher? This is beyond wild. I feel like you're in some sick and twisted romance novel."

"This is a mess. It feels like a fantasy, but sadly, this is my reality," I said, free falling tears sprung from my eyes.

Why do I always get caught up and blindsided by the sex? He showed me his true colors, and he told me clear as day on the first day we met. But deep down, I knew he was capable of love—it wasn't all gone. I could see it by the way he looked at me. He saw me, but whatever this Melinda chick did screwed him up.

I need to take some space. There's no way I'm going through this again. Especially the way he snapped at me. His voice boomed—still echoing in my head like thunder.

"Tay, you like him, huh?"

I nod my head in agreement, a rush of heat hitting my heart center.

"And that's okay. We can't always choose who our hearts connect with. It's almost as if it's predestined to happen, which is why it always catches us by surprise. All you can do is trust your gut—it will never steer you wrong. You can sulk, whine, cry, and hope. Your feelings are valid, but don't stay in it. Feel them, experience them, and let them go. Dwelling on the what-ifs won't serve you. You are in school to learn, so make the best out of it. Get in touch with a tutor—stay sharp. And whatever is meant to be yours will be yours. You're smart, and your heart won't fail you this time, I promise."

I know I had told Anna not to say anything, but I guess I needed her advice since Liz was married now. She was a few years older than the rest of us, intelligent and intuitive. And when it came to relationships, she always knew the right thing to say and made it make sense.

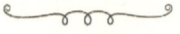

A few weeks had gone by, and I had gotten in contact with a tutor named Braeden. We were scheduled to meet after school by a diner near the school called Marcelle's.

I sat down on an ornate iron bench, pulling my phone out of my bag to check the time, and reread the last text he had sent to make sure I was at the right place. I had no idea what he looked like, so hopefully, this wouldn't be awkward.

"Taylin?" a raspy voice grabbed my attention away from my phone. A tall guy with a light dusting of stubble on his jawline, a mustache and chin strap combo, olive-skinned, and an athletic build underneath a flannel shirt and jeans stood before me. His gray eyes were piercing mine. *Fuck.*

"Yes," I said hesitantly, placing my hand in his for a handshake. He gently helped me up off the bench and grabbed my backpack.

"Shall we?" He motioned for the front door, opening it for me to walk through. A nice Hispanic woman was standing there, greeting us with a smile.

"Welcome to Marcelle's. Table for two?"

"Yes, please," we both said in unison.

She sat us at a table by the window and handed us both menus. I will give you a few minutes to decide, but I'll bring you both some water, and our house popped popcorn."

"Thank you," Braeden said.

"Everything looks so good, but I'm really wanting this Spanish-style meatloaf with rice, beans, steamed veggies, and seasoned potatoes." My mouth watered in anticipation.

"I'm digging the country fried chicken and gravy with mashed potatoes," he replied.

"Oh, that sounds delish."

"Yea, wanna share?" he asked, and the thought brought a smile to my face.

"Sure."

We had devoured our meals so fast that I had gotten sleepy from the amount of food I had eaten in such a short amount of time. "I don't think I'll be able to stay awake enough to study," I joked.

"You'll be fine; it'll be used as extra study fuel," he said with a smile. His teeth were perfectly straight and white—except for the little something I pointed out.

"How embarrassing. Let's head to the library." He laughed, placing money in the check folder.

"You didn't have to do that."

"It's cool. You can get the tab next time. I'm sure we'll be working together for a while, at least I hope."

Me too.

As we made our way back to the school, Braeden still holding all my belongings except my purse, a weird feeling came over me. I looked around, but nothing out of the ordinary caught my attention. *Well, that was weird.*

As we rounded the corner, I noticed the library wasn't far from Cas's office. We were near the door, and he walked into the hall. Our eyes caught for a moment, stopping him dead in his tracks. He glared at Braeden and me, and I rolled my eyes, continuing to follow Braeden into the library.

I don't know why he's staring, but it felt kind of nice to see him jealous of seeing me with another man.

We found a table large enough to sit at, but not too long that we couldn't sit near each other.

"So, what subject do you need help with? I'm pretty good with numbers, so I mainly help people with math. I'm also good with English and creative writing," he said.

"Wow, well, math is good. I haven't written much in a while, and that was an old passion of mine."

"I have a feeling you're a great writer. Maybe you can journal a day in the life of Taylin and all of your feelings like a grown-up version of a diary."

I hadn't thought about that, and with all of these conflicting thoughts I'd had, it would be nice to put pen to paper.

"I have a sheet of linear equations to do for homework. They are usually pretty easy, but sometimes I forget how to check my work."

"Okay, let's try this equation. $5x+7=42$."

I took in a deep breath and tried to see the equation unfold before my eyes. "Okay, so we subtract the 7 and 42 by 7. Then we bring down the 5x because the 7's cancel each other out, and $42-7=35$, leaving $5x=35$. Divide both 5 and 35 by 5, which would leave one if you divide the 5's, but you don't use it. You bring down the x. $35/5=7$, so $x=7$."

"Good, now how do you check your work?" he asked.

Come on, Tay; you can do this.

"You plug it in. So $5x+7=42$. You'd put $5(7) +7=42$. $35+7=42$. $42=42$."

"Perfect, let's try radical expressions."

Brae made math easy. He had a way of explaining things that calmed me down and helped me focus without overthinking or being in my head, which was much appreciated.

We had been in the library for hours, and I looked up at the door a few times because it felt like we were being watched, but I hadn't seen anyone.

"Wow, we've been in here for three hours, and it hasn't even felt like that much time has passed," I said.

"Hey, you're good company and a damn good student. So, of course, time flew by; there wasn't much I had to do. You're the superstar here. Did you drive in?"

"I did."

"Okay, let's wrap it up for the night, and I'll walk you to your car. It's pretty late."

"Thank you." *Such a gentleman.*

We grabbed our things and walked through the side door of the building. The lot my car was parked in wasn't far away. He helped me load my stuff into the passenger side and shook my hand. "Text me when you're ready for our next session. I've heard Mr. Wyatt can really pile on the work," he commented.

"That he can, and I'll be in touch soon. Thank you again."

I slid into the driver's seat, and shortly after Brae left, an SUV pulled up beside me, and I immediately locked my door. Looking behind me I backed out quickly without making eye contact with whoever it was.

"You're home late," mom said as I walked through the front door.

"Yeah, I was solving problems with my new tutor, Braeden."

"Braeden, huh? Is Mr. Braeden handsome, by any chance?" she joked, waggling her eyebrows.

"Yes, he is," I said, cracking a smile. "Not my type, though."

"Oh, so he must be a nice guy. Hey, it never hurts to give it a shot."

"We'll see."

Chapter Twenty-Four

Caspian

THE PAST FEW WEEKS had been a shit show. I could not get over the Melinda and baby thing. No matter how much I tried to let the entire situation go, I felt like I was trapped in my own personal Hell. I knew I couldn't reach out to Taylin because I thought she was pissed at me for some reason. And the guys would not understand because none of them have kids yet. Carlos's woman just sprung pregnancy on him, so he was still a fucking mess. And as much as it would suck, the only other person I could reach out to was my sister, Lyra. I had not spoken to her in years, but she was close to my situationship with Melinda.

Me: Call me.

Lyra: Is this a joke?

Me: Fucking call me.

The phone rang, and I could feel my blood boil and blood pressure rise. The relationship with my sister had always been a rocky one. She was two years younger than me and developed early. And no, I don't mean her rack. I mean mentally. She was always smart as fuck, and solutions to problems always seemed to fall into her lap. That wasn't as easy for me growing up. Although I was older, she always thought she was in charge and it caused us to butt heads a lot.

"Hello, Lyra."

"I'd like to say that this was a pleasant surprise, but it definitely wasn't. What do you want, Cas?" she snarled. Her words were bitter and cold.

"Melinda," I muttered under my breath.

"Oh, shit. What happened? Are you alright?" Her tone softened.

"No, she showed up at my fucking job a few weeks ago. The whole, I *miss you* spiel bullshit, and I'm sure no other man has been able to deal with her since."

"Okay, but that's not all—continue."

"She was pregnant." The word stabbed me in the chest.

"Oh no, I'm on my way over. Scotch, right?"

"You still know me so well."

An hour later, my doorbell rang, and I saw my sister outside through the doorbell camera. I ran down the hall to open the door, and she looked at me like I had two heads.

"Well, you look like a bag of dicks." She laughed.

"Thanks, that was the look I was going for," I replied, reaching for the paper bag she was carrying.

"Dude, I got it," she said, stepping through the door, shoving me out of the way. "This place is a wreck. Very unlike you."

"No shit."

"We've gotta clean this place up, and why is there broken glass everywhere?"

"No comment."

Two years ago

"Cas, get off the ground! What the fuck are you doing? You know I can't carry you," Lyra yelled.

"Just let me die," I replied.

"No, I'm calling the police."

This was it, the moment my life would end. Nothing mattered anymore. The woman I thought I'd spend the rest of my life with was a cheating cunt, and there was no reason to be here. I had invested so much into the relationship. I was vulnerable, and I fucking hated being vulnerable with anyone. That was something I'd never do again. No one is getting close to me if I make it through this.

Blue and red flashing lights lit up the sky, and a man came rushing into my face, flashing a light into my eyes.

"Ma'am, what's going on with him?"

"Oh, ya know, a depressed man in his late twenties, an entire bottle of scotch on the grass over there—alcohol poisoning, most likely. He gets that from our dad," Lyra said.

"Who are you in relation, ma'am?" the EMT asked, loading me up onto a stretcher.

"His sister."

"Okay, ma'am. Sir, did you drink that entire bottle this evening?" he asked, but I couldn't respond. My mouth stopped working, and everything started fading to black.

Beep.

Beep.

Beep. I heard as I opened my eyes. My stomach was in so much pain. A tube was shoved up my nose, and cool air flowed up my nostrils.

"Glad to see you awake, asshole. I thought you were really a goner this time."

"What happened?"

"Let's see, you drank yourself into oblivion. They had to pump your stomach, give you an IV to rehydrate you, and give you oxygen. Cas, she isn't worth losing your life."

"Says you."

"I never trusted her. She had bad vibes written all over her."

My sister may have been right, but I was in so deep with this woman that the red flags were fucking non-existent.

Melinda was the second girl I had ever been in love with. Before that, it was just experimenting, and I was okay with that. I always went back and forth with the thought of being in love or just fucking. And after I get through this, fucking is the way to go.

I decided that day in the hospital that I wouldn't let this kill me. My father was an alcoholic, and there were many times I had to pull his sorry carcass off the floor and send him to the hospital. My mom left him many times but always came back because she felt sorry for him. I vowed not to fall into a pattern of saving someone from their own bullshit, and I was pretty successful until recently. Melinda and I had our ups and downs, and I was constantly saving her because I was in love. I had to pick her up from her drunken excursions with her friends after she was either left behind or that one time where her friend crashed the car in the club parking lot. She was very bipolar at times and told me she couldn't handle the love I'd given her because it was too strong. Which I thought was pure bullshit because everyone deserves to feel some sort of love—at least I fucking thought so.

"Cas, the doctor said you can go home tomorrow. They want to monitor you a little while longer, and then a head doc will come in and make sure you're stable and let you go. I'll come and stay with you for a bit to make sure your dumbass doesn't do anything else stupid."

We arrived back at my apartment, and my sister looked mortified at what she'd seen. "Cas, what did you do? You know you're not getting your deposit back, right?"

I'd dented the walls, and the fridge handle was missing. My bed was flipped upside down, the frame broken. Glass was scattered all over the living room, and I ripped all the cushions off the couch.

"I don't care. I'll pay for the damages. I need to get the fuck out of here. Everything reminds me of her. She paid for half the shit in here. Her sister called me asking me to pack up her stuff, and I decided to destroy it. If she wanted it, she wouldn't have been such a slut. Or she would have gotten it out before she decided to be on her fucking back with another man."

"Cas, I get it. You're pissed off, but this isn't a good look for you. I have never seen you act like this before."

"You're acting like Mom right now." I rolled my eyes.

"What do you mean?" She stopped in her tracks, gaping at me.

"You're being annoying as fuck, and I don't need a lecture on me acting out of character. Just help me clean the shit up, so I can move to the condo I put a deposit down on."

"Fuck you," she yelled, tossing a box of trash bags at me. "You start in there, and when we're done, you can kiss my ass, Cas."

"Nah, that's your boyfriend's job, or maybe your girlfriend's. I can never tell with you."

She flipped me off and started sweeping up the kitchen.

In the midst of cleaning, I'd decided to crack open a bottle of Jameson that I'd been saving for a special occasion. I didn't want to feel anything. I tried to get rid of the rest of that shit that belonged to her in the apartment without committing murder. The liquid was a temporary numbing agent for the flood of emotions bubbling to the surface.

As I placed the couch cushions back on the couch, flashes of Melinda popped into my head. I envisioned Chauncy in the middle cushion and hammered it with my fist in a fit of rage.

"Fuck you, Chauncy! You ruined my family. She was everything to me!"

"Cas, chill! It's okay; he's not here," Lyra screamed, wrapping her arms around the back of me, holding me as tight as she could. I had lost my entire shit. Tears were continuously flowing for a woman—scratch that, a bitch who didn't deserve a goddamn bit of my emotions.

"It's moving day!" Lyra smiled. "Are you excited about this next chapter?"

"Yes, and no, but either way, let's do it," I replied, placing the last box onto the moving truck.

We pulled up to the new condo that I had purchased with a check from my mom. "To get me started," as she proclaimed. But she felt bad for me, and deep down, she didn't want me to end up like my father by making the same mistakes.

"This is nice," Lyra commented. My friends Carlos, Brian, and Jeremiah agreed.

One by one, we loaded up dollies with the labeled boxes. My sister was a very organized person and made sure the corresponding boxes went to the correct part of the condo.

After a long and tumultuous day, everything was unpacked. All the boxes were broken down and stored in the basement. Everyone left, and I felt so isolated. The new furniture that I had ordered was scheduled to arrive the next day, and I had to sleep on a futon I bought due to them telling me everything that I ordered was out of stock in the warehouse. So, I was pleasantly surprised when I got the call; it was coming so soon.

I'd awakened to my phone buzzing behind my head with a number I didn't recognize. I usually wouldn't have answered, but something made me. "Cas, it's Melinda. Can we talk, please?" I know I shouldn't have, and I was a jackass for this, but I gave her my address to the new place. After we hung up, I'd seen a few texts from Lyra saying she was grabbing food and coming over. Shit, this isn't gonna be good.

The doorbell rang, and Melinda was outside with coffees and a bag from the bakery we both loved by the old place. Her curly locks were pulled back into a ponytail, and she was dressed in sweatpants and a top, which she only looked like that when she was going through one of her depressive phases. Otherwise, she was well-dressed.

She followed me into the living room, and we sat on the floor across from one another. Tears streamed down her cheeks as she handed me a coffee and a cheese-filled pastry. "Thank you for letting me come over. I was convinced you would never see or speak to me ever again. I remember how easily you told me you'd cut your ex, Megan, out of your life, and I certainly didn't want to go through the same."

Rage swept over me. Gripping my knuckles until they were white, I said, "You deserve a fate worse than Megan. You cheated on me, and I wanted you to be my wife. I don't understand how you didn't pick up on that! Especially after cohabitating for four years!" It took everything inside of me not to start throwing shit.

"Cas, I did, and I panicked, okay? The thought of being with one partner. One man for the rest of my life—freaked me out.

It shook me to my core, but I realize now that spending the rest of my life with you is not scary. It's a blessing. You have always loved me for me and cared about me. You support my goals and dreams, and you never made me feel less than. I was such an idiot. Chauncy caught me at a moment of weakness. He caught me when I was vul–" Wow, she panicked at the thought of being with me forever. I had been so sure I wanted to be with her. Was I that fucking naïve?

"Stop right there! I don't need to hear your fucking excuses! You want closure, well, here it is." As I was about to let Melinda have it, my doorbell rang, and the door opened.

"Cas, I brought you–what the fuck is going on here? Why is she here?' Lyra asked, her grip tightening on the bags in her hand.

"I can explain," I started, knowing exactly where Lyra's mind was going.

"Explain what, Cas? She fucking hurt you." Lyra placed the food and drinks on the floor. I looked over at Melinda, and the next thing I knew, my sister was on top of her. Her hands clasped around Melinda's throat. I enjoyed the show for a moment, but I knew I couldn't let this continue.

"Lyra, cut the shit! Get off of her," I growled, yanking her off of Melinda.

"Cas, are you serious right now? She shouldn't be here."

When it came to my relationships, my sister was always overprotective. Anyone who even remotely caused me any pain she was on them like a fly on shit.

"I know, but I'm a grown-ass man, and I am capable of making my own decisions. I was going to handle this, but then you just had to burst in here like the Superman of saving hos. I can take care of myself, and you can leave."

"You know what, Cas? You're right. Excuse me for caring about my brother and his well-being. Excuse me for saving your ass the night in the yard. Did you forget about that? When you almost died of alcohol poisoning over this stupid bitch?" she yelled, pointing at Melinda.

"Cas, I am so sorry. I had no idea," Melinda cried.

"Of course, you had no idea. Because you didn't give a flying fuck about him. You just wanted to get railed one last time before you settled down. I know how persnickety bitches like you operate. You knew my brother was your meal ticket to the perfect life, but didn't think you'd get caught whoring around."

Lyra lunged at her again and slapped her so hard, her hand was imprinted on the side of Melinda's face. I snatched her up, and her body slid across the room.

"Really, Cas? Are you choosing her? You know what, you can go fuck yourself. When she wrings you dry, don't fucking call me, you idiot. You deserve everything she's ever done to you and more!" she said, storming out the front door.

I looked at Melinda, who was still holding the cheek that my sister had just slapped. "I deserved that," she cried.

"Yes, you did. Now get out, and I never wanna see you again. I got all the closure I needed."

"I came here to tell you something."

"I don't care what it is. Get out!" I roared, kicking over the coffee she had brought.

"It's something you've always—"

"Out, now!"

As she stormed out of my house, I went into the cabinet in the kitchen and grabbed the last bottle of scotch I had. Never fall in love, Cas. Never again.

"Cas, I have been thinking a lot these past few years. I should have called you and apologized that night, but I was so pissed that you had her over after we had just broken you free of her wrath."

"I know, and there's no need to apologize. She had it coming. I don't hit women, so I appreciated the gesture. I kicked her ass out of my place immediately after that, by the way."

"I know."

"How do you know?"

"I was still sitting in my car, talking to Tommy. He was always able to calm me down. I saw her storm out. She was such a klutz and tripped over her own feet and fell. It was like instant karma." She chuckled, and I couldn't help but laugh along with her.

"That's hilarious. Yeah, after your little fiasco with her. I didn't need to hear anything else that she had to say. She told me she had something to tell me that day, but I didn't wanna hear it."

"Do you think she was trying to tell you she was pregnant then?" Her eyes widened.

"Shit. I was so bent out of shape that I didn't even care. And honestly, if she had gotten it off her chest back then, I wouldn't have believed her anyway."

"So, what else is going on? I don't believe that's the only drama in your life right now," she stated, grabbing a glass and sitting down on the couch, filling it with Merlot.

I hate how easily she could read me.

"Well, let's see. I fucked a student."

"Cas, what the entire fuck?" she yelled, her eyes widening and jaw slacking open.

"It was before she became my student."

"Explain?" she demanded with narrowed eyes, gulping the rest of her wine.

"Long story short, we met in Vegas at Brian's party. Fucked, I kicked her out, then she ended up in my class the next week."

"I swear, your life is like a living soap opera. The Jerry Springer show doesn't have shit on you." She laughed.

"Touche."

"Well, how do you feel about this girl?"

No matter how I said this, Lyra would call my bluff. She knew I couldn't hide my feelings, especially when it pertained to another female.

"She's special."

"Wait a minute," she said, walking over to me and grabbing my face with her hands. "You love her, and that's why you're such a mess right now. Yes, Melinda caught you off-guard, but this girl—whose name is?"

"Taylin."

"Taylin...sounds exotic. I bet the looks match the name?"

"Yes, and then some. She's beautiful inside and out."

"And how are you fucking that relationship up?"

"Can we not do this right now? I just want to move past all of this external bullshit and focus. I don't need a therapy session right now. If I did, I would call Doctor Calvin."

"Alright! But you're the one who wanted me to come over."

"Yes, to make amends and vent. Not be castrated by my own feelings."

Having my sister over did make me feel better. I needed to talk to Taylin and come clean. I did care about her a lot, and I knew the way I had been treating her wasn't fair at all. I didn't need to lose my job over this, but I was stuck in a conundrum. I never let a student get this close to me, so I didn't know how much I could actually trust this woman seeing as I've been burned so much in the past by my heart. I did end up telling Lyra everything, and although she always busts my balls, she helped me to come to my fucking senses.

Chapter Twenty-Five

Taylin

CAS TEXTED ME AND pleaded with me to talk to him, and I agreed to meet up with him after school somewhere far away that no one would recognize us. He had me meet him at some diner in the boondocks of Connecticut just outside Rhode Island. It was a small mom-and-pop diner, but the food smelled amazing.

I had gotten there before him, but a woman greeted me and told me to have a seat once I arrived. She confirmed that my date was indeed on his way, which sounded so weird, but surprisingly made me feel good at the same time.

As I took a minute to gaze over the menu, the door flung open, and he came right in, sprinting over to the back table to meet me. "Sorry, I'm late," he breathed out. He handed me a bouquet of lilies, and they smelled amazingly fresh. I placed them down beside me on the seat and looked over at him; a genuine smile formed on his face as our eyes locked.

"What?" I asked nervously, completely thrown off-guard by his demeanor after the last time I saw him. *What the hell is with this man?*

"You're beautiful, Taylin. I just want you to know that. I wanted to apologize for being a total prick to you. My actions were not a reflection of you by any means. I was trying to face my demons on my own and realized that's not always easy. People need help, and I have to let people in if I want that help, so I wanna let you in," he said, picking both of my hands up one by one and placing them inside of his, gently squeezing them. His hands were warm and comforting, but his eyes showed a hint of sadness and vulnerability for the first time as he pressed his lips against the palm of my hand.

"I can't promise you that I will forget everything you have put me through, but I can forgive you, Caspian Wyatt. Since the first time in Vegas, I knew there was something neurotic but special about you. There was this—"

"Magnetism," he interrupted.

"I guess you could say that, but I couldn't stop thinking about you. Every day after that, you were on my mind, and knowing I'd never see you again hurt me to my core. I knew I would never have a love so freeing and so passionate and powerful."

"You gathered all of that about us just from one night?" he asked, perplexed, his brows pulling together as he looked at me with awe.

"Yeah, I knew in my heart of hearts that this was meant to be something special. Underneath that asshole posterior, I knew there was a man that had the capability to love."

"Are you ready to order?" the waitress asked, breaking the eye contact between us.

"We just need one more minute, please. Thank you," he replied, letting go of my hands and gesturing for me to look at the menu.

We both skimmed the menu and decided to get the meatloaf with glazed carrots, mashed potatoes, and a vegetable medley with homemade gravy.

It felt so good to be on the same page as Cas...finally. No fighting, no bullshit, just openness and sincerity. He admitted his fears and flaws, but hey, we all have them. This wasn't the time to point fingers, although I wanted to. We agreed to let things flow between us and see what happens. Communication on both sides will be open, and if things don't work out, we can resume professionality until the semester is over.

We'll see how this goes.

A month had passed, and things were going well for Cas and me. In school, things remained normal. I went to class, did my work, and hung out with him at night. He invited me over and would cook for me some nights. He was sweet and attentive, and we both agreed not to have sex for a bit. So that way, we could get to know each other on a deeper, more emotional level, and not just a sexual one. Which was hard, I had to admit, especially when he had his plaid low-hanging pajama pants on.

It was nice. Fernando still wanted to be more, but I told him honestly that I didn't see things working out between us, and I couldn't continue to string him along. I knew Cas was what I wanted, and it wasn't fair to either man if I gave anyone false hope.

As I made my way to algebra class, I noticed an extra chair and desk combo added to the front row. Cas had yet to arrive, which was weird because he was always in the class before us. It was like he lived in that room. A few others were sitting on the far side of the room that had shown up early as well.

A few moments before the bell rang, the masses filed in, and everyone was here except for Cas. I texted him to see where he was, but he never replied.

Mr. Wyatt's secretary came in and addressed the class. "Today's class has been canceled due to personal reasons, which I cannot disclose. So feel free to hang here until your next class since this was last minute. We couldn't get a substitute to cover."

What the hell is going on? Everything seemed fine last night when we were together. And there weren't any red flags presented at all, so I was genuinely concerned.

The door opened before his assistant left, and a new girl walked in. She had dark shades on and an oversized gray hoodie and sweatpants. "Is Mr. Wyatt not here?" she asked.

"No," Debbie replied.

"That's good. I wouldn't want him to see me like this," she said, motioning to her casual ensemble.

"Like what? The hot mess express that you are right now?" another girl named Ivette said—another Caspian Wyatt groupie.

"Ha, you'll see, bitch," the new girl retorted.

I had a weird feeling about this new girl. Although she was hiding underneath these clothes, I could sense she was up to no good. *I'm watching you, bitch.*

The rest of the day had gone by, and I hadn't heard a word from Cas. I called, and it went right to voicemail. At the diner, we had promised to have an honest and open line of communication, and we had thus far, so I was worried. I didn't want to be a creep and show up at his place, but if I didn't see or hear anything by the next day, I would.

I had the biggest room in the house. Almost everything was purple and had a place. You could say I had a touch of OCD with the way my books were neatly stacked on the bookcase in alphabetical order. I made my bed every day and never brought food in there. My mom always thought I was weird because I always ate at the kitchen table. No matter how late it was.

As I sat in my room, alone with my thoughts, I looked over at my desk, at an old stack of journals, and flipped through one. It was filled with lots of my poems and articles. I used to be so passionate about love and feelings that I had forgotten about it. Seeing these inspired me, so I took a moment to clear my mind and my space and jot things down. It was almost as if my hand had a mind of its own. Next thing I knew, I had four pages worth of thoughts down.

"Tay?" my brother said softly.

"Yes, Tine?"

"I'm glad to see you writing again," he said, popping his head in the door.

"Thanks, it was much needed." I smiled.

After my session, I went and laid down in my bed, the soft purple comforter wrapping me in warmth as I drifted off to sleep.

The next day, Mr. Wyatt was sitting in the class as we all arrived. He didn't appear to be sick, hungover, or anything, but his energy was off. He wouldn't make eye contact with me at all.

As the second bell rang, a girl came flying into the class. She had flawless light caramel skin, and her brown curls were perfectly cascading down her back. Her slender frame was sporting a crop top and low-rise jeans, with a pair of leather boots. She skipped to the same seat as the girl from yesterday, and everyone's jaws hit the floor—including Cas.

"Looks like you have some competition now," Debbie whispered loudly. I cut my eyes over to her like daggers, and she retreated into her notebook.

"And you are?" the teacher asked.

"Chantelle Octavious," she answered with a slight Spanish accent.

"Ah, you're the new transfer student. Do you have your paperwork with you?"

"Yes, I do." She grabbed her belongings out of her bag and sashayed over to his desk, carefully placing the papers down so that her tits were right in Cas's line of sight.

Oh, this bitch wants to die.

Cas seemed to keep his composure during class, even though Ms. Octavious kept interrupting and could barely understand a y-slope or what an integer was. It perplexed me how dumb she was at math, but there she was, pining after what was mine.

As the bell rang, she walked back down and said something in his ear. His eyes caught mine as I jammed my things back into my backpack and stormed out. I didn't need to attend any more of the slut production she had going on.

This is complete and utter bullshit.

Me: Anna, there's a new bitch in my class, and she's hot and pining for the professor.

Anna: Oh no! Do I need to cut a bitch?

Me: One of us will, I'm sure.

Chapter Twenty-Six

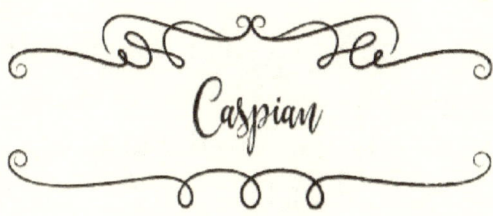

Caspian

"CAS, OPEN THE DOOR. It's important!" Lyra yelled, pounding on my door at 5:30 a.m. as I was getting myself prepped for school.

"What the fuck? Are you trying to wake up the entire neighborhood?" I yelled, ripping the door open.

"It's about Dad."

"You couldn't have called me?"

"No. This is an in-person conversation." She paced back and forth in the hallway.

"What about the old prick?"

"He's dead." I couldn't even move. Couldn't breathe.

This wasn't happening.

"He's *what*?" I questioned. No, this couldn't be right. She was joking with me. That man was damn near invincible, and there was no way he could be dead. However, I hadn't seen him for the better half of four years.

I fell to my knees on the floor, the air compressing from my lungs. Hearing that my father died was like a sucker punch to the gut.

"Cas, are you alright?"

"He's dead? D-e-a-d?" The words stung as they left my lips.

"Shit, I didn't think you'd take the news like this," she said, kneeling beside me.

I got up and walked right into the kitchen to grab a glass, tossing two pieces of ice in, followed by Jameson.

"That's exactly what killed him. He was found unconscious on the floor in the halfway house he was in, with pills and a bottle of alcohol beside him."

"Last I heard, he'd gone to rehab and got his shit together?" I said, tossing the liquid back.

"Cas, we haven't talked in two years. So much had changed, and I'm sorry I didn't keep you in the loop, but I was kind of afraid that you'd be unstable if you knew how bad he was doing. Although you hated him last, I recalled."

"Yes, but I didn't want the old bastard to die."

"What have you been doing with yourself, son?" my father asked. I hadn't told anyone I was visiting him in rehab, but I needed to see him.

"I'm going to be a teacher soon."

"That's good, but what else do you wanna do with yourself besides teaching a bunch of bratty kids?"

"I don't know. I did find a girl that I liked, back in college. I hope things progress further because I feel like she's the one I wanna marry."

"That's too bad. Marriage is overrated, son. You have so much potential to be anything you want, Caspian. You're a good-looking guy, and you should be out there fucking multiple women in different countries and continents at this time. That's a regret I had, but don't tell your mother I said that. If you aren't living, you're a loser in my eyes, but hey, what do I know. When I get out of here, I'll try to get my shit together, but probably not. There are a few ladies here who will do anything for a little attention, if you know what I mean." He winked and elbowed me in the side.

"What about Mom?"

"What about her? She can do better than me; we all fucking know that. I never deserved that woman."

"So that's why you get drunk all the time and constantly harass her? You're a dick and I hope I never end up like you."

"Sorry to say, but you probably will. We Wyatt men are known for two things; our dicks and our money." A shit-eating grin formed on his face.

I stormed out of the room. That day made me realize how disgusting my dad was, and I didn't want to see him again.

"We all have to die at some point, Cas. That's the only thing that's guaranteed in this lifetime."

I tossed back two more glasses and stopped hearing my sister's voice entirely. I grabbed my phone to let my assistant know that I wouldn't be coming in today due to personal reasons. The last thing I needed was for the class or Taylin to see me like this. I don't do grief well. I never have. When I lost my grandma as a kid, I never quite recovered from the trauma of finding her on the floor. She looked like she was asleep, but I had learned that she had a heart attack.

Lyra's phone rang, and I could tell by how she rolled her eyes that it was someone she didn't want to hear from.

"Hi, Mom. How are you holding up? Yes, I'm with him right now. I told him." She placed the phone on speaker so that I could hear. I hadn't heard my mom's voice in years either.

"Caspy, are you there?"

"Yes, Mom. I'm not a kid anymore; you don't have to call me that."

"You'll always be my little Caspy; how are you holding up? I know how you felt about your dad."

"I don't know how I feel, Mom."

"He's already started drinking, Mom. So if that's any indication of how he's doing—the prognosis is not good."

"Shut the fuck up, Lyra," I snapped. I didn't need her bullshit judgments right now.

"Language. Well, I need both of you to come to my house today so we can figure out a funeral or celebration of life. He didn't want to be buried, but I know he had a few friends that still cared about him, and they would like to pay their respects."

I'm glad someone does because I had no respect left for him.

The ride to our mom's place in Tiverton, Rhode Island, felt like it took an eternity. Even in Lyra's BMW, it felt like we were moving in slow motion. I hadn't seen mom's new place since she moved out of Mass a few years back. We pulled up to a small two-floor townhome with a large driveway. Mom was sitting on the porch as we arrived, talking to a lady with black hair in a suit.

Her eyes widened as she laid eyes on me. "There's my boy," she shouted as we approached the front steps. She hugged me and ran her hand down the front of my shirt. "Hi, Mom."

"I have missed you so much. Have you been okay?"

"As good as one could expect."

"How's the condo?"

"Fine, everything is where it should be."

"Good, and have you found a girlfriend?"

"Mom, can we not do this right now? Let's get dad's arrangements over with. I took a personal day from school for this."

"Okay, okay. Are you two hungry? I'll fix some breakfast. This nice lady here is my lawyer, Ms. Pierce, and she'll be helping us with the planning and splitting the rest of your father's assets."

As we went inside, my phone was blowing up with messages from the guys and a call from Taylin, but I couldn't deal with any of that right now, so I turned my phone off.

It took most of the day to get things sorted out. There was a lot of paperwork done, and I had never had any experience with a will before, but from what I heard, everything was ironclad. My sister and I would split the money, and my mom could sell anything else he owned and keep those proceeds for herself since they were still married. Knowing my mom, she wouldn't want to keep anything and would still give it to Lyra and me.

"Today was hellacious," I commented as my sister drove me back to my place.

"I know, but everything is done. We get to have his celebration of life and move on from this."

"The sooner, the better," I said, climbing out the passenger side. "Thanks for the ride."

"Cas, please reach out if you need to talk. Or talk to your therapist."

"Yes, *Mom*." I shook my head. I'm a grown-ass man. If I want to drink, I'll fucking drink myself into a stupor.

"I'm serious! Don't drink yourself into oblivion tonight; you have to go back to work tomorrow."

"How do you know I'm going back to work tomorrow?"

"Because I know you. You hate missing work. Even if you are grieving."

She will always know me so well.

All night, I dreamt about my dad. I wouldn't call them pleasant occurrences; it was more like nightmares and guilt? He seemed proud of me but pissed off that I was drinking so much. Could people be pissed beyond the grave and haunt your dreams? I wonder.

I had to get myself together to make it to school on time. As I walked into my office, there was a plethora of notes on my desk.

I quickly skimmed them and made my way to the classroom.

I had nothing planned for the day, but at least I showed up, and I didn't drink before coming in. So that's a win-win in my book.

As my first class of the day started filing in, I knew I would face the wrath of Taylin for not responding to her yesterday. When I'm ready, I'll tell her what happened.

She sat down at her desk, and I could feel her eyes on me, but I refused to make eye contact with her. I was on edge, and I didn't need to act emotionally in front of everyone.

As the second bell rang, a girl came flying into the room like a bat out of hell. She was a gorgeous girl, and everyone noticed. She was the new transfer student that I had read about in my notes that morning, but I didn't expect her to look like that, and I knew this would be a problem.

As I gave the class an easy assignment, she asked so many fucking questions. It was pretty annoying, even for me. I usually can deal with it, but she was very needy, and I was in no mood for it. I slightly snapped at her but tried to keep things as professional as possible. After class, she came to my desk to bother me, whispering how we should be alone to get more acquainted with one another. I laughed, dismissing her, and glanced over at Taylin as she furiously packed her stuff up and stormed out of the classroom.

Fuck.

After many hectic days and sleepless nights, it was the day of my father's end-of-life ceremony. My sister grabbed me from my place, and we were both silent the entire ride to the funeral home. I had this sick feeling in the pit of my stomach and drank a nip of Fireball to settle my nerves.

"Cas, really?"

"Shut up, Lyra. You cope your way, and I'll cope mine."

There were a bunch of cars filling the parking lot of The Burch Funeral Home. We decided to have an open casket viewing before we cremated our father. He used to be in the military, so a few guys from the service honored him as my sister took her place at the podium to acknowledge everyone for coming. My mom sat in the front with my aunts from both sides of the family, and I sat in the back because I couldn't be that close to his dead body. My sister asked if I wanted to say a few words, and I said I would, but I couldn't bring myself to read the eulogy, so we had my dad's sister, Shelly, ready to read it.

The ceremony was excellent; the military played music and folded a flag to give my mom. I said a few nice things that I could remember about my dad, and my aunt's deliverance of the eulogy was perfect. Everyone wanted to get together afterward for the repast, but I wasn't interested. I just wanted to go home. I walked up to my dad's body to say my final goodbye. He looked peaceful for someone whose liver gave out on him. He still had a full head of brown hair, with salt and pepper sprinkled in. He was clean-shaven but had scars all over his face. He had picked up a lot of weight over the years, and last I knew, he had a whole host of medical problems, diabetes being a huge one. I refused to be like him, even though I hated to admit the drinking problem he passed down to me. He had given me my first shot of whiskey at twelve. It was our secret bonding time when mom was at work late at night.

As everyone was distracted and talking about linking up after, I called an Uber to go home. I couldn't stand being around all of these people anymore. I did my due diligence and mingled for a bit, but this was beyond excruciating being in this energy.

I had ignored everyone for so long that I was sure everyone hated me. I did tell the boys what happened, and they did come by and pay their respects, and since I disappeared, everyone was calling me to see where I was. I just couldn't deal with it anymore. I needed to be alone.

As I walked in the door, I found a bouquet on my doorstep from Melinda. She was paying her respects. I was glad she hadn't shown up because I would have lost my entire shit, and there was no telling what condition I would have been in after seeing her, but I did appreciate the friendly gesture.

I sat down in the kitchen and finished the liquor I'd left in a glass from the night before. If my sister were here right now, she'd smack the shit out of my hands.

My doorbell rang, and I looked on my iPad to see who was at my door, and it was Carlos. I buzzed him in because I didn't feel like fighting.

"Cas, why did you leave? Everyone was looking for you."

"You know how I feel about that, man. I couldn't stomach another minute being fake and pretending like we had this glorious relationship."

"I know, but I would have given you a ride. I didn't wanna be stuck there either. Your mom broke down by the casket, and it was a mess."

"Glad I missed it."

"I wished I had. Anyway, where's the alcohol. Might as well numb the pain, right?" He joined me at the table.

Although Carlos pissed me off most times, I did appreciate him being here with me and not being a pain in my ass.

I awoke on the floor, my head banging, and Carlos was right beside me. "Guess we drank a little too much."

I looked at the clock, and it was after midnight. My doorbell was ringing. Who the fuck was at my door?

I checked the app and buzzed my sister in. "Cas, have you heard from Mom?"

"What do you mean? Wasn't she with you?"

"After the party, she disappeared, and no one can get ahold of her."

Shit. I was too hungover to be a part of a search party.

"Carlos, wake up. We gotta go find my mom," I said, pushing him with my foot.

"Do we have to?" he whined.

"Yes, I have an idea where she might be, though."

I made Lyra drive since she was the soberest of all of us. "I didn't even realize she was hurting this much; she put on such a brave face," Lyra stated, her tone somber.

"Well, I think that deep down, the old man was still considered to be the love of her life. He put her through the wringer with his drunken antics, but she always came back to him in some capacity."

"True, so where do you think she is, Cas?" Carlos questioned.

"She's at the lake or lake house in Barnstable."

"Oh, yea, the Wawa place," Lyra said.

"Wequaquet, yes. That's where they spent their first date. Dad told me that story a billion fucking times. How they went fishing on the lake, and she caught a bigger fish than him on her first try."

"That's so cute," Lyra said. "But It's so late and dark. How did she even get there?"

"Was Aunt Sue MIA?"

Lyra paused for a moment to wrack her brain. "You know what? After mom had her breakdown at the funeral home, she was there, but after a while, at the party, they both disappeared, leaving Aunt Patty to clean up the mess. I don't know why that hadn't dawned on me until now."

"Well, I was always able to see beyond what's in front of me," I joked.

"Bullshit, Cas. You are lying right through your fucking teeth," she replied.

It was a gorgeous fall evening. The wind was calm, and the weather was perfect. It wasn't too warm or too cold. I couldn't remember the house number, but I could feel we were close by the familiar smell of the water. Dad had brought me up here a few times to teach me how to fish as a young boy.

"There's her car," Lyra pointed out. The ugly yellow box-shaped Range Rover was parked right out front.

The lights were still on inside the cabin, and we could hear inconsolable sobbing coming from the other side of the door. Lyra lightly knocked, and Aunt Sue questioned who it could be at this hour.

"It's my kids; it took them long enough to find me." We heard as the door slowly opened. Our mom was sitting on the floor, wrapped in a blanket. Her face was soaked with tears. My mom had aged quite a bit since the last time I spent time with her. Her once long dark hair was now full of gray and cut just above the nape of her neck. She'd lost a considerable amount of weight, at least down 80 pounds from what I remembered. The brightness of her blue eyes had been dimmed, I'm sure, for quite a number of years, but I wasn't around to notice. But looking at her now, she was hurting. That man was her soul mate, and I know she feels guilty for trying to move on a few years back, but she needed to get rid of Rich's toxicity. Richard Elliot Wyatt, the name plastered on the front of the program from the funeral, lying on the floor beside my mom. A photo of him from the service was used—back when he looked good.

Lyra lay on the floor beside her, placing her head in Mom's lap like a little girl. I could tell Carlos was slightly uncomfortable here, but taking everything in stride. "It's late; you should all get some sleep. It's been a rough couple of days for all of us," Aunt Sue said, pulling out the rolling bed and some extra sheets for the pull-out couch.

Carlos and I crashed on the pull-out and Lyra and mom laid on the rolling bed, while Aunt Sue slept on the small queen bed, and I drifted off to sleep as soon as my head hit the pillow.

Chapter Twenty-Seven

Taylin

CAS HAD BEEN ACTING weird for weeks on end. I couldn't even go near him at school because Chantelle occupied his time whenever I wanted to, and he wouldn't answer any of my texts or calls. So, I was starting to think this was a lost cause. Something shifted, and I couldn't quite put my finger on it, but frankly, it was pissing me off.

Although I had told Fernando I didn't want anything serious, he had been begging to hang out with me lately. And tonight was a night I was going to give in. Call it spite, call it loneliness, but I couldn't deal with being ignored like this. *Something I definitely need to heal.*

I pulled up in front of Fernando's dorm, and butterflies laced my stomach. I had no control over what went down between us tonight, but I needed something from him.

"Hey stranger," he said, opening my car door. "Long time, no see."

"I know, I'm sorry. I just—"

"You don't have to explain, Taylin. Even if it's just as close friends, I chose to wait for you because I knew you'd come back to me. I couldn't see myself not having you in my life."

I did not deserve this man. He was so sweet, so caring, so *present*, all things I hardly felt from Cas. I wish I could be a better woman for him, but I could only be myself, and right now, my heart was in agony because I didn't know what the fuck I wanted anymore.

"I ordered pizza and wings, and it should be here soon. I wasn't sure if you wanted to drink or not, but I did grab some white Moscato wine."

"Thanks, that's sweet of you."

My phone buzzed as I followed Fernando through the kitchen. I pulled it out to see a name I hadn't seen in a while replying to me—Cas.

Fuck off, jerk.

I had forgotten how great of a time Fernando and I could have together. It was like a refreshing breath of air to hang out and watch movies, eat and drink. Fernando felt safe to me. There was hardly any drama involved with him, and I appreciated that for its weight in gold.

The wine was starting to kick in, and I felt buzzed but so relaxed. Fernando placed his arm around me, and our eyes met as I turned my head to face him, and he pressed his lips against mine. Our tongues connected harmoniously, hungrily craving more as I climbed into his lap and straddled him. His erection grew, pressing up against me. My core heated, wanting something I hadn't had in a while.

I pulled back, holding either side of his face in my hands. "Fernando, are you sure you wanna do this?" I asked, his hazel eyes meeting mine.

"Taylin," he said my name in a breathy moan, turning me on even more. "I've been wanting to do this since the first time I laid eyes on you."

He gently grasped the back of my head, pulling me into a kiss. His hands were caressing my upper body. In one fell swoop, my shirt was off, and he unclasped my bra. *Thank God I had a matching set on.* He looked up at me in amazement as he buried his face in between my breasts, inhaling the scent of me there. He cupped my right breast as his lips took the other nipple into his warm mouth. He was so gentle, unlike Cas, who commanded my body. After giving them both equal attention, he picked me up and carefully placed me back down on the bed, pulling my black leggings off. He spread my legs apart, settling himself by my feet. As he placed a trail of kisses up my right, then left leg, my sex demanded attention. He slid my panties off and smiled. "Wow," he whispered before kissing the creases of each thigh. He teased me, running his tongue over my mound before settling in between my wetness. My clit pulsed in anticipation.

The release that erupted from my body left me in a state of euphoria. He told me that he didn't want to have sex just yet, but he was dying to know what I tasted like and that he was not disappointed. Neither was I. I guess we had to do things at his pace, and I think I was okay with that.

He lay beside me and handed me one of his shirts to put on before pulling a nice plush blanket over us both. Then he wrapped his arms around me, placing a kiss on my forehead, and we both faded off to sleep.

The next day, as I made my way to school, I couldn't stop thinking about the way Fernando had made me feel. I had several messages and texts from Cas, and I didn't care. I made sure to ignore him all night. How dare he forget me and brush me off for weeks on end, then demand I talk to him as if nothing was wrong. I tried to push my feelings aside and revel in how Fernando made me feel last night. *He felt safe.*

I pulled into the student parking lot and walked up to the door, noticing Chantelle clicking her heels up the sidewalk. Her skirt molded to her body, making her ass pop. It was short, and if she bent over, it would leave nothing to the imagination.

She dropped a book in front of a group of jocks and waited for one of them to dive for it before pretending like she was going to pick it up herself. "Oops, clumsy me, thank you!" she said to the jock in the letterman jacket—football player.

She turned around, and our eyes met. "Hey, classmate!" *Great, just what I needed.* "Let's walk to class together, shall we?"

"Can I ask you something?"

"Sure," she replied.

"Why are you dressed like this? Are you partying after school or something?"

"No, silly. It's to get the professor's attention."

My blood pressure instantly rose, hearing those words fall from her stupid lips. I attempted to keep my composure. "What makes you think it'll work on him?"

"Well, it depends on the 'him' you're referring to, but this outfit has never steered me wrong."

Curiosity began to kill me. "Is it Mr. Wyatt?"

A devilish grin began to form on her face. "Maybe you seem a little jealous. I was warned that he doesn't usually mess with his students, but I feel like he's gotten to you in a way. So, I'm up for the challenge." I couldn't even think; I just acted.

Slamming her head into the lockers, she begged for me to stop. "Professor Wyatt is off-limits!" I yelled as blood trickled down the side of her head.

"Ms. Bradford?" a voice said, pulling me from this dark vision. Chantelle was nowhere to be found, but somehow, I ended up in front of Professor Wyatt's office. "The Professor will see you now."

How the hell did I end up here?

I walked into his office, and he was sitting down behind a wooden desk seething. "You ignored me last night," he growled.

"Aw, you poor thing. Sucks, doesn't it?" He grasped his tie in frustration, freeing it from his neck and opening the top few buttons of his white-collared shirt. His chiseled abs showed as he turned sideways in front of the blackboard, hanging behind him with algebraic equations written in chalk.

"What do you want with me, Cas? You have been acting weird. Ignoring me, brushing me off, not returning my calls or texts. What was I supposed to do?" I felt his gaze travel to my neck, and he pounded his fist on the desk.

"So, I see you've moved on already." Confused, I turned, facing a small mirror he had on the wall, a small hickey visible on the side of my neck. *Shit.*

"What I do is none of your fucking business. You do not own me, and I am not your property. If you cared about me, you would have honored the promise we made at the diner that day. So fuck you! Besides, your newest treat is waiting for you in class," I said as I stormed out of the office.

Tears sprung from the corners of my eyes. Fernando was coming from the opposite direction and immediately ran to wrap his arms around me. "Are you alright?" he asked, but quickly paused as heavy footsteps stopped behind me. "Mr. Wyatt?" he said on a breath as Cas continued to walk past us toward the classroom. *Fuck my life.*

"What happened, Tay?" Fernando asked, wiping my tears away.

"I don't want to talk about it."

"Okay, well, maybe we can hang out again tonight? And if you want, I'm all ears if you need it." *At least someone wants to be around me.*

"Maybe," I said, placing a hand on his cheek.

Chapter Twenty-Eight

Caspian

FUCKING FERNANDO.

Last year, he was a sharp student in my class, but boy did I want to snap his neck just then when I saw his arms wrapped around Taylin. Yes, I had been distant. My whole existence was in disarray after the loss of my father, and it was so hard to cope with it, even though I hated the bastard.

The hickey on her neck, the mark of another man claiming her...it made me see red. She was mine to have, and I was gonna get her back come hell or high water.

As I stormed to my classroom, not giving a fuck who saw or heard anything as I flung the door open, Ms. Octavious was standing at the whiteboard behind my desk with a skirt so short that if she bent over, you could see what she ate for breakfast.

"Mr. Wyatt, I need you. Well, your help, please?"

"You need to dress more appropriately for my class."

"I can wear whatever I want!" she scoffed.

"Yes, you have that right, but I don't need you parading around my desk like that. There are math tutors available at your disposal and would probably complete your assignments for you," I said, a mortified look plastered on her face at my response. Which I could tell she wasn't expecting.

"I heard you were an asshole."

"Glad the name precedes me." Taylin came in, walking hand-in-hand with Fernando. I couldn't tear my eyes away.

"It's obvious you want her, Mr. Wyatt," Chantelle whispered in my ear. "Such a shame. I bet I would make you happier than her," she said, twirling a strand of hair around her finger and puffing her breasts up.

"Get out! Get the fuck out of my classroom this instant. You will be transferred to Mrs. Connors's class."

"I will not! I have every right to be here just like your little flavor of the month up there!" she yelled and looked at Taylin.

Taylin and Fernando both froze in place, staring back at me. The entire class gasped, and all eyes were burning into my skin, waiting for my response.

"I would be the luckiest man on earth to have a chance with Ms. Bradford; at least she's smart and has class. Unlike you. You've been in my class all of what? Five minutes. And you already have your tits and pussy lips practically dragging across my desk like a cat in heat. If I wanted a scantily clad whore, I have a few to choose from at the drop of a hat, so your services are not welcomed here. Now, as I said, get out!"

"This won't be the last you see of me, Mr. Wyatt. You'll see. I'll make your life a living hell! You chose wrong."

"I'm already in Hell, so you'll just be adding more fuel to the fire."

The entire class erupted in a fit of laughter, and I knew I had taken some of the heat off Taylin and me. *Thank fuck. That bitch is nuts.*

"Cas, slow down, man!" Jeremiah yelled.

"Let him do his thing, man. Remember, he just lost his dad, and he has not been in the right state of mind since," Carlos said.

"Yeah, no. I'm not gonna sit here and watch him destroy his liver over this. That's how his dad died in the first place," Jeremiah replied.

"All of you can stop staring at me like that. I am a grown-ass man, and if I wanna drink, I can drink. I thought you said there were gonna be bitches here?" I snapped.

"Cas, what's going on? I thought you were dealing with the girl from class?"

I smacked the beer out of Carlos's hand, and it spilled all over his shoes and onto the floor.

"Shit, this is worse than I thought. He's a man scorned right now," Carlos huffed, grabbing some napkins to clean his shoes off.

The guys told me about a party tonight at Jeremiah's other best friend, Mitch's, house. He was a successful divorce lawyer and known bachelor. We had a conversation a few years ago, and he told me he would never settle down because he had seen how messy things could be when you fall out of love. He always knew how to throw the best parties, and after the drama with getting Chantelle out of my class earlier and seeing Taylin with *him*. I didn't wanna feel shit. I had enough.

Fuck. Her mouth feels so good. No, wait, hers is way better—more enthusiasm.

Mitch slipped me an edible, and I was on cloud fucking nine. I had two girls on their knees in the bathroom taking turns taking my cock in their mouths. I wasn't fucking anyone, but I was overdue for a release or two.

After I covered them both in cum, I zipped my pants and walked out of the bathroom without a word. The music was thumping all over the house. Mitch lived in what felt like a mini mansion. There were a shit ton of rooms, a pool out back, speakers set up from all angles, and half-naked bitches everywhere.

"Hey there, handsome." A sexy redhead caught my attention on the way to the bar. Perfect pair of tits in a barely-there top and miniskirt. Not my type, but she was hot in her own right.

"Want a drink?" I offered, knowing this wouldn't go anywhere past small talk.

"Sure, I'll have whatever you're having."

"So let me get this straight. You had a one-night stand with someone who showed up in your life a week later? Your ex came back to drop a bomb on you about your past, and you recently lost your dad? I don't know how you could even be remotely sober right now," Candi said, shaking her head in disbelief.

Somehow, she kept my attention, after all, due to the truth serum that must have been slipped into these drinks. I never told a stranger my whole life story, but I felt like I could trust her. This was better than talking to my therapist, and it was free.

"Yep, my life is a shit show."

"I wouldn't say that; maybe it's time to turn those thought patterns around. So, the girl, do you like her?"

"I more than like her," I admitted, feeling more like an ass now than I did earlier.

"Does she know that?"

"Probably not. I've been nothing but a raging dick to her as of late."

"Andrew, is it? Have you been honest with her about what's going on?"

I'd given her a fake name in the event some of this truth I'm spilling comes back to haunt me. "No, she's younger than me and probably doesn't care."

"From the vibe I'm getting. I don't believe that. I feel like she would care, and she would understand. If I'm being honest with you, I feel like she's hurting because she can't connect with you right now like she so desperately would like to."

This woman seemed so wise. She wore those bracelets made of crystals, used words like manifesting and destiny in our conversation, and talked about the moon.

"I'm sure I already fucked everything up. She started messing with another guy due to my fuckery."

"Yeah, I don't believe that. You need to sit her down and have an honest fucking conversation with her. Stop burying your feelings in alcohol to numb the pain and talk to her like a man. You'll see she'll flock right back to you, I promise. And by the way, your father says he's proud of you, but he doesn't want you to end up in the same place as him. Here's my card if you ever wanna talk again."

Candi Teagan, Psychic Medium.

Ah, that explains it.

"And, Andrew?"

"Yeah?" I replied, sticking her card into my wallet.

"You need to be honest with yourself about your feelings. If you can't admit them to yourself, how could you admit them to her? There's something you're getting from her, a need—a want, fulfillment. And there's nothing wrong with that." For the first time in a long time, I agreed with almost everything a woman says. *This is weird.*

After Candi left, I pulled out my phone and sent a text to Taylin.

Me: Taylin, we need to talk.

Taylin: Cas, it's 2 in the morning.

Me: Please. I'll explain everything.
Taylin: Where?
Me: My place. I'll be there in an hour.

I had just pulled into my driveway as I saw her Corolla pull up. "Hey," I said as she walked up the walkway.

"Hey," she replied. She was dressed in a sweatsuit. It was freezing out.

"Come inside. It's freezing out here." As we walked inside, I turned the fireplace on and pulled the recliner a little closer to it for her to sit in.

"Would you like something to drink?"

"Coffee preferably. And you reek of booze and cheap perfume."

"I had a bad night."

"Clearly," she said, rolling her eyes.

I went into the kitchen and popped a mocha latte pod into the Keurig, placing a small mug underneath. I then popped a vanilla one in after for myself. I handed her the coffee and excused myself to take a quick shower. I felt like a disrespectful asshole smelling like this if I was going to have an actual real conversation with her.

"Cas, why am I here?" she asked, sitting up on the couch. Her hands clasped tightly around the mug I had given her.

I sucked in a breath and remembered what Candi said about being honest. "I have not been okay lately." I sighed, sitting down on the carpet in the middle of the living room.

"Clearly, what else is new? You flew off the rails in class, but I have to admit...it was hilarious to see you put Chantelle in her place."

"I know. Seeing you with him did something to me, and I had no time to regroup before going into class. Then Chantelle, dressed as a slut, sent me over the edge. She has been so needy and fucking driving me up the wall ever since she joined my class."

"That's nice, but why am I here?" I could see the irritation in her eyes, but also the hurt I'd caused. I had to fix this.

"I lost my dad, and I haven't been the same since we had his celebration of life ceremony."

She placed the mug down on the floor and knelt in front of me. "Cas, I am so sorry."

"Between that, Melinda, you, Fernando, Chantelle, I couldn't keep my fucking head on straight. And my mom didn't take this well, so we had to go on a search mission after the funeral. It was just a mess."

Chapter Twenty-Nine

WHEN MY PHONE PINGED at 2 a.m., I knew it could have only been one person, and, of course, I was correct. Cas. And as much as I wanted to fight the temptation, I obliged and went to meet him at his place. He handed me a cup of coffee and went to shower the stench of asshole off himself and actually sat down to have an honest conversation with me. When he told me he lost his dad, I felt a ping in my chest because I lost my real dad when I was younger, and it's a wound that still hurts me to this day. I did not do well with loss, and I could tell at this very moment that neither could he.

"Cas, I wish you would have been honest and let me in instead of going through this by yourself. That is a lot on top of trying to teach a bunch of bratty college kids every day. I don't know how you're even functioning at all right now." I knelt in front of him and placed a hand on his cheek, wiping his tears away.

"I lost my dad when I was younger, and it still hurts me to this day. Were you close with yours?"

"No, he was an alcoholic prick and didn't give a fuck about my sister and me after we hit puberty. Before the age of thirteen, he was great."

"I'm sorry. I lost mine when I was eight, and he was my best friend. My mom did marry again, and my stepdad is great, don't get me wrong, but I do miss my papa."

He gazed into my eyes; both of ours were tear-stained. He took my hand and climbed on the couch, placing me on his lap. While straddling him, I swiped his hair away from his face and leaned in for a kiss. It was a tender moment until he gently pushed me back in frustration. "Taylin, I haven't been sure of anything ever in my life, like I am sure that I don't deserve you. I haven't been fair to you at all, and there was no reason for that. You are a fucking gem, and I toss you away at any chance I get. I can't deal with the emotions that come along with being around you. Plus, I don't need the school board finding out about us. Teaching is the one thing that never fails me, and I can't risk losing that." His eyes shone sadness.

"Cas, I would never jeopardize your job. I know how I feel about you, and there's nothing that I wouldn't do to be with you." My hands rested on his shoulders, my thumbs rubbing soothing motions round and round to try and comfort him the best I could.

"Have you slept with Fernando?" he asked bluntly, but quietly. He shouldn't be pissed if I did...he would be, though.

"No, but we did fool around a little, hence the hickey you saw. You?" I said honestly.

"Blow jobs from some bitches at the party I was at." I nodded with a deep breath, appreciating him telling me the truth, but hating it all the same.

"I see, so now what?"

Standing us up, he took my hand and led me down the hall to his bedroom. He picked me up over his shoulder and tossed me onto his bed, ripping at my clothing. I didn't have anything on underneath the sweatsuit, not because I was hoping for this, but because I had literally crawled out of bed.

"Cas, stop," I said, adjusting my clothing.

"Why, what's wrong?"

"We can't keep ending up like this. You ignore me and pull me away from Fernando and my friends. All to fucking treat me like garbage because some kind of trauma or bullshit happens. Maybe it's a sign that we shouldn't be doing this!" I yelled, tears falling from my eyes.

He was silent for a moment, running his hand through his hair. "Tell me you're mine, Taylin."

"What? No. I can't. Not until you prove to me that I'm more than just a random notch on your belt. If you can't, you're going to lose me forever."

Frustration was apparent by the way he looked at me. I could sense he was thinking hard about the next decision he was going to make.

"I can't promise you that there will be no more drama. I also can't promise you that I won't flip-flop with my decision-making; the only thing I am sure about is how I feel about you. Seeing you in class is the highlight of my day. Seeing how smart you are and how fast you can solve equations is like a huge boner alert for me. No matter how many students try to get my attention, you're the only person who can have me without even trying. Sometimes I see you sitting in your little car after school and wonder what you're thinking. When my phone beeps and your name flashes across my screen, it brings me joy even when I'm in agony. I never meant to hurt you and ignore you. I just don't deal well with grief, and all of this trauma that Melinda resurfacing brought up is killing me inside." He ripped his shirt over his head and flexed his muscles without even trying. *Damn, why does he have to make this so hard?*

That was the most honest thing I think he had ever said to me. As our eyes locked, I couldn't stop the tears from falling. I almost felt sorry for him because I knew deep down that he didn't deserve any of this. He was a victim of circumstances, and that had the power to change even the nicest of people.

"Cas, let me help you. Let me be by your side. We can resume things as normal at school, but when it's just us—be open and honest with me, okay? Just like you promised before."

"Okay. So now what?" he asked, wiping the tears away from my eyes.

"Let's get some sleep. We both have school in a few hours."

"Deal." He moved closer to me, ready to place another kiss on my lips, and I put my finger over them, stopping him in his tracks.

"From now on, we do this on my terms, and I want it to be slower. Let's build a friendship first, then maybe we can progress to something else."

I was having a hard time sleeping and decided to take a look around his place. I knew I wasn't gonna have time to go home and change, but then I remembered I had an emergency bag in the trunk of my car. For nights when I couldn't make it home, and I didn't want to look like shit all day. I grabbed one of his robes and then the bag out of my car, running back inside. I had a pair of jeans and a nice shirt that I could put on now. With a travel bag of face wash and creams, a small perfume bottle, and a toothbrush to make my night feel more normal.

I decided to take a quick shower and get changed and then continued exploring. The last time I was here, there was broken glass all over the place, and everything was in disarray, and I was here to comfort him. I had no idea how long he lived here, but everything inside looked new. The appliances in his kitchen were all stainless steel. He had a small dark cherry table with a few chairs and some bar stools by the island. All the walls were a neutral beige color, and the floors were hardwood.

I made my way downstairs and saw he had a weight room. A large punching bag was attached to a slot on the floor, and I went and punched it. One strike after the other. It felt good to hit something. I hadn't realized how much frustration I needed to let out, and this was the perfect way to do so. "Feels good, doesn't it?" a voice startled me.

"Yes, real good."

"Here, give me your hands. Let's tape them up so you don't hurt yourself. More often than not, unless you're a boxing pro, you want to at least put tape around them, so they don't swell. Your hands are too precious to damage."

The act of him wrapping my hands in these bandages felt very intimate and sacred. After he taped my hands up, he showed me the proper way to strike the bag. After a few more hits, I felt like a pro, and the release felt phenomenal. Not quite as good as sex, but pretty close.

My alarm went off in my pocket, and I knew I had to get myself to school. "Fun's over; see you in class later," I said, hugging him. I tried to walk away, but he pulled me back and devoured my lips. I felt like he was leaving his mark on me so that another man wouldn't dare stand a chance. *How do I break this to Fernando?*

The day had gone off without a hitch. I saw Cas in class, and things resumed as usual. I was so glad Chantelle was gone because my vision may have come true. It wouldn't have been the first time I caused harm to a woman trying to disrupt something that was mine. Another fun fact about being with Miles. I always had to fend for my life. But the past is the past. I met up with Fernando after school to give him the news. "I think we should remain friends, Fernando. Things get too complicated and messy every time I think about us being together, and I don't want to ruin our friendship."

"I understand, and I agree with being friends. And although it sucks, I still wanna wait for you."

"Don't," I said. "There are a million women in this city that deserve you. Don't wait for one that doesn't."

"They all fail in comparison to you, but I'll do as you wish." I could see the pain on his face from the harsh reality that we could never be, but I couldn't bring myself to keep playing with him. Even if Cas and I don't work out, I won't go back to him. I truly wanted him to find the love of his life because he deserved it. No man that delicate and sweet should be alone, especially as cuddle season was fast approaching.

After letting Fernando down, I decided it was a good idea to meet up with Anna. We hadn't had the chance to catch up in a while, and I had an earful to tell her. We were going to meet up for dinner at a restaurant her uncle worked at, so of course, free food and drinks were always a good time.

As the bright colors of the red, white, and brown signs of the Milano's Bistro caught my attention, my stomach immediately started to growl. Anna was waiting outside with a huge smile plastered on her face. "Bitch, I've missed you," she said, throwing her arms around me and giving me a tight squeeze.

"I've missed you too."

"Let's eat." She grabbed my hand, pulling me through the front door. "Hey, Uncle Milo!"

"There's my beautiful niece, and wow, is this, Taylin?"

"Yes, Uncle Milo."

"You have turned into an even prettier young woman," he said with a friendly smile. I have always had a little bit of a crush on him since we were younger. He was tall, with short brown hair, one dimple in his cheek, with the prettiest blue eyes I'd ever seen. And he was always in shape. And although the gray in his hair showed that he aged, nothing else had.

"Thank you." I blushed.

"Okay, where should we sit, Unc?" Anna asked.

"Anywhere you like, princess."

We found a booth in the back of the restaurant and Anna slid into one side and I slid into the other. We both picked up the menu and quickly put it down because we both knew we wanted his world-famous chicken and seafood alfredo and margaritas, placing our order with the waitress without hesitation.

"So, what's going on?" she asked.

"I don't even know where to begin," I sighed heavily.

"You can either start or end with Cas." *I was afraid of that.*

"Well, he was pissing me off per usual, so I gave up and started dating Fernando again."

"How did that go?"

"Not so good. I quickly ended it as soon as I started it."

"Why?" she questioned.

"Because it never felt right, and I knew Cas was all that I wanted—even if I had no clear shot at having him. He was being a dick after that night I went to his house, and it had just been one thing after the other, and I was tired of it. Fernando was safe, but he wasn't forever."

"Well, I knew that. Hence why I told you to hook me up!"

"Girl, no." I laughed. "I'm not doing that to him. You're more unstable than I am."

She laughed, "You're right. So did anything else happen?"

"Well, there was this stupid girl, Chantelle, that was in my class, and she tried her hardest to get Cas to notice her, but it backfired, and now she got kicked out of his class. She caused a scene and actually called Cas out on his feelings for me, and instead of denying it, he said he would be the luckiest man on Earth to have a chance with me."

"Wow, that was huge of him."

"I know, and then we talked last night and made up."

"Okay, that sounds good, but, Tay, we know his patterns. He's fine one minute, and then he's nuts and drinking until his liver should explode."

"I know, and his father died of alcohol and other reasons."

"So, he needs to get help in more ways than one, it seems," she said as the waitress placed our plates down in front of us with a large basket of breadsticks. "Thank you, Kila."

After my catchup date with Anna, I had this weird feeling in the pit of my stomach, and soon after, my phone buzzed in my hand.

CW: Taylin.

Me: Yes?

CW: Why do bad things keep happening to me?

Me: What happened now?

CW: Melinda.

What does this bitch want now? I rolled my eyes. I was so tired of hearing and seeing that woman's name. I wish I could wave a magic wand and make her disappear forever.

Chapter Thirty

"HELLO?"

"Is this Caspian Wyatt?"

"Yes, who is this?"

"Julie, Melinda's sister." *You have got to be fucking kidding me right now.*

"What now?"

"It's Melinda."

"What about her?"

"She tried to commit suicide this morning."

"Okay, and what does that have to do with me?"

"She left a note, and I wanted you to have it. Can we meet somewhere?"

"Sure, I guess. Where?"

"How about the café near your old apartment."

"Sounds great." *Fuck my life.*

Julie did not look good. Her hair was short and frayed all over her head. Her eyes had bags and dark circles underneath, and she had put on a shit ton of weight.

"Well, at least one of us still looks good," she said, laughing as she handed me the folded piece of paper.

"Did you wanna get something to eat?" I offered.

"No, I have to go back to the hospital and check on her. But, Cas, I just wanna say on behalf of her and myself, sorry. I know the way you broke up wasn't good, and the fact that she had cheated in my house was unfair and cruel. I always did like you, but Melinda is, well, she's Melinda, and she always has to have her cake and eat it too. She's never been right since you two split, so you did do a number on her."

"Too bad it wasn't for good," I said, holding the note up. "Thanks, and take care of her."

"I'll try," she replied, a tear falling from the corner of her eyes.

I turned back and went to sit in my car. I placed the note on the dashboard, and my palms started to sweat. *Should I read this now or later?*

As I sat down on the couch, I pulled the note out of my pocket and felt a stabbing sensation traveling down the right side of my gut. My body started to heat up, sweat poured out of me profusely, nausea crept up on me, and the pain became almost unbearable.

I grabbed my phone out of my pocket and shot a text to my sister and Taylin before everything faded to black.

I awoke to my sister and Taylin staring at me in a hospital room. "What the hell happened?"

"Well, it appears that the karma bus has finally started to run you over," Lyra said with a smirk on her face.

"What do you mean?"

"Your appendix was inflamed and infected. It was about to rupture, but the doctor removed it before it could do any serious damage," she answered.

I looked down at my stomach and saw the small bandage on my lower right side. "Hm, I would have expected it to be a larger incision." I ran my hand over the sore spot.

"They performed laparoscopic surgery. So, you have a few small cuts instead of a large one."

I noticed my sister was doing all of the talking, but Taylin had been quiet the entire time. Knowing my sister, she probably gave her a hard fucking time for even being here.

"Taylin, why are you so quiet?"

"I thought you were gonna die."

"He probably should have, would have served his sorry ass right!" Lyra said.

"Do you have to be a cunt all the time?" Taylin asked, and my eyes widened at her boldness. "I don't even know you, but I have a strong feeling that your friends must hate you. I know your brother can be an ass, but he can't help it. He needs attention. What's your excuse?"

For the first time in twenty something years, my sister was silent for a moment. "I like this one, Cas. You need to keep her around; she'll take good care of you and keep your ass in line," Lyra told me while looking right in my eyes, then she picked up her stuff and walked out the door.

A doctor came in as Lyra exited, and I saw her stop outside the door to listen. "Mr. Wyatt, you are quite the lucky man. If you had gone on any longer, your appendix would have completely ruptured."

"Well, luckily, it didn't. How long is the recovery for this?"

"About 1-4 weeks and you should be able to return to work if you take care of yourself and follow these instructions," the doctor with the name Thomas across his white coat said, handing me a paper with a long list of numbered shit on it.

"Great. Well, I'm a teacher, so I won't be lifting anything heavy—at least not for a while," I joked, smiling at Taylin, but I was met with a stone face. *Ouch.*

The doctor looked at Taylin and handed her a copy of the instructions as well. "Make sure he stays out of trouble. We're going to monitor you for a little while longer, and then you're allowed to go home tomorrow."

"Thanks, doc." I could feel my sister's presence still outside the door, but she never came back in.

"So what do we do now, Cas?" she asked, pulling her hair away from her face.

"You have to take care of me now, doctor's orders," I said, wagging my finger at her.

"Only if you promise to listen and take it slow." She held her hand up, rolling her wrist slowly.

"I'll try, no promises."

The next few weeks sucked ass. I could barely get around my own place and had a nurse come in. Taylin offered, but I couldn't subject her to this. She often came over and kept me company, letting me know how boring my substitute was—some old man with a weird accent and glasses.

"So, he's not nearly as hot as me, you say?"

"Not even a little." She laughed.

"How old are you?"

"Twenty-one, why?" *Fuck, I'm almost a decade older than this girl.*

"Just curious."

"Well, are you gonna tell me how old you are?" Her eyebrows wiggled.

"Twenty-nine. Taylin, I know you love math, but what is your end game after college? What career are you interested in?"

"I would love to be a financial analyst." She beamed.

"Ew, why?" I joked.

"Because my stepdad taught me about stocks and investments when I was younger. He bought my brother and me stock in Walmart and Exxon Mobile. He also bought us each a savings bond that I have yet to touch. I keep an eye on what is trending and where I should invest in the future, so I would love to help companies do that too."

"That's pretty cool."

"Yeah, how did you end up being a college math teacher?"

"I went to school for my bachelor's degree in science, and then I also got one in early education because I initially wanted to teach high school. Then, when it was time to take my teaching internship, I changed my mind, and the rest is history. I love my job. I love crunching numbers and solving complex equations."

"Me too!" she replied. It was refreshing to talk to a woman who actually had similar interests. That was something Melinda and I did not have. It was mainly a sexual attraction, and Taylin was much more than that. I hated to admit it, but Taylin was growing on me a lot and part of me really regretted the hell I had put her through. But it was hard for me to trust and let someone see me like this. Call it a lesson learned from my dad, but he always pushed my mom away when he was going through his shit, and the older I got, the more comfortable that felt. Especially the more people got close to me and hurt me.

"Cas?"

"Yeah?"

"Where did you just go?"

"What do you mean?"

"You definitely weren't here just now."

"Don't worry about it. Just know you'll never see that side of me ever again."

Chapter Thirty-One

Taylin

DEAR CAS,

I hope this letter finds you well. By now, I am hoping I was successful in taking my life this time. These past two years have been a fucking nightmare for me. I lost my job at the firm. I lost my baby. I lost my mind. And most of all, I lost you—the only man who ever truly cared about me. I don't know why I was so stupid all those years ago, but maybe it was all for a good reason. You needed to be set free. If we had gotten married, I don't know if I would have been as happy as you would have been. I did love you, but the thought of being married so early into my twenties freaked me out. I never told you because I saw how happy you were when you did talk about marriage, and I didn't want to ruin the magic for you. And I know me fucking my best friend did more than ruin things for you, and for that, I am sorry. I will take that regret to my grave because that's the one thing I wish I did right. When I found out I was pregnant with the baby a week later, I was a ball of emotions, but you wouldn't talk to me. I know how much you wanted kids because you wanted to be different than your father. You wanted to be there, be present and teach them what love is, and I wanted nothing more than that for you. I wanted you to be happy with me, but you couldn't. I was able to carry the baby just shy of nine weeks when I miscarried. And it devastated me.

I can't even tell you what that loss did to me. I felt like my body failed me. My one job as a female was to breed and make babies, and I couldn't even complete the task. I never even attempted to try that again because if it wasn't yours, I didn't want it. I refused to shack up with some deadbeat and end up raising them all alone. My mom raised me better than that. I know some people end up single parents, but I wanted to try my best to have a healthy relationship.

When I reached out to Brian, a part of me was elated to know you were just as broken as I had been all this time. I had hoped that when I saw you, you would forgive me, but you didn't. You seemed just as angry as you were that day, and I knew then that you hated me. I'm sorry for hurting you, Caspian Elliot Wyatt. If I could take it all back, I would. If I could have been at Julia's watching TV by myself instead, I would have. The days and months passed, but the pain never went away.

I heard whispers that you might have found someone else, and I hope she takes care of you and treats you well. You deserve someone who has the same goals as you and has ambition and drive. Molds you into the promising professor I know you are meant to be. You have a big heart, and you need someone with the energy to match that. You've always been brilliant, and I just wish I had smartened up sooner. I hope you'll remember the good times we did have long ago.

I love you. Before, now, and always.

Xoxo,
-Melinda Johansson

A part of my soul hurt reading that later from Cas's ex, as he was being sent to the hospital. A woman showed up simultaneously and told me she was his sister. We found him on the couch blacked out, and a piece of paper was on the floor in front of his body. I grabbed it before his sister could see it just in case it was his suicide note.

As the ambulance rode away, I sat down on the couch and read that letter, wondering if he had even read it himself. It seemed like no matter what this man did; things just kept happening to him. Now I was beginning to understand. He wasn't always this cold and shut off. He was once able to love, believe in marriage, and wanted a family— all things we never had the chance to talk about yet, but they were things I wanted too.

I had gotten all the information from the EMTs about where they were taking Cas, but since I wasn't his immediate family, I knew I didn't have to rush right to the hospital. I decided to walk around his place and snoop around. I looked under his bed and found a weird, unlocked box. Inside were a few pictures, and I assumed the lady inside was Melinda because she vaguely looked familiar. Brown hair, high cheekbones, tight body, and he looked happy. I hadn't had the chance to see him genuinely happy yet, and I hope things will change after whatever is happening to him. He deserved to be happy, no matter how much of an asshole he had become.

"So, who are you again?" His sister interrogated me as soon as I walked through the door, her arms crossed at her chest.

"Taylin, you?" I gulped.

"Lyra. So how do you know my brother?" Her eyebrows lowered and pinched together. I hated the way she looked at me.

"We ran into each other a few times and seemed to hit it off." It was sort of the truth. I figured it would be best I let him tell her how we met. I knew he could get in trouble if I said the wrong thing—sister or not.

"Ah, I see. Well, I'm not sure how long you've known him, but this is typical Caspian. I'm sure this is alcohol-related as usual. He gets the obsessive drinking from our dearly departed father." *Wow, they must both get the bluntness from him too.*

"I see. Where is Cas right now?" *I wish I didn't have to talk to her.* She made my stomach feel queasy.

"The nurse said he should be out of surgery soon."

"Surgery for what?" *How serious is this?*

"She said he had a small rupture in his stomach."

"Oh my God! He could have died."

"Probably. Oh, well," she said, shrugging her shoulders nonchalantly.

I don't like you. And if we weren't in a hospital, I would smack you.

I wasn't sure what his mother was like, but I sure hoped she wasn't a sarcastic bitch like his sister. She was pretty.

She had long dark hair and the same eyes as Cas, but her personality was trash. "So you wouldn't have cared if he died?"

"Not really. More money in the inheritance for me."

"Wow, you're really a piece of work."

"I am, but you didn't have to lie to me, you know, Taylin."

"About what?"

"I know you're his student. He told me all about you."

I swallowed hard, choking on the air as she called me out. *I'm surprised he told her about me. Maybe I was important to him after all.*

Cas finally woke up a few hours later, and I couldn't help but stare at him as he came to. His sister was already starting with her shit, and I quickly gave her a piece of my mind. She stormed out of the room, and the doctor came in and filled us in on what had happened and his recovery. I knew immediately that I would be there for him, whether he liked it or not. I was also glad this wasn't an alcohol-induced issue or a suicide attempt. He had a lot to live for, and it would have been sad if his life had ended on that couch.

After the doctor left, Cas looked over at me and smiled. "Guess what, Taylin?"

"What?"

"As soon as I'm able to, I'm gonna fuck the shit out of you."

"Cas, quiet down; we're in the hospital," I said, placing my finger up to my lips.

"So? Half the people are in here because of something sex-related, I bet you."

"You're a mess." I giggled, rolling my eyes.

I worried about Cas a lot. It seemed like every time he was able to change, something terrible happened. I am a firm believer that what goes around comes around, but when is it enough? Even he didn't deserve so much pain and anguish. I was so glad his surgery was minuscule, but it could have gotten so much worse, and he might not have been here. I don't know what I would have done if he was gone forever. His sister was such a bitch, and I don't see how he could even deal with her. He hadn't mentioned her much up until recently, so I had a feeling their relationship was estranged.

A stray tear rolled down my cheek as I made my way back to his place with him, thinking about what I'd do if I could never see him again. Asshole or not, I was in love with him.

It took Cas an extra week to feel comfortable walking around and taking care of himself. He had a nurse who came to help him out every day, and I made sure to stop by as often as I could after school. School seemed so dull without him there. The sub they had replaced him with was old and frail and made math seem so boring. His voice was so melancholy and drab. He sounded like that guy from the Clear Eyes commercials back in the day. And since Chantelle was gone, I had no drama to start either. Although I did spot her a few times in passing in the hallway, she gave me a colossal side-eye, and I would smile. Sometimes I wish she would have tried me because I was looking for a good reason to smack a bitch.

I had given him a day or two to himself, and I decided I would visit him and bring him dinner. Before I left the house, I made some roasted broccoli, baked lemon herb chicken, and basmati rice. I realized I had never cooked for him before because he usually did all the cooking, so he was in for quite the surprise.

As I rounded the corner to his place, I saw a weird woman standing in front of Cas's driveway. She was covered from head to toe in black, her face was covered with a cloth, and her eyes with sunglasses, so I couldn't make out her features. When I parked my car and shut the door, she turned around and walked off. *Because that wasn't weird or anything.*

I rang the doorbell, and he opened it shirtless, his abs still intact with a small scar adorning them, but I felt it gave him more character. I traced my hand down the middle of his chest, and he smiled. "Like what you see?" he asked, grabbing the Tupperware containers out of my hand.

"Always. So a weird thing just happened. A woman was posted in front of your driveway. When I pulled up, she turned around and walked off." His brow furrowed.

"Did you see what she looked like?"

"No, she was completely covered up."

"Hmm. Let me check the doorbell cam."

He pulled out his iPad and rewound the footage until right before I showed up. The woman had been outside his place for quite some time, and she didn't move or touch anything. She just stood there posted like she was his bodyguard or on the lookout for something suspicious.

"Fuck, this isn't good."

"What's going on?"

"I would say it's Melinda, but that's not her MO. When she is hella depressed, she will dress in sweats, but that definitely wasn't her, but I think I may know who it was."

"Who?"

"Her other best friend, Andrea. I haven't seen her in a long time, but she was just as crazy—if not crazier than Melinda."

"Well, shit, that's not good. Have you noticed anyone else outside your place like this before?" I asked.

"No, but you bet I'll be looking back through the footage to see if I notice anything else out of the ordinary."

"Speaking of Melinda, did you ever read the letter she left you?"

"No, wait. How did you know about the letter?"

"When I got here, it was on the floor, and I thought it was your suicide note. So, I grabbed it and held on to it until everyone left. I didn't want to risk you getting locked up in the nuthouse or something."

"I appreciate that, and honestly, I had forgotten all about it. But I'm guessing I should read it."

I had such a bad feeling in the pit of my stomach. I just knew something else bad would happen, and I didn't like it one bit. *I sure hope I'm wrong.*

Chapter Thirty-Two

Caspian

I WAS STARTING TO feel like a cat with nine lives the way the universe kept trying to take me the fuck out. I was trying my damndest to be a better person, especially regarding Taylin. The nurse the hospital sent over to help me out was hot but differently. Her mind stimulated me more than anything, and usually that would have been grounds for me to slide my dick inside of her, but I couldn't do that to Tay. The way I felt about her was unlike any other woman who came before her, and I wasn't going to mess it up. *Not this time.*

When Taylin came over with containers of food, it was a nice gesture. I was going to order her favorite Thai food, but this was even better. I honestly didn't even know she could cook because she rarely talked about it. I noticed that we spent more time together, but we still didn't know the meat and potatoes of each other. We didn't know jack about each other's lives growing up, which needed to change.

"Taylin, what did you want to be when you were younger?"

"An astronaut," she replied right away with a smile.

"Why an astronaut?"

"Because I was obsessed with space. My dad bought me a telescope when I was three, and every night I looked up at the stars and the moon. I wanted to learn everything I could about our solar system and how the planets worked beyond what we could see down here. I loved watching the rocket launches, even the ones that didn't make it. What about you?"

"I wanted to be a firefighter. My grandpa was a fire chief, and I thought it was the coolest thing ever. He took me on a ride and a tour of his station when I was five, and I just knew that's what I wanted to do. I always wanted to help people, but I shifted into teaching as I got older."

Although I thought the conversation was a good distraction, I had a weird feeling that the girl on the video was Andrea, and I didn't want to scare Taylin, but she was dangerous. Do you know those women who aren't afraid to put sugar in a man's tank, burn his clothes, or throw Molotov's? That was her. One time, Melinda and I got into a fight that wasn't even that serious, but she told Andrea, and she lost her shit on me and tried to run me off the road coming from work one day. Not many things scared me, but that girl was close.

After dinner, I brought Taylin back to my room. I slowly undressed her and grabbed her hand so we could take a shower together. I knew she liked her showers on Hell setting, so I tried to get it as hot as I could stand it without bitching out. She put a scarf around her curly locks and took a step in, moaning as the water hit her skin. My cock twitched as I stepped in behind her. She turned to face me, wrapping her arms around my neck. Her body swayed from left to right as if there were some type of magical music only the two of us could hear. I joined in and moved with her. Her eyes locked on mine, and I could see tears forming in the corner of her eyes, not from sadness but from joy. She seemed happy to be around me, and I wanted to see more and more of it. She jumped, and I caught her legs as she wrapped them around my waist. "Are you on birth control?" I asked.

"Yes," she moaned against my ear.

"Good to know for future reference."

"What do you mean?"

"Tay, you know we can't do this right now."

"Oh, right, because of your surgery."

"No, because the next time I get to fuck you, I want you to feel that no other man can make you scream the way I do. I want you to handle all of me, and I want to feel all of you. And I don't want any hesitation. No interruptions, just us."

"I'd like that. Cas, I hate to admit this, but I feel like I'm falling for you," she said quietly. Her eyes never left mine.

"I'm falling for you too. Let's get cleaned up, so I can eat some of that delicious food you brought me."

"I hope you like it!"

"If you made it, I know I will."

As I lay in bed with Taylin, I heard a loud booming sound and glass breaking down the hall. *What the fuck?* I jumped out of bed, and she followed right behind me. The window beside the front door was broken, and a rock was on the floor with a note attached. *Fuck, here we go.*

"Who the hell could have done this?" Taylin asked, mortified.

I freed the note from the rock and opened it.

She doesn't deserve you. I was the better choice, and you blew it.

"Okay, now I don't know who the fuck this is. This doesn't make any sense. This is a level above Melinda and her friend, so I don't know what to do."

"Cas, I hate to say it, but I'm scared," she said, her body visibly trembling. I wrapped my arm around her shoulders and pulled her close.

"Don't worry; this doesn't scare me. I will always keep you safe. You hear me? I'm two for two, aren't I?"

A half-smile turned up at the corner of her mouth, but I could tell she was still afraid.

"I think you should call the cops."

"I don't think it's that serious, Tay. If anything else happens, then I'll call them. Besides, I still have the camera footage for evidence."

"Okay, but I still don't have a good feeling."

"We'll just have to keep an eye out, okay?"

It was my first day going back to Warren University, and I was a little on edge. After the bullshit that happened a few days ago with the rock going through my front window, I wasn't sure who to fucking trust. Anybody could be watching me or have it out for me at this point. As much as it pleased me to torture my students, I figured I'd give them a pass this week, but next week things would resume as normal.

As I climbed out of my SUV, the Dean was waiting for me outside, but he didn't seem like his usual happy self. "Something the matter?" I asked.

"How are you doing, Cas?"

"I'm alright. Not too impressed I had to have minor surgery in the middle of the first semester, but I'm glad to be alive."

"Good, so there have been some whispers around campus that you may have a stalker."

"Oh? And what makes you think that?"

"Well, once you see the door to your office, you'll understand."

Fuck. What now?

As I followed him inside, I saw someone had desecrated my door in red lipstick. Written across the bottom was the same thing as the note that came through the window of my place.

"Is there any way to get this cleaned before the students show up?" I asked.

"Yeah, the janitor is already here, but we just wanted you to see it for yourself. Is there any student of yours that tried to push anything too far? Or may have gotten the wrong impression that you can recall?"

I had to wrack my brain, and nothing came to mind at the moment. "Not at the moment, but if I can think of someone, I'll report to you as soon as I can. Also, I wanted to tell you that a note with this same thing written on it came through my front window a few nights ago."

"If you haven't yet, you might want to call the police, Caspian."

"Okay," I replied, snapping a pic of the door to show Taylin later.

I walked into my office, and the inside was untouched because I always made sure to lock my door and Gina was the only other person who had a key, but she always took them with her when she left for the day. Thank *fuck* because this could have been much worse.

As the final bell rang and my students all filed in class, most were shocked to see me but seemed relieved. Taylin was late, which was unlike her. I pulled my phone out to see if I had a message from her.

Taylin: So, I woke up to my tire being flat. There was a nail inside of it. I'll be a few minutes late.

"So, did you guys and gals miss me?" I asked, sliding my phone back on the desk.

"Yes, Mr. Thadd was boring as fuck!" Debbie yelled out, and the class erupted in laughter.

"Well, now I'm back to making your lives a living hell, so you should have enjoyed the break while you had it. It's almost the end of the first term, and I need you all to be ready for this first-trimester test."

As I finished talking and catching up with the class, Taylin finally arrived and took her seat. She was shooting me a smile as she unpacked her things.

I turned around to draw up some equations for the class and heard the door swing open. "You bitch, how did you get lucky enough to fuck the professor? I saw you two together." I heard as Chantelle marched into my classroom, grabbing a handful of Taylin's curls, yanking her onto the floor. "He should have been with me," she yelled, hammering her fists into Taylin's body. I ran up the stairs, and before I could get to them, another classmate beat me to the punch and pulled Chantelle off her. Taylin exacted her revenge immediately. I watched as Taylin choked the living shit out of her until campus police came storming my classroom. Everyone's phones were out, and I knew this was going to be a total shitshow.

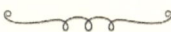

We were all instructed to follow the police into a small room, and I was not prepared for this at all. "So, Mr. Wyatt, care to explain?" the Dean and police officer asked. I looked over at Taylin, and she gave me a nod before taking over the conversation. *Well, now I think I know who the stalker is.*

Chapter Thirty-Three

FOR DAYS I HAD a bad feeling in the pit of my stomach, and I kept feeling like no matter what I did or where I went, someone was watching me. That night at Cas's place when the brick came flying in, was one of the best nights I had ever had with him. We could talk, eat, and just be—almost like an average couple.

I begged him several times to file a police report because none of this was making sense. But being the typical male that he is, I knew he wouldn't do anything until the shit hit the fan.

What the hell? As I went outside to hop into my car for school, my front right tire was flat. I examined it and saw a weird nail sticking out of it, and I called my stepdad outside to check it out.

"Hmm, I see the nail, but there appears to be a tiny slash mark near your hubcap too, Tay." My stepdad, Mark, was really good with cars, and luckily, I always had a full-sized spare tire in the trunk of my car. I sent a text to Cas letting him know I'd be a few minutes late for class as my car was being lifted into the air by a jack.

I went inside and grabbed something to eat since I wasn't going to be able to go anywhere for at least twenty minutes.

"Hey, sweetheart," my mom said.

My mom was so beautiful. I looked just like her, only she had more gray than brown in her hair these days. Her eyes had slight wrinkles at the corners, she had these little black freckles all over her cheeks, and she lost a little bit of weight from trying this juice cleanse and clean eating regimen. She raved all about it and wanted me to try it out, just to be healthier. Not that I had a problem with my size, but I did eat a lot of junk and survived off lots of caffeine.

She handed me a smoothie and told me that it was packed with lots of vitamins and other good-for-you items in it, and my stepdad came inside to let me know my car was all set.

Mark was handsome for his age; short salt and pepper hair adorned his head, and it was tapered at the sides. We had a running joke about his hands, and I always teased him about them because they were big and calloused. He liked to call them workingman's hands. He was tall and in shape, and I know a lot of it had to do with his and my mom's pledge to be healthier.

"Thanks for the drink, Mom."

"You're welcome," she said with a bright smile. "Hey, Tay?"

"Yes, Mom?"

"Are you seeing anyone? You seem rather cheery these days."

I smiled, not hesitating to answer but knowing I couldn't tell her everything. "Yes, but it is rather complicated."

"Of course, it is. It wouldn't be your life if it weren't." She laughed.

"Exactly! I gotta go. I promise to chat more later."

"Tay, before you go, can I talk to you for a minute?" Mark asked.

"Sure, Dad. What's up?"

"Be careful. I feel like someone purposely did that to your tire." A concerned look was on his face, and I knew he was serious.

"Okay, well, I'm not sure who would do such a thing, but I'll keep my eyes peeled."

"Good, and I hope you're getting your grades up. I'd hate for you to lose the bet and have to come back to the garage and work with me for two weeks straight."

"Never! I want my trip to Hawaii like you promised!" That garage was fun during the summer when he had the intern Jimmy there, but otherwise I couldn't stand that place. I *miss Jimmy.*

"Love ya, kid."

"Love you too."

As I rushed into class, I felt like I had seen Chantelle in the hallway, but I had no time to stop and glare at her like I usually do.

I opened the door and flashed a smile at Cas, quickly taking my seat and unpacking my things. The next thing I knew, the door was flying open and I'm being yanked to the floor by my hair. Katrina pulled Chantelle off of me, and I saw red. I choked and clawed at her face until the force of a strong man freed her from my grasp. I would have tried to kill her if I hadn't been interrupted. She was embarrassing not only her but also Cas and I, and I knew this wouldn't be good. He hadn't even done anything with her, to my knowledge, so I had no clue why she had such a vendetta against me. And how and where did she see us? Was she the one who was standing outside of his house? Was she the one who tossed the brick through the window? How the hell did she even find us. *Why is she stalking someone she just met?*

The campus police had Chantelle, Cas, and I go into this room and have a seat on different sides of a long table with the Dean of the school at the head.

I could tell Cas was nervous because his job was on the line here. His biggest fear was practically flashing before his eyes. So, I couldn't burn him at the stake, at least not now. The Dean started questioning him, and I could see the sweat forming at the top of his brow. It's not like we had time to rehearse any of this. And it wasn't like we had expected anything like this to have happened.

"Hi, Dean Shulman. So, from what I have observed, Mr. Wyatt has been nothing but professional with all of his students. When Chantelle transferred in, she immediately moved her desk down by his, and I knew she was going to be a problem then," I stated with confidence, hoping they would take my word over hers.

"Of course, you did, because I was trying to steal your boyfriend from you," she snarled. "Nobody else seemed to care."

"He's not my boyfriend. Shut up, you stupid—"

"Ladies, this behavior will not be tolerated," the Dean interrupted.

"Sorry, but the first day she arrived, she had asked about him, and he wasn't there. So the next day, she wore the skankiest outfit she could find and pranced around the entire room trying to get his attention, but he reacted how he normally did and told her to have a seat. She caused a scene a while back and whispered something in his ear before pointing at me and spewing lies in class."

"They're not lies. I've seen them together outside of school quite a few times," she said.

"How would you see something like that unless you were stalking him?" I asked with a raised brow.

"I have proof." She pulled out her phone and had a video of me walking out of Cas's condo.

"His father died, and I had come to drop off some flowers. But if you weren't stalking him, you wouldn't have that evidence, now would you? Creep."

"A week ago, someone was standing outside of my place at the end of my driveway. And the other night, someone threw a brick through my front door window with a note attached to it," Cas added.

"And someone wrote on his door with the same thing that was on the note I was informed," the Dean reported to the cop.

"So let me get this straight, Ms.?" He pointed to me.

"Bradford."

"You are a student in Mr. Wyatt's class, correct?"

"Yes."

"And you have his address?"

"Correct."

"Why would he be contacting you about his dad?"

"Because he wasn't himself."

"Again, why would he be contacting you? And how did he even get your number?"

The cop had a stern look on his face, and he was not the nicest-looking guy. He seemed overworked, and I could tell he hated his job by the scowl on his face. The days-old stubble on his face, the bags and dark circles under his eyes, and the stench of cigarette smoke that was coming off of him was not pleasant at all. He did have a nice body, though. So I assumed he lived, ate, and breathed the gym between shifts.

I looked over at Chantelle, and she had the most giant shit-eating grin on her face. "I gave it to him so he could help me find a tutor. I was sure he was texting someone else, and by accident, he texted me and told me that his dad had passed, and I felt bad because I lost my dad at a young age, and no matter how old you are, it hurts. So, the video you have is of me dropping flowers and food off because he was upset. There was nothing more or less and doesn't prove anything. I just feel like you got rejected by him and are making things up to make yourself seem less crazy. When in the interim, you should be in jail for damaging someone's personal property."

"Mr. Wyatt, do you have anything to say?" the officer asked.

"Yes, Ms. Octavious tried to make several passes at me. After last period, she would come into my classroom and say inappropriate things to me and try to give me pictures of herself. I could see her stare at Taylin when she would leave class but had no idea what it was about because I have never done anything out of the ordinary in my class regarding anyone. I would never be intimate or involved with a student—period. Chantelle did cause a huge scene in class one day, and I'm sure some of the students have video evidence of that as well."

"You should have filed a report, Mr. Wyatt," the officer said.

"If I had known things would escalate to Defcon 1, I would have."

He never mentioned the picture incident to me.

I was excused from the room while the others stayed behind. Another officer entered the room, and I saw that the officer named Smith was filing an actual police report with him, which made me quite nervous.

It pissed me off to no end that she had a video of Cas and me together. It also made me nervous because how did she even know where he lived? She hadn't been here that long.

Part of this felt like a setup, and I would soon get to the bottom of it. *Things are not adding up.*

I wanted to text Cas and tell him to let me know when everything was all over, but I knew it would have made things look worse. So I tried to send out a signal that he would pick up telepathically. *Please let me know that you're okay.*

"Anna, it's been hours, and I haven't heard from him," I sighed, checking my phone for the hundredth time.

"Just chill. I'm sure they had to do a thorough investigation due to crazy pants McGee. Since the bitch was probably trolling his house and stalked him from the school," she replied, taking a sip of her vanilla chai tea.

"I know, but something just feels off about this." I tossed my phone on her bed and wrapped her plush blanket around my shoulders.

"Want me to look her up?" she asked, placing her pink laptop on top of the small table in her room.

"Yes."

I gave Anna her information, and it was crazy how fast she was able to dig into her. She found a few social media profiles, but what freaked me out was a video I saw of her driving by Cas's place. Anna clicked play, and she was saying all kinds of things about Cas. She was saying how she found the hot professor's home and that she would make him hers. I screen-recorded it so I could show Cas. I felt like I was going to throw up after seeing it. She had a few pictures of him on her page with her face photoshopped next to his. I could tell some of the photos were very old, by the youthfulness in his eyes, and the lack of facial hair, so she must have stalked his social media for quite some time, but why. She had just gotten transferred to our school. "Dig more. I know there's another connection here," I said to Anna.

"You got it, boss!" she said, tying her hair up into a knot on her head.

After a few hours of scouring and going through endless posts, I saw something when I was getting ready to give up. "Oh my God!"

"What?" Anna questioned.

"That's Cas's ex, Melinda!" I pointed. Under the picture's caption, it said, hanging with mi Madre and Auntie Melinda.

"Okay, so what am I missing here?"

"He told me Melinda, his crazy ex, had an even crazier friend, named Andrea, and that must be her daughter!" This was unreal.

"Holy shit. So momma bear and baby bear are both batshit, and maybe they both secretly wanted him too?"

"Maybe they all wanted to share him." I shuttered at the thought.

"Dude, that's gross." She scrunched up her face.

"Well, he also told me that Andrea got pissed and almost ran him off the road once when he and Melinda got into a fight before, so maybe they sent her after him because he wouldn't recognize who she was?"

"This is fucked. I feel like you're roped into some kind of Lifetime romance serial killer movie."

"Seems like it, but it all explains the weird feelings I kept having. I knew something fucked up was coming, and I just didn't know what or how to decipher it."

"Well, now you know, but you have to be careful, Tay. Who knows what else these crazy bitches have up their sleeves? I mean, if the woman sacrificed her own kid, who knows what she's capable of!"

"True. Thanks, girl. I'm gonna head home now."

"Are you okay?" I started to shake my head before she even finished.

"No, I'm not. This is reminding me of the Xavier situation."

"Oh no, Tay. I don't think Cas is gonna have to move across the country. And I don't think he has anyone pregnant."

"It's not that. It's the fact that there are other women around. He did get someone pregnant way before my time, and I know it's not the exact situation, but it still sucks."

"I'm sorry, just have a little faith. Things will work out, and I don't think the universe would do that to you again. You don't deserve it."

"Thank you. I'm gonna go and cry now."

"I love you!" she said, embracing me in a tight squeeze.

On the drive back home, tears fell from my eyes. This overwhelming feeling of guilt and sadness washed over me. I still hadn't heard from Cas after the meeting earlier that day, and I was so confused. I felt like he would have at least messaged me and told me everything would be okay, but nothing. I wasn't sure why I was feeling this way, but I felt like there was going to be another short period of silence between us, and it sucked so bad. We had been working so hard to communicate and make things work. Our sexual chemistry had raised off the charts to new levels, and I finally felt at ease. It just seemed like the universe was trying to send me a sign. Maybe I wasn't supposed to be with Cas after all. Maybe I was just supposed to focus on my studies, learn everything I could from him, then move on with my life. Perhaps I should just fall back and let things play out for a bit. I knew it would be hard deep down, but it was a sacrifice I was willing to make to keep my sanity. I didn't need another Xavier problem.

Three years ago

"Xavier Aaron was every girl's dream, and this bitch just so happened to snag him! How did you do it?" Patrice asked me.

Patrice was one of my teammates on the girls' soccer team. We nicknamed her the loudspeaker because she couldn't whisper for shit, and she was always so animated when she heard gossip.

"I'm just lucky, I guess."

Xavier was the love of my life. We had been together for over a year, and things couldn't have been any better. He was attentive to my needs, and he was able to sense when things were wrong with me. He always had the right things to say, and he was always there for me. In a way, he seemed to be the perfect guy, but in my experiences, perfect did not exist. He was over 6'1, with an athletic build, and he was an amazing lacrosse player. He had rich brown hair that was always in a disheveled mess on his head, but it worked for him. It enhanced his square jaw and perfect green eyes.

He had his arms wrapped around me as we were sitting around a bonfire one Friday night. We did this on nights we didn't have games, which wasn't often. It was our hangout spot to unwind from the stress of high school drama and relentless practices. It was our senior year, and I wanted to make the most of it. We only had a few more nights like this left before graduation. Scouts were watching Xavier so he could get a full ride in college the next year, but I knew I needed to take some time off from this. I wasn't sure what I wanted to do with my life. I thought about being a CPA, but it took hours of studying and required a bachelor's degree. I wasn't sure if I was ready for that yet.

"Taylin, you are the most beautiful girl I have ever seen. From your curls to your curves, I love every piece of you and everything in between," he said, placing a kiss on my lips.

Everyone else went to their respective tents, and we were sitting by the lake looking up at the stars. It was rather chilly this night, but it was refreshing to be by the water.

There wasn't anything wrong I could say about Xavier. He never gave me any reason to distrust him, and seeing as I was still a virgin, I felt like this was the time to give myself to him fully. Not by the lake, but sometime this weekend.

It was our graduation day, and I was a bundle of nerves. Xavier and I finally sealed the deal, and it was not what I expected. It hurt, but felt better the more we kept doing it. He told me he had big news, but I had to wait until after graduation. He knew how much I hated secrets and surprises.

"I can't believe we did it, guys!" Patrice yelled as we all tossed our caps into the air. Her dyed red curls bounced as we all scrambled to find them on the ground.

"Hey, babe. Can I talk to you?" Xavier asked, pulling my hand and leading me toward the back of the bleachers.

"What's up?"

"Well, I got an acceptance letter from one of the top-performing schools in lacrosse in the country!"

The way his eyes lit up was like a kid on Christmas. I was so happy for him, but I knew the hammer was about to be dropped by the pit in my stomach.

"That's great, and where is that?"

"North Carolina. The University of NC."

"Wow, that's a fourteen-hour drive from here." I took a step back, my head dropping to the side.

"I know, but their team is legendary, and I know that's where I need to be," he said, placing his hands on my shoulders, trying to pull me closer to him.

"I see, but where does that leave us?" I was trying to be supportive, but couldn't help the frown forming on my face.

His eyes softened, and then reality set in. "I was so excited about the school that I didn't think about what would happen to us. I know you've been undecided as to where you wanted to go, so maybe you could come to North Carolina with me? Find a community college nearby until you decide what you wanna major in?"

He was always thoughtful and tried to include me in everything, but I knew this was where our journey had to end. I knew I couldn't move so far away from my family, and I couldn't leave my mom and brother up here. Tears flowed from my eyes, but I was thankful for the waterproof makeup I had decided to wear.

"Tay, don't cry, honey. It's our special day. I didn't think you would be upset."

"I don't know what to feel right now, but I am happy for you. You get to live your dream, and I don't wanna stop that."

He wiped the tears away from the corners of my eyes and kissed me on the forehead. "You could never stop anything but my heart, Taylin."

It was the night before Xavier had to leave. He had to move down there, settle in his dorm, and start practice soon. His new coach wanted everyone to work as a team in all aspects of the sport. I had the chance to go with Xavier to check out his school and meet his coaches a few weeks back. North Carolina was such a beautiful place. The mountain scenery, the long roads, the smells. The country was lovely. However, we did get a lot of stares when we were in certain places. No one gave us any trouble, though. Most people were kind and friendly and showed us southern hospitality. The smoked pork brisket sandwich had quickly become one of my top five favorites.

"Are you sure you don't wanna come with, Taylin?"

"I can't." I shook my head, my heart breaking all over again.

"So, this is goodbye?" he asked, a tear rolling down his cheek.

"It has to be. I thought we would be together forever, but our lives are going down different paths, and we have to respect that."

"I can respect it, but that doesn't mean that I have to accept it."

"I'm sorry." My gaze dropped from him. I couldn't look in his eyes anymore.

"Can we just try? Maybe do the whole long-distance thing? I don't want to throw this all away, Tay."

"Are you sure you're gonna be able to do this? I mean, I'm sure it's easier for us to just split now, before all those hot college girls get ahold of you."

"Don't say that. If you're my girl, you're my one and only."

"Okay. I love you."

"I love you too."

I hadn't seen Xavier in months, but we still talked occasionally. The texts started to come few and far between, and I didn't like it. I knew he was busy with practice, and the coach was putting them through vigorous and strenuous workouts. But things had gotten weird when I called him, and a female picked up his phone. Not once, but twice. Then after I confronted him about it, he became silent for a week or so.

I decided I was going to go down and surprise him. I brought my best friend, Anna, with me and stayed at a nearby hotel.

"Tay, what happens if we are in there, and you see something you won't like?"

"Then my suspicions are right. I told him we should have broken up after graduation, but he insisted we make the long-distance thing work."

The campus was huge, and since we looked like college kids, no one asked us any questions. I remembered Xavier's dorm room, and the nerves set in my stomach as I neared his floor. As we approached the door, I heard a female moaning loudly and heard Xavier moan too. I turned the knob, but the door was locked. So I banged on it.

"Jeff, fuck off, man. I told you I was busy," he yelled as the moans resumed.

I banged on the door again and heard him stomp to the door. "Jeff, what the—oh shit, Taylin. I can explain," he rushed to say, slightly closing the door and looking back at the half-naked chick in his bed. I felt like I was going to be sick.

"There's nothing to explain. I told you this wouldn't work, and you should have just left me the fuck alone. I told you these hot college chicks would get to you."

"I wouldn't say she's hot," Anna retorted. "Hello, what's your name?" Anna yelled to the brunette in the bed.

"Kasey," she replied shakily.

"Is that the voice you heard, Tay?" she asked with a hand on her hip.

"Sure is. Hi, Kasey, I'm his girl—well, former girlfriend. You are more than welcome to have him now, since he's a lying sack of shit. I can't believe you would do this to me!" I yelled the last part only for him, my hand connecting with his face.

"Taylin, wait. Can we talk, please?"

"Go and talk to him, Tay. If you don't, you know you'll regret it," Anna said, stopping me from leaving.

"Fine, get dressed. You have ten minutes."

"I know there are no excuses or explanations I can give you, Tay. I was lonely, and I had needs. I don't like Kasey like that, but she was filling a void I was missing."

"So, why were you trying to hold on to me? You're the one that wanted to do the whole 'long-distance' thing, remember? I wanted to end things because I was afraid this would happen."

"Because my heart still belongs to you." I rolled my eyes at that.

"But your cock belongs to other women, apparently."

He ran his hand through his hair in frustration. "How about you get one free pass back home, and then we try this one more time? I will wait for you to come down and see me, and on breaks, I'll come and see you. That way, I have something to look forward to, and I won't fall into this trap again."

I knew I should have trusted myself, but no. I thought Xavier was different. I wanted to believe him. I thought our life would be exempt from the bullshit, and it wasn't. I don't know why the universe did this to me, and I went against my better judgment and got shot in the foot because of it.

"Fine, I'll give you one more shot. But if you can't handle it, just be fucking honest with me, Xavi. I don't wanna deal with the back-and-forth bullshit, and I also don't want to have to fly down here and surprise you to see you cheating on me."

"You won't, I promise."

A *few months had gone by, and Xavier and I seemed to be doing well. I never hooked up with anyone, but I let another guy eat me out. Xavier and I talked every day; we would FaceTime and do everything to stay connected as best we could. Sometimes we would mutually masturbate with each other. I felt like I could really trust him again. I was planning another trip to visit him for Christmas break, and he seemed very excited.*

He had to go back to practice at the end of the week. Otherwise, he would have come home. As I boarded the plane with Anna, I got a text from an unknown number.

Unknown: Xavier isn't as faithful as you think he is.

Me: Who is this?

Unknown: Kasey.

There is no way. This has got to be a joke.

As *we made our way to Xavier's floor, we heard people shouting. "Tell her the truth about us, or I will!" I heard as we stopped in front of his door. Tears fell from my eyes as I stepped back, and Anna banged on the door.*

"We can hear you, asshole. Come on out and fess up."

The door opened, and Kasey appeared; her stomach had a slight bloat to it. Xavier was sitting on the bed with his hands on either side of his head.

"You're pregnant?" Anna asked.

"Yes, and it's his. We have been together off and on for months. I told him to tell you the truth, Taylin. He told me all about you, and how much he missed you. I told him he should

work out whatever his issues are, but he lied to me too. I made him show me his phone and saw all the pictures and videos of the both of you. I told him I would expose everything to you, hence why I texted you."

"If you weren't pregnant, I'd slap you. Why would you be with him if you knew he was a liar?" Anna asked. Just the look of her had all the air leaving my lungs.

"Because I knew I was pregnant, and I grew up without a father and I couldn't do it to him," she replied sadly, pointing to her stomach.

"I have to go. I can't breathe."

"I'm sorry, Tay. You don't need to expel any more energy on this piece of shit. I can't believe you, X. You lost a good woman. I hope your dick falls off. Good luck being a dad."

"And, by the way. I'm not the only girl he has been sleeping with. I was just the only one dumb enough to get pregnant," Kasey added.

My heart felt like it had been jabbed by a hundred tiny needles and could explode in my chest at any moment.

"Well, since we're here. There are plenty of other single, available hot men to choose from. I'm sure you won't have any problems hooking up with any of them. Even if they are liars, it'll only be one night," Anna said.

"You know I can't do that, Anna."

"Well, I'm gonna have some fun while we're down here."

"You go ahead. I'll go back to our hotel."

"No, Tay. You're going to go out with me and not let this ruin your fun. You are a majestic queen, and I'll be damned if *that peasant dulls your sparkle,"* she said, *kissing me on the cheek.*

"Thanks, girl."

I should have never given him a second chance, but now that he was bringing a child into this situation, I knew there was no way to repair this. He lied to me so much, and he told me I was everything, and clearly, I wasn't—because now he's going to be a dad.

I will never go against my better judgment again.

Chapter Thirty-Four

Caspian

"I KNEW IT. I fucking knew it!" I screamed, slamming the thick glass cup on the counter.

"Cas, I don't even know what to say," Carlos replied.

"I mean. I never break my fucking rule—ever, and the one time I let shit slide, it gets me a stalker, and now I had to file a restraining order."

"So, what exactly happened?"

"For starters, this girl transferred into my class, right? Okay, no big deal. Then she shows up in the shortest dress I have ever seen on a college campus and gives me the fuck me eyes in front of everyone. There were times when I was so uncomfortable, and that's saying a lot. She would show up after my last class of the day and bother me about personally helping her."

"Did she ever touch you or anything?" he asked warily.

"Nope. Not at all. And I for damn sure wasn't touching her with a ten-foot pole."

I could not believe that Chantelle was most likely behind all of the bullshit that had happened. I had no idea how she even knew where I lived. She was a new level of crazy; she literally reminded me of Melinda's friend, and I couldn't stop thinking about it.

"What did she look like?"

"Tan skin, green eyes, long curly hair. I can't quite put my finger on it, but she did seem familiar. I also can't stop thinking about Melinda's crazy friend lately."

"Oh yeah, what's her name again?" he asked, pulling his phone out. "Doesn't she have a daughter?"

"Yeah, but I don't think she'd be old enough—wait. The mom's name is Andrea."

Carlos scrolled on Facebook, looking through Melinda's friend list. I had no idea why he was even friends with her still, but I pretended not to care.

"Uh, Cas. Does she look like this?" he asked, flashing me a photo on his phone.

"Oh my *fuck*," I said, spitting an ice cube out of my mouth. "That is her!"

"So, do you think Melinda had something to do with all of this?"

"I didn't before, but I do now. This is some pure fucking crazy shit."

"Why would Melinda do such a thing?"

"To scare me into getting back with her or 'needing her.' It was her last-ditch effort before the attempted suicide,

I'm certain."

"Uh, Cas," Carlos started to say, a look of concern on his face.

"Yeah?"

"Look at this?"

Carlos went onto Chantelle's page and saw a video of her driving by my house on multiple occasions. She had also photoshopped pics of herself with me. *What the entire fuck?*

"You should save all of this and send it to your lawyer asap."

I was granted a temporary leave of absence from work due to this whole ordeal with Chantelle. The police officer told me it was best I lay low for a while to make sure Chantelle wouldn't do something else stupid. The whole ordeal perturbed me. What was so great about me that made these women and their children lose their minds?

I had decided to stay in a hotel in the next town over from my place for a bit. I had new cameras installed around my property, so I could keep watching just in case. I was furious with Melinda, and there were so many things I wanted to do and say, but I decided to wait. The next time she or her sister reach out, I'm unleashing holy hell on them and then severely cutting ties. I also knew that I had to stay clear of Taylin as well. The Dean and the police officer didn't seem to expect too much between us since Chantelle only had one isolated incident on video, but I wasn't going to take any more chances. I never wanna get caught having sex with a student, and I for damn sure don't want people assuming I'm doing so. *Even if I am.*

As days went by, I realized how much I did miss Taylin, but I couldn't speak to her. Not now. I knew she was worried by the number of texts she had sent me, but I couldn't bring myself to respond. I didn't want to get her hopes back up, and I didn't want her thinking I was going to go running back into her arms for comfort. I had to end that shit, too, no matter how messy it would have become.

It killed me inside not to say anything to her. I could feel the sadness from the texts coming through less and less. She just wanted to make sure I was alright, but I had to admit it; for the first time I was actually scared. All of this was grounds for me being fired, or worse, never teaching again, and I couldn't live with myself. Teaching was the one thing that made me happy. Teaching never cheated or gave up on me. When I was feeling low, teaching was there to pick me back up. Teaching was like the lover I never had, but always wanted.

"Welcome back, Mr. Wyatt," my assistant Gina greeted me.

"Thanks. It's good to be back, Gina. If Melinda steps foot here, calls, leaves a message or anything—notify me immediately, okay?"

"You got it."

As I made my way to my classroom, I looked at the old equations on the board from my substitute and wanted to hurl. He was teaching them basic baby shit. I knew the class wasn't expecting me to be back so soon, but now that I am I had to be better than ever.

My phone buzzed in my pocket with a message from Carlos.

Carlos: Hey, man. Emilia took me back, and we are having a little girl!

Me: No shit? Congrats, man. Don't fuck this up, okay?

Carlos: I won't, but we're definitely going to celebrate later.

I picked up the spray bottle and washed the marker off the whiteboard. I grabbed Clorox wipes and sanitized my desk and everything else the sub may have touched. Luckily, I locked all of my things up and put my things away, but I still didn't like my space being disturbed.

As the first bell rang, the students filed in little by little. Everyone came in by the end of the second bell, including Taylin. She looked at me in a way I'd never seen before, but I tried not to let it bother me. I've seen worse.

After class ended, Taylin stormed down the stairs toward my desk. "Before you even start-stop. I don't want to hear it, and I don't want to see it, and I don't want to acknowledge it. You can just turn around and go straight to your next class, Ms. Bradford."

She stood on the last step with a horrified look on her face, as if I'd just shot her dog. "Wow, just wow. You are un-fucking-believable. After everything? This is how you treat me?"

"After what? A couple of fun nights? What did you expect? A relationship out of me?" I said incredulously, but it was false and I was feeling sick to my stomach.

"A couple of fun nights? Have you lost your fucking mind? I expected respect, you piece of shit," she seethed, throwing the book at me.

"I respect you, but you need to respect my decision. Let me spell it out for you, student, teacher." I motioned, pointing between the both of us. "This *cannot* happen."

"I don't care! You could have at least let me know you were alright. I was worried sick! But clearly, you're just fine. And to think I thought maybe—" I didn't let her finish.

"Maybe, what?" I crossed my arms, willing them to stop shaking.

"Nothing. Forget it. I'm going to finish this semester, and then you'll never have to hear from me or see me again!" she bit out, storming out of the room.

I sat down at my desk, placing my hands over my eyes. I didn't even know what to do anymore. I just knew that this was wrong, and I should have run after her, but I couldn't. *What the fuck do I do now?*

Chapter Thirty-Five

Taylin

"WOW. AFTER EVERYTHING WE have gone through these last few months. He just dismissed me like I was trash."

"Tay, do you think that maybe he isn't the man for you?" Jalia asked.

Jalia begged to hang out with me because we hadn't had our girls' night in a while. She used a Groupon to get us a hotel for the weekend in Rhode Island. Jalia was the quieter one out of the group. She was also the shortest, with a thin frame, massive afro, and glowing brown skin with a huge butt.

"I'm starting to believe I was an idiot in general. I know it was just sex in Vegas, but I promise you I felt so much more, Lia. There was a spark I'd never experienced before, and when we saw each other again the next week, it was still there, although he was being a jerk."

"Maybe he's afraid of love? Why else would he act like this?" she questioned, pursing her lips.

"Well, because he's been cheated on, and the last ex he had is batshit crazy, which made him crazy as well. But every time we're together, even though we haven't had sex since New Hampshire, the chemistry is there. When it comes down to it, one of us always stops because we both know we're gonna get stuck, and we both know that this is wrong, but it feels so right."

"Have you talked to anyone else since you started school? You don't tell me anything anymore." She pouted.

"I was talking to this guy, Fernando, but he is way too nice for me. I know I'll hurt him, and that's not what I want to do."

"I see. So my advice for you is to do nothing. Go to school, and while you're in his class, either make sure you look nice, but not too slutty. Or be in places you know he'll see you and hang with another dude. That'll either make him get his shit together, or he'll leave you alone and let a real man have you."

"He is a real man," I stated, hating that I felt so strongly about him.

"Yeah, but he keeps playing with you, and we don't have time for that kind of stress. It gives you wrinkles!"

It was refreshing to hang out and chat with Jalia all weekend. She made me feel better about myself and empowered me in a way. It had snowed, and we decided to go to Lincoln Woods state park to have some fun. We started a snowball fight with a couple of cute guys there, and we all made plans to grab dinner before we all went back home. They were visiting from Vermont, so I didn't expect anything serious to happen with either of them.

"It's been a long time since we both went on a double date," Jalia said.

"I know. It should be fun, though."

"How do I look?" she asked. She wore a pink sweater dress with thigh-high black boots and a puffy coat. Her makeup looked professionally done, and I could never get my eyebrows to look as good as hers.

"Ya look good, gyal!" I said in my best Jamaican accent.

"Good. Do you want me to help you with your makeup?"

"I thought you'd never ask. Yes, please!"

We pulled up to a Mexican place called Xaco Taco and were greeted by the hostess inside. The guys had texted us and told us they already had a table and were waiting for us there. She grabbed two menus and led us to the back, where Felix and Chadwick were sitting.

"Hey! There are the two lovely ladies who pelted our asses with snowballs earlier," Felix said, standing to hug us both. Felix was the more outspoken one of the two. He was caramel-skinned, tall, with short black hair and a dark mustache goatee combo. And Chadwick had a darker complexion, with no facial hair, but he had a long curly hair that went down his back.

⁓

We talked with the guys for hours, had delicious empanadas and rice and beans, kicked ass on the skeeball machine they had, and then went home. I didn't see myself with either of them, but they were both chill.

As I lay in bed at home, scrolling through silly videos, a text from Anna came through.

Anna: Guess what?

Me: What?

Anna: I met someone.

Me: Deets?

Anna: Are you back home from your playdate with Jalia?

Me: Yes.

My phone rang, and Anna was calling me on FaceTime. "Wow, this must be serious if you have to see my face," I joked.

"Girl, he was so fine! His name was Jay."

"Where did you meet?" I twirled my hair around my finger like a valley girl.

"At the bank, surprisingly. He held the door open for me then ended up in line right behind me. It was so busy that we both kept making jokes to pass the time."

"And?"

"And we have a date tomorrow night."

"That's great. What does he look like?"

"Tall with long dark hair on the top and the sides shorter. Tan skin. I'm pretty sure he has some Italian mixed in somewhere. He smelled so good, and he was def in shape. I could tell by the muscle indents through his coat."

"Oooh, well, have fun on your date! Where are you going?"

"I don't know. I think he said some Italian place, but I'm sure I've never been there before."

"Awesome. Well, have a good time. You deserve it, and he better treat you right, or I'll kick his ass."

"I know you will. How was your weekend?"

"Good. Jalia and I went on a double date with some guys. And before you ask, no, there wasn't anything memorable. We had some laughs and good food, but they both live in Vermont."

"Aw, that's too bad."

Another month had passed, and Cas was still acting weird. I didn't bother entertaining him anymore. I was numb over the whole situation. I went to class, turned in my assignments, and kept it moving. Although I could tell he wanted to talk to me some days, I didn't give him time to.

I had a tutor session scheduled with Brae, and we both met up at the diner for dinner again. I told him we could stay at the library after as long as we needed to. I had nowhere to go and no one to rush home to.

"I was so glad you texted me. I thought you didn't need me anymore," he teased.

"No, I just had a lot going on, but I've decided I'm going to focus on what truly makes me happy, and that's math."

"That sounds like music to my ears. Well, let's begin, shall we?"

I felt like I was able to be myself around Brae, and it was very rare that someone just got me without any ulterior motives. It had gotten pretty late, and we both were yawning. "Maybe we should wrap this up," I said.

"Yeah, it's well after midnight. It was nice to work with you. Tay, I know this may be frank of me, but do you think maybe we could grab lunch or coffee sometime?"

"That sounds nice. Just text me when." A vast smile formed on his face, and his eyes sparkled.

Chapter Thirty-Six

Caspian

JERM BRAGGED ABOUT SOME hot chick he'd met and wouldn't stop talking about her. I was happy for him because he'd been single for quite a while, but, man, was I tired of hearing about her. *Now I know how Carlos felt.*

"What are we gonna do for your birthday, Cas?" he asked.

"Nothing. I want to chill and get drunk in peace. If I have to leave the house, at least make it a bar or club far the fuck away from here."

"You got it!" he said, leaving my place. I knew he was up to something, but I couldn't quite figure it out. As long as he didn't throw me a party, anything else would be fine. I despised turning thirty, and it made me feel like I was getting old, even though I knew I looked damn good.

Carlos dragged me out to the bar because he wanted to celebrate the fact that he was bringing a baby girl into the world, and as emotional as he would get, I was glad it was a girl too. The world couldn't handle another mini version of him.

"So, how does it feel?" I asked, taking a sip of Jack and Coke.

"What?"

"Bringing a human into this world."

"It feels scary as fuck. The thought of creating this tiny human who's totally dependent on you freaks me out. I'm just glad Emilia took me back, man. I was miserable, and I wouldn't have been okay if she had that baby, and I couldn't be there. I know what it's like not to have your dad around, and I couldn't live with myself if I couldn't be there for my little one."

"I understand that in many ways." It had been a long time since I'd seen Carlos this happy. After the whole depressive phase with Emilia, he finally brought his ass back to work. He worked as a mechanical engineer at a school in Boston. They knew how valuable he was and gave him his job back after explaining what had been going on.

As we sat and vibed to the music, a couple of college-aged girls gave us the eyes, and we ignored them, finishing our drinks. "I think it's time to go before you get in trouble," I said, my stomach in knots. *There is no way in hell I'm falling for any of these teeny boppers here.* They looked younger than the girls from my school. *No way.*

"Nah, I'm not interested, but by all means, Cas. You can stay."

"No thanks. We can go. Congratulations, though, man. I truly am happy for you." I patted him on the back.

"Thanks, Cas. That means a lot. I do wish you happiness in the future, and I can't wait for you to call me and tell me you're expecting your bundle of joy."

"Yeah, I don't foresee that happening anytime soon, if ever," I retorted.

It was the day of my birthday, and I was being inundated with texts and calls. They were wishing me a happy birthday, but I didn't want the reminder. All I wanted to do today was get drunk, but I felt the guys were up to something. Carlos had come over, brought me a suit, and instructed me to be ready by 9:00 p.m. sharp. My birthday was always a weird time because it was literally the day after Valentine's Day. Girls always tried to take advantage of that by getting me to book weekend getaway trips to celebrate both, and I grew tired of it quickly.

I booked myself an appointment with my barber to line me up and trim my beard for me. If I was going to celebrate being thirty, I had to make sure I looked great. Either way, I was ending my night fucking someone.

Carlos: Be outside in five minutes.
Me: Okay.

I gave myself a once-over in the mirror before spraying myself with cologne. I tossed on the navy-blue suit and white-collared shirt Carlos dropped off for me. He also gave me his uncle's old gold cufflinks, which were high quality.

I walked outside and saw a limo in front, shaking my head as I approached it.

Chapter Thirty-Seven

Taylin

"ANNA, YOU LOOK BEAUTIFUL."

"Me? Girl, have you not looked at yourself in the mirror? You're gorgeous!" she replied.

We both looked in the floor-length mirror at ourselves and smiled. Anna's hair was in long waves over her shoulders, and her dress was long and sparkly, with a high split on the side. The maroon-colored gown molded to her body perfectly and accentuated her breasts. I was wearing a similar dress, but royal blue with a plunging neckline. My hair was in voluminous spiral curls just above my shoulders because of shrinkage. Our makeup was done by Jalia, who was definitely a master at her craft. She worked part time at Sephora, and it showed. Jalia had to work her second job that night, so she couldn't make it, which bummed us out, but we understood. "You girls look great, have fun!" she said before rushing out the door to Anna's apartment.

Anna's place was a small and quaint one bedroom. Her father was a fireman and had money saved up for her to go to college, but she didn't want him to spend a lot on an apartment. She was always good at saving up her own money and only reached out to him when she needed to.

We were on our way to a surprise party for Jay's friend. We never learned his name, but he was turning thirty and informed Anna that this would be a night to remember.

"I bet he has some hot single friends," Anna said, throwing some extra clothes in a bag for the both of us.

"I sure hope so. I haven't gotten laid in months. I could use a night to remember, for sure."

"No matter what happens, just be yourself. You're young, smoking hot, and any man would be lucky to be in your presence—even if it's for only one night!"

Jay had a driver come and pick us up to drive us to the party, and it was almost 10:30 p.m. when we arrived. The place was somewhere in the boonies of New Hampshire, and I was having a case of déjà vu when we arrived because the cottage looked like the place I went to with Cas, only it had a second story above. There were cars parked everywhere. On the grass by trees, a slim strip of the driveway was left for our car to bring us to the side door. "We have arrived, ladies, and I'll be outside whenever you're ready to leave. Even if it's not until tomorrow," the driver said.

"Wow, thank you," we replied in unison.

The bass from the music was thumping on the pavement as we walked inside. The party was already in full swing when we got there. The live DJ was up on a small platform with lots of flashing lights behind him. There were people taking pictures in a photo booth with all kinds of Valentine's Day-themed props. *Shit, it is around the day of love, isn't it?*

As we explored more, there was a bartender making drinks. We were informed that the drinks were free, which was not good for me, but great for Anna. That girl loved her margaritas and martinis.

"Hey, beautiful!" We heard as we approached the bar.

"Oh my God, Jay!" Anna said, throwing her arms around his neck. He placed a kiss on her lips and gave her a once-over as he twirled her around to get a good look at her ensemble.

"You look fucking amazing!" he said. His eyes never left hers.

"Thanks, babe. This is my friend, Tay," she said, beaming. Jay was even hotter in person. A well-tailored suit fitted his body, and I could certainly see the muscles she spoke about before. It was refreshing to see her this happy. The energy flowing between them felt good, and I knew he was a good guy.

"Hi, this place is massive," I said, looking around.

"I know. Just wait till you get upstairs. I have two hot tubs. Make yourself at home, ladies, and the birthday boy should be here at any moment. He has no idea I'm even throwing this, so it should be an interesting night for sure." He laid a kiss on Anna's lips before greeting a few more people that walked in.

"Aw, he seems sweet," I told her.

"I know, right? I wasn't sure what to expect, but we have been taking things pretty slow. Tonight, though, I feel things are going to shift. If you know what I mean." She smiled, elbowing me in the side.

The music stopped, and Jay grabbed the microphone from the DJ booth. "Attention, everyone, the birthday boy will be here in five minutes. We're going to turn all the lights down and be very quiet. He's going to be blindfolded, so he'll be in for a big surprise as soon as he walks inside." He looked down at his phone. "Shit, he's pulling up now. Quiet, everyone!"

A few moments passed, and the side door opened, but I couldn't see who was coming in. I found a spot behind the bar while Anna crouched by a table. She was able to see more than I could. I watched her face when she saw who was coming through the door and her excited expression changed to one of concern.

"Surprise!" everyone yelled, and as I stood to my feet, my heart sank in my chest. There he was—looking sexier than ever. He ripped the blindfold off and laughed.

"What the fuck is this? Guys, I told you I didn't want a party," Cas yelled.

"Who gives a fuck what you want. You only turn thirty once! Now enjoy yourself, asshole, you've been a pent-up douche for months now!" Jay said, laughing.

As Cas went through the crowd, laughing and greeting everyone, I froze in place. Anna ran over to me and pulled me to the other side of the bar. There was a door leading outside, and although it was freezing out, she brought me to the small porch.

"Are you okay?" she asked, and I just stood there, unmoving. "Tay, speak to me!"

"I don't know how to feel right now."

"I swear I didn't know he was friends with him. What are the fucking odds!" she yelled.

"You know what, Anna. It's okay. Let's go back inside. Jay said it would be a night to remember, and he is right."

I ran back inside and went straight to the bartender. "I'll have two tequila sunrises with Patron, please."

"Oh shit," Anna said.

"Make it three; my friend would like one as well."

The bartender smiled and placed three tall glasses on the counter. He put all the ingredients into a shaker and quickly filled all the glasses, adding some pineapple skewers before sliding them over. I mouthed thank you since the music had gotten louder. I inhaled one and sat down on a stool for a moment.

"Tay, please pace yourself. I know you're feeling some sort of way right now, but I don't need you to black out."

"Fuck it. If I black out, I black out," I said, slowly sipping the second one.

"Low" by Flo Rida came on, and I lost my shit. I had gone to the second floor where another live female DJ was playing music. As I danced in a circle, my eyes caught with another man. He was tall with a well-groomed beard; broad shoulders and his blond hair was pulled back into a low man-bun. He smiled and approached me, placing his hand out for mine. We danced together and laughed as we both got low.

"It is the season of love, after all, so let's slow things down a notch!" the DJ said over the microphone. She put on "Perfect" by Ed Sheeran. The gentleman asked me if it was still okay to dance with me, and I obliged.

"What's your name?" he asked, his deep voice sending chills down my spine.

"Taylin, yours?"

"Raphael. Nice to meet you, Taylin. You look perfect, by the way."

"Thank you." I could feel my cheeks heating from his compliment.

"How do you know the birthday boy?" he asked.

"I'm here with my friend. Her date is his best friend," I replied, directly avoiding the question but still giving him an answer. "You?"

"We all went to college together, but I was closer to his best friend, Carlos. I didn't interact with him much, but I hung out with them all from time to time."

"Nice." I nodded, putting my head on his chest and the gap between us closed.

The DJ continued to play slow song after slow song as Raphael and I kept dancing. Not saying a word, and it felt nice.

Raphael and I had spent quite a bit of time together. We laughed, joked, grabbed some food, and drank. It was nice just to let my guard down and have fun. I found out that Raphael had his CPA and had a job as a financial analyst in downtown Boston. We exchanged numbers because he told me he might be able to get me an internship with his company.

I hadn't seen Anna for quite some time, so I pulled my phone out to text her.

Me: Where r u bitch?

Anna: On the top floor with Jay. U should come up here 😊

Me: I'm with someone.

Anna: Even better.

"Wanna go upstairs?" I asked.

"Sure," he replied, grabbing my hand.

As we went upstairs, the sounds of Electronica EDM were swirling in the air, and I knew I'd found my happy place. I loved old-school techno and house music from the 90s.

I spotted Anna sitting with Jay, Cas, and a few other men. I was hesitant to go over but said fuck it.

As I approached Anna, Cas looked at me. His eyebrows raised, his jaw went slack, and his mouth opened. He looked me up and down, then looked at Raphael behind me.

"Hey, Cas. Happy birthday," Raphael said.

"Thanks, man." His jaw was tight as he responded.

"Let's dance," Raph said in my ear. He grabbed my hand and led me to the dance floor. An old song, "Mr. Vain" by Culture Beat, played, and I closed my eyes, remembering how this song always made me feel when I was younger. I remembered having dance parties with my brother, Tine when I was little and he recorded tons of CDs with that type of music. We used to have so much fun together, before he got a stick up his ass as an adult.

There were times when Raphael and I danced together, our bodies twisting and turning together as more songs continued to play. I could feel Cas watching us, but I didn't care. I was having a good time with him. At least he wasn't an asshole. The DJ announced she was taking a few-minute break, so I walked back over to Anna.

"Anna, where's the bathroom?"

"It's back there," she said, pointing toward the back of the room.

"Thanks. I'll be right back, Raph."

As I went inside the room and closed the door behind me, locking it, so no one else barged in, someone pounded on the door as soon as I finished.

"Sorry, occupied."

"Taylin, open the door right now." The familiar voice stopped me in my tracks.

"Go away, Cas," I said, washing my hands and looking at myself in the mirror to buy me some time.

"Open the door before I break it down!" he yelled. *Is this guy for real?*

I unlocked the door, not wanting him to cause a huge scene.

"What do you want?" I huffed, shocked by the audacity he had.

He pushed his way in, locking the door behind us. He cornered me and placed his hands on the walls beside me. "What are you doing here?" His eyes narrowed at me.

Having him this close did something to my body. I wasn't afraid, but slightly turned on.

"I don't have to tell you shit."

"Answer me!" he demanded.

I held my ground with him, looking him in his eyes. I wanted to give him such a hard time, and make him pay for everything he had done, but something inside of me obliged. "Your boy, Jay, is dating my best friend, Anna. He invited her, and she brought me. Not that it even matters."

He went quiet and looked me up and down. "It fucking matters. I've missed you," he admitted. His head hung low.

"I don't care. Get out!" I said, tears blurring my vision.

"No." He tilted my chin up, staring intensely into my eyes. "I won't. You shouldn't be here with him."

"Then who should I be here with, Cas?" I pushed him back, trying to create some space between us.

"Me." *What a joke.*

"Well, you've ignored me for how many months now?"

"I had to."

"Who told you that you *had* to?"

"It's complicated, Taylin. Fuck! I just—"

I cut him off. I didn't even want to hear whatever excuse he was getting ready to say to me. "A simple text would have sufficed, but no, you couldn't even do that!" I yelled, tears sliding down my cheeks.

"I'm sorry, but I'm gonna take back what's mine. Tell me to stop if you don't want it." His eyes darkened with desire.

I couldn't tell if it was the alcohol or me craving his touch, but I choked out, "I want it."

Our lips crashed together as his hands roamed freely all over my body. He clasped my hands together behind my back and propped my ass up on the sink, moving my dress out of the way for easy access.

"You will never dance with another man ever again. You got it?"

"Then don't piss me off," I sassed with a raised brow.

He tightened his grip on my wrists behind me. "Do you understand what I said, Ms. Bradford?"

"Yes." I nodded, completely breathless.

"Good girl."

Chapter Thirty-Eight

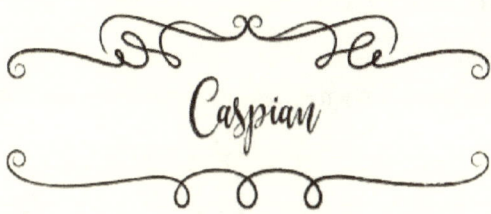

I COULD TELL THE guys were up to something when a limo showed up in front of my place. Carlos came to the door to get me, and Brian waited inside. "Where the fuck are we going?"

"Can't tell ya yet, birthday boy. Just enjoy the ride," Brian said as he handed me a shot glass full of liquor.

After what felt like a ride to never-never land, we finally arrived in the boondocks of New Hampshire. "Here, put this on," Carlos said, handing me a blindfold.

"You guys are royally a pain in my dick."

"So what. You'll have fun. Live a little. I don't know when the hell you became a stick in the mud," Brian said, shaking his head.

"Since he stopped fucking with that Taylin girl," Carlos remarked, his lips pressing together.

"Shut up right now, or you can take me back home," I bit out.

"Chill. Just put it on!" Carlos interjected.

The guys led me inside a building, and it was quiet. As soon as I went to rip off the blindfold, I heard, "Surprise! Happy birthday, Cas!"

I'm gonna kill you. I mouthed the words to Jeremiah.

As we made our way upstairs to the second floor, Jerm had brought a young girl with him—introducing her to the group. Her name was Anna, and she was hot. Another girl had brought over a round of shots and given them to all of us. I took two and tossed them back. I knew I needed to loosen up, but it was hard. I had so much shit flowing through my mind over the past few months that I'd forgotten how to have fun. I hadn't even gone to the club; I was so miserable. And let's not even talk about the lack of sex. My balls were so blue, I thought they would have detached from my body by now.

As the music played, I looked over at the door, and Taylin walked through with a guy I used to know back in college, Raphael. Seeing her with him made my blood boil, but I knew I had to keep my composure for now. Anna waved them over, and then I realized why the name felt so familiar. She told me quite a bit about this girl a few months ago. And flashes of the last time I saw her at the club flew into my mind, and I remembered I had seen her before, but vaguely.

Taylin came over and said hi, but then walked off and danced with him. Seeing her dance with him both made my dick hard and filled me with rage. She should be with me; it's my fucking birthday.

After the music stopped, she asked her friend where the bathroom was, and I followed her. This bullshit ended now. I needed to feel her. I missed everything about her.

As I barged into the bathroom, she looked slightly afraid but still stood her ground. I grabbed her by her neck and kissed her. I clasped her hands behind her back as I lifted her onto the sink. I was sliding the material of her dress out of my way to run my hand over her mound. I pushed her panties to the side and paused, holding my finger against her clit. "Tell me how much you missed me," I demanded.

"So much," she panted. I slowly began rubbing circles around her nub, and her eyes darkened as she began to squirm against my finger. Her wetness coated me as I added another. Her soft moan was like music to my ears. I released her arms and pushed the top of her dress to the side. Pulling her taut nipple into my mouth I continued to apply pressure to her G-spot.

I watched as her eyes rolled into the back of her head as I briefly looked up at her. Her midsection moved as she rode my fingers into ecstasy. I took my fingers out and sucked her juices into my mouth. "Come with me," I demanded as I fixed her dress.

We both walked out of the bathroom and right past everyone. I knew of a spare bedroom in the back hall and took her there. We went inside the vast room with a massive king-sized bed in the middle of it. I grabbed her face and kissed her deeply, passionately, reclaiming everything I had forgotten in the past few months. I unzipped her dress, and it fell to the floor. She wiggled out of her panties and stood before me as she broke our kiss.

"Are you ready for me?" I asked, needing her more than anything right now.

"Yes," she replied breathlessly.

"Good. Because you are going to feel all of me tonight."

I shoved her against the floor-length mirror and quickly unbuttoned the top of my shirt, ripping it over my head. Then I released my belt from my waist, loosely placing it around her neck, as my pants fell to the floor. She looked at my boxers as I removed them, and her eyes widened. My tongue traveled down the back of her, landing in between her ass cheeks. I placed a hard slap on each one twice and rubbed the marks I'd left behind. Biting them as she yelped loudly made my dick even harder. "Spread your legs apart for me," I said as my tongue dove into her folds from the back. I helped her spread her ass apart as my tongue traveled from top to bottom. Her moans grew louder and louder. This woman's pussy felt so good in my mouth, and I couldn't get enough of her juices as they ran down the sides of my mouth. Eating ass was usually not my forte, but man, I couldn't stop myself from sticking my tongue in deeply. I took my time with her, thoroughly enjoying every part of her, before I stuck a finger in her asshole. That sent her over the edge as an orgasm rippled through her body. I spun her around and bent her over, demanding she climb on the bed on all fours. She braced herself on her elbows as I wasted no time climbing on the bed behind her. I released the belt from her neck and placed it on the bed.

My dick was throbbing, and I gave it a good pump before pressing it against her entrance. She moaned as I pushed myself inside roughly. I grabbed her hips and thrust into her. Her walls clenched against me as she screamed.

"That's a good girl. Let everyone hear how good I'm fucking you."

She moaned louder as my strokes picked up intensity. I pushed her head down into the pillow and placed her arms together above her ass, tying them up with the belt as I fucked her. I slid the tip of my pinky into her anus, and she screamed even louder.

"This pussy is mine! You are mine, and I better never see you so much as speak to another man without my permission. Do you understand?"

"Yes," she whimpered.

"I can't hear you," I said, slapping her ass.

"Yes!" she cried out.

"What's my name?"

"Cas," she moaned.

"Repeat it!" I demanded, as my hand connected with her other cheek. As my orgasm tore through me, I could feel hers happening at the same time. As we both climaxed together, something shifted, and I knew I couldn't keep this façade up any longer.

We lay in bed together in silence. She had fallen asleep, and I watched her. She looked so peaceful after being thoroughly fucked by yours truly. My phone was buzzing in my pants, and I got up to grab it off the floor.

"Hello?"

"Uh, are you gonna come back to the party? Everyone is looking for the birthday boy!" Carlos exclaimed.

"Yeah, be back in a few. I had to handle some business."

"So, we've heard." He laughed.

"Taylin, you gotta wake up so we can go back to the party."

"I don't wanna," she whined, curling into my side.

"Why not?"

"I wanna sleep."

I ripped the covers off of her, her naked body on its side. My dick hardened at the sight of her, and I knew I had to have her one more time. I rubbed my cock against her lips, and they parted, letting me slide in effortlessly. Her eyes flung open, and she gagged as I slid in deeper. I reached over and played with her pussy as she sucked me off. She was so wet.

I pulled my dick out of her mouth and lay on the bed beside her, commanding her to climb on top of me. I wanted to taste her as she sucked me off. She rubbed her pussy all over my face as I sucked on her clit. I flicked my tongue up and down, dipping it inside, and she cried out in ecstasy. I felt my orgasm build as she moaned. I pressed down on her ass, suffocating myself with her pussy as I felt myself come in her mouth. *Happy birthday to me.*

"Are you ready to go back to the party now?" I asked.

She looked at me in shock as she shook her head no. She was pretending like she was still sleepy.

"Okay, well, I'm gonna send your friend in here to check on you."

"Okay." She was being such a brat, but she was a cute one. I placed a kiss on her forehead and covered her up, as she drifted back off to sleep.

I tossed my clothes back on and looked over at her in the bed once more before leaving. I knew I couldn't keep playing coy, and I couldn't continue to fight what I was feeling deep down. I was in love with Taylin Bradford. *I've missed you.*

"There he is!" Jerm said as he patted me on the back. "Drink this," he stated, handing me a shot glass.

I looked over at Anna, and she smiled. "You should go check on your friend down the hall."

"Okay."

"Keep the drinks coming, boys. Tonight's gonna be a good night."

"Finally, he's back! Glad you got some ass." Carlos laughed, clinking his shot glass with mine.

Chapter Thirty-Nine

"TAYLIN? YOU NEED TO wake up so we can go have some fun," Anna said, gently shaking my body. I could hardly move after what Cas and I had just done.

"Fine," I huffed. "Where did Raph go?"

"He's still out there, but he's been hanging with another girl."

"That's good." In a way, I was relieved. I knew if I went back out there and sat with Cas, it would have been awkward, and I'm sure the entire floor heard us having sex.

"So?"

"So, what? Don't you even start with me," I said to Anna.

"Listen, no judgment. All I'm gonna say is...*finally*, and maybe he'll stop being a dick now?"

"One can only hope, but I won't hold my breath," I said as I slipped back into my dress. I was so sore, but in all the right places.

Anna and I returned to the party, and it seemed like there were even more people there. The DJ was still spinning out tunes, and everyone either had on some neon glow lights or was holding something that glowed in the dark. A girl handed me a glowing necklace as I walked by, so I slipped it on over my head. Cas was standing by a pool table, watching as his friends played pool. Our eyes met, and he gave me the biggest smile, one different from any I'd seen before. He was waving me to come over and stand by him. As much as I wanted to be happy about this, something didn't feel right in my gut. No, I didn't think something terrible was going to happen, but we had a lot of things to address once the party was over.

"Are you any good?" he asked me, watching as I walked around the table.

"I don't know. Maybe you should rack em up, and we'll find out," I said, grabbing a stick and chalking the tip of it.

"Oh, I love me a girl who's competitive." He licked his lips and smiled, grabbing the triangle from the side of the table.

After kicking his ass in the game multiple times, his friend turned his attention to the middle of the room where a big ass cake with the number thirty on top was. There were multiple layers covered in black and white frosting, and his name was on the bottom tier. He grabbed my hand and brought me over as he blew out the candles on the top. I grabbed a little frosting, placing it on his nose, and everyone laughed and took pictures. He looked at me, put frosting on my lips, grabbed me in front of the crowd, and kissed me. "I don't care who sees us together. You're the woman I want to be with."

"And you're the man I want to be with," I cried out.

"You know you could have just told me the truth, right?" Raph said in passing as I went to the bar for another drink."

"I didn't lie to you. I just left out a minor detail because honestly, Cas and I weren't on speaking terms, and I didn't know this was his party until I got here."

"I see. Well, I'll still put in a good word about the internship, but I don't want any problems from him. I vaguely remember how possessive he can be."

"You won't. Thank you so much."

"Ow," I said aloud as I sat up in bed. My head banged, and the light from outside made my eyes hurt. I looked around the room, and Anna, Cas, and Jay were all in the room with me. *What the hell happened last night?*

I decided to brave the pain and try to find caffeine. This place was like a mansion, so I knew there had to be coffee somewhere. I could have ordered from Starbucks if I knew where I was, but my phone was dead.

I walked through the hall, and trash and confetti were littered everywhere. There was no one else in sight, which honestly was a good thing because I felt like shit, and I'm sure I looked like shit. I went down to the first floor and into the kitchen. It was beautiful. Open, with an attractive backsplash and granite countertops. All the appliances were top-of-the-line and stainless steel. I spotted a Keurig and a metal carousel next to it full of different types of pods. *Thank God.*

"You scared me half to death." I heard as I grabbed two mugs out of the cabinet and nearly dropped them onto the floor.

"Cas, you scared me! I needed some coffee, my head's killing me."

"I have a solution for that." He grabbed the cups out of my hand and placed them on the counter, leading me into another side room. *How many rooms were in this place?*

He tossed me on the edge of the bed, shoving my legs up by either side of my head. "Hold your legs," he ordered as he sunk into me. I guess he had to make up for all the teasing we had been doing to each other over the past few months. He placed his hand around my throat and moved slowly, calculated, taking his time with me. I felt so full, and he rocked his hips back and forth, hitting my G-spot with his curve. He knew how to make my body react in ways it never had before. The sounds of our sexual escapades were like music to my ears. He rubbed and pumped, rubbed and pumped until he felt my orgasm building, and he pulled out. "No, no, you can't come yet."

"Please, you make me feel so good."

"I know, baby. But you have to wait." Cas was taking everything he needed from me. In Vegas, it was different. We didn't exactly know each other, but that's what made it fun. This time, I felt like we belonged together, and our bodies were meant for each other. I wanted no one else but him, and there was no way I could even imagine allowing another man anywhere near me after this. He gave me a look and smiled, releasing my neck as he fucked me intensely. I came several times as he smiled, making sure I was pleased before his own orgasm took over.

"How does your head feel now?"

"Much better." He placed a kiss on my lips, and his fingers slipped between my legs again.

"I'm just making sure," he said, and an orgasm tore through me once more as he kissed me on the head and told me to get dressed.

"Thank God, he has food in here for once," he sighed as he looked in the fridge.

"This is Jay's place, right?"

"Yeah, his name is Jeremiah. I call him Jerm, so it's weird to hear you say the name 'Jay.'"

"Well, that's the name I know him by, sorry. Anyway, we need to talk."

"Can it be after breakfast?" he whined, and it almost made me laugh.

"Fine, but not a minute later!" As much as my body felt so good, I knew we had to have this heart to heart. There was no way things could go back to normal after this weekend. I refused to let that happen.

Cas was quite the chef. He made a stack of pancakes, eggs, bacon, and sausage. We put our plates aside and left the rest for the others whenever they decided to wake up.

"Why have you been ignoring me?" I asked bluntly.

"Taylin, a lot of shit went down after the bullshit with Chantelle."

"Like what?" I asked, taking a bite of bacon.

"Well, I had to file a restraining order against her. I also had to make a deal not to speak to you either because it warranted me losing my job if I did outside of class, obviously, but I didn't want to take any chances. I also got a summons to court about Chantelle damaging my property. They DNA tested the brick, and sure as shit, it was her. I didn't tell them you were there, so you don't have to come."

"Oh, okay. Is this why you were gone for a bit?"

"Yes. It killed me not being able to talk to you. And when I saw you here with Raph, I couldn't handle it. I don't know how this is going to work, but I don't have to. I know you're the one I want, and I don't care. If I lose my job, then I'll find another," he said with sadness in his eyes, and there was no way I could ever let him do that.

"But you love teaching!"

"I also love you." My jaw dropped.

Hearing him say that made me choke up. Tears flowed from my eyes, and my heart sped up in my chest. "You love me?"

"Yes, I've known it for a while, but dismissed it because I thought I was crazy."

I ran over to him and wrapped my arms around his neck. "I knew for a while too."

"Alright, lovebirds, where's the food? I can smell it all the way downstairs," Carlos said.

"Over there," Cas replied, not taking his eyes off me.

After everyone ate and sobered up, we all went home in our separate ways. I was sad I wasn't riding back with Cas, and Anna was sad she couldn't ride back with Jay, but since he had already paid for the ride, there was no use in wasting it.

"You seem happy," Anna remarked.

"I am. You do too."

"I am. This is the happiest I've felt in a long time. Last night, Jay and I had the best sex of my life, and I just know I'm gonna marry that man."

"That's wonderful!"

"Don't worry, you're gonna be my maid of honor. I've known that since we were seven." She grabbed my hand, squeezing it tightly.

"Aw, you're mine too, if the day ever comes."

"It will." She smiled.

Cas and I agreed to meet up later to talk things out, and I was nervous, but we had to put some things into place before anything else got out of hand.

Chapter Forty

Caspian

ON MY WAY TO school the next day, I knew that I had to make a hard decision. I loved my job, but women like Taylin only came my way once in a lifetime, and I couldn't risk losing her. We had a long talk the night before about how we would act at school. We would keep things nonchalant in the public eye, but once we were alone, there were no restrictions. We decided to meet up at different hotels miles away so that no one could follow either of us. It was safer that way. We had lots of fun, roleplaying, and dressing up. I always reimbursed her for her travels, since it was such an inconvenience for both of us.

As my first class of the day filed in, everyone dropped off their homework packets. This was the last week I was there before taking a two-week vacation, and I needed a break to clear my head. I hadn't quite gotten over my father's death, and I told my mom I'd come up and stay with her a bit. I *need this escape.*

❧

"Cas!" Carlos yelled in my ear.

"What?"

"Melinda is dead." *Say what?* I nearly dropped the phone from my ear.

"What do you mean?"

"She was in some sort of accident." I should have been upset to hear that, but I was numb. "And guess what?"

"What?" I asked, still trying to process what he had just told me.

"Andrea has also been arrested."

"For what?"

"Arson, amongst another host of charges." *How did he even know all of this? Serves her right, though, crazy bitch.*

"I don't even know what to say, to be honest with you."

"There's nothing to say. Although it's sad about Melinda, you can move forward with your life now."

"I still have one more problem, though."

"What?"

"Chantelle," I sighed.

"I'm sure she'll be taken care of soon, too. Keep me posted and good luck today!"

That was not the phone call I expected to get on my way to the courthouse. Although Melinda was a cunt, I didn't expect to hear she had died. I know she tried to take her own life multiple times, but I guess she got her wish anyway. But to be fair, I wasn't at all surprised.

Last night, I caught Chantelle on video in front of my property and clearly violated my restraining order. My lawyer was able to get an emergency hearing, and I had to bring the footage as evidence.

As I pulled up to the courthouse, I saw Chantelle walking in with handcuffs. *This girl has a host of problems.*

Chantelle was sentenced to 2.5 years in the house of corrections. She was also charged with stalking, and damages to personal property. I knew there was more coming, but the judge asked me to leave the room because she was being convicted for something else that had nothing to do with my case. From what I heard; she was going to be put away for a very long time. *Guess that's karma for you.*

Chapter Forty-One

Taylin

CAS TOLD ME WHAT happened with Melinda, her friend, and Chantelle, and it was a lot to take in. I knew Melinda kept attempting to kill herself, so I wasn't quite sure how to feel now that she was actually gone, but a sense of relief washed over me. He also let me know that he was going off the grid for two weeks to be with his mom and to grieve his father. I told him to check in with me when he could and that I would give him space. I knew he was under a lot of pressure, and he needed this break. He also told me that he had a surprise for me when he got back, and I was excited yet nervous. I couldn't stop thinking about his birthday weekend and how good he made me feel. How good it felt to be in his arms. I hated not being able to be with him, but I understood.

After the first week, all I could do was look at pictures of us from his birthday party and relish in the memories. I wanted to reach out, but I couldn't go back on my promise. I spent some time writing my feelings down in my journal and talking to Jalia. She told me she met a guy at a dance class she was taking, and they were going on their first date. I loved that all of us had someone in our lives that made us happy. It had been a long time since that happened.

The school was so boring without Cas there. This time, they brought in a younger sub, but her voice was annoyingly high-pitched. I wanted to claw my eardrums out when she spoke. Everyone in the class looked just as miserable as I did. The only fun I had was when I went to my art elective. There was some drama between two of the girls and a guy in the class and I had a front-row seat to all the tea they were spilling.

I kept up my tutoring sessions with Brae, but I let him know that I was seeing someone and that this would just be to learn and nothing else, and he was content with that. He had told me he and his ex-girlfriend got back together, and he was happier than ever.

Anna and Jay's relationship was really taking off, and I couldn't be happier for them. She told me they were getting ready to go on their first big trip together to meet his mom's side of the family back in Washington State.

Fernando checked in with me occasionally, but I let him know I didn't feel comfortable talking to him much since I was seriously seeing someone now. He understood and told me that he had his eye on a girl in his biology class that he started talking to. *Good for him.*

Everything seems like it's finally coming together.

It was a long two weeks, but I was on my way to meet Cas at the Omni Hotel in Providence. He sounded much happier, and it seemed as if his spirits were lifted. I guess a little time away with his mom was just what he needed.

As I walked through the doors, the place took my breath away. There was a large crystal chandelier with gold in the middle of the ceiling, and large support beams surrounded a pristine red and white carpet with sets of plush red chairs. There was a large window with a water fountain on the other side that I knew I'd be taking lots of selfies in front of. I checked in at the desk. The agent gave me a key and told me to head to the tenth floor. This hotel was very fancy, and I was even more nervous about whatever it was that Cas had to talk to me about. *Here goes nothing.*

My palms started to sweat as I approached the tenth floor, and I followed the signs to room 1029 and went inside. There were rose petals all over the floor when I turned the lights on, balloons and a box of heart-shaped chocolate were in the middle of the bed with a bucket of what looked like champagne on the desk to the left.

"Surprised?" Cas said as he slid out of the bathroom, dressed in a white button-up shirt and slacks.

"Yes!" I jumped back, holding my mouth with my hand.

"Taylin, I know things have been rocky this entire—I don't even know what to call this, but the entire time we've known each other. I know I was a complete asshole most of the time, and quite frankly, I don't deserve you. You kept giving me chances, you fought for me, you've comforted me during loss and drama, and for what reason I'll never know, but I am thankful. Because before I met you, I was an empty shell of a man." *What was happening?*

He knelt on one knee in front of me, and my heart dropped. "Taylin, this is a promise ring. And with this ring, I promise to be loyal to you. I promise that I'll always be open and honest with you, no matter how hard things get. One day, if you'll have me, I'd love to make you my wife, but until then, I am yours. Will you be mine?" he asked. My eyes were a blurry mess from the nonstop tears flowing.

"Yes, I will be yours." He slid the beautiful ruby ring on my right ring finger. Ruby was the color of my birthstone, which made it even more special. He smiled and lifted me, twirling me into the air before placing me back down on my feet.

"I also have to tell you something else." My heart raced in my chest; I wasn't sure how much more I could take.

"What is it?" I asked, a little nervous all of a sudden.

"I quit my job." No.

"You did what?" I stomped my foot, raising my arms over my head.

"I quit my job," he repeated himself calmly, and I couldn't have been more confused. *How could he be so calm right now?*

"Why the fuck would you do that?" I was perplexed.

Searching his eyes for an answer. He smiled at me and said, "Because of you." Tears glossed his eyes.

"Cas, oh my God, why? I'm nothing special."

"On the contrary, you're exceptional. Taylin, I quit for us." *He did this for us? This can't be happening.*

"Are you crazy? No, take it back! You can't quit. What are you going to do?"

"I'm still teaching."

"What do you mean?"

"I took a job at a college in Rhode Island. That's why I was gone. I had an interview set up and spent some time with my mom. They called me yesterday and told me I got the job, so I'll be starting in the summer." He beamed with excitement.

"Why would you do that?"

"So, I wouldn't keep breaking my two rules."

"And what were those?" My eyes searched his for an answer.

"Never fall in love and never get caught having sex with a student."

"I'm confused." *It was sad that he never wanted to fall in love, though.*

"Since I've met you, I've fallen in love and had sex multiple times with a student, which complicated things at Warren University. Now that I'll be at a different school, my rules have changed."

"And what are they now?"

"Fall in love and have sex with the most beautiful girl in the world." He brought my hand up to his lips and kissed it. A stray tear fell on them. I was completely at a loss for words, but I knew this was the man I was meant to be with forever. *I guess the one does exist.*

Epilogue

Four years later

"PUSH, BABY! YOU CAN do it."

"I can't do it, and it hurts too much," I yelled, my face contorted with pain.

"One more push, Taylin, and he's out," the midwife said. At that moment, I regretted my decision to have a natural birth, but I knew I had to tough it out. *You got this, Tay.*

"He's here," Cas cried out. I'd never seen him like this before, but it was cute.

I sat in the water as they laid my son on my chest and heard his cry for the first time. I couldn't help but cry as he took his first few breaths. "We did it."

"Yes, we did, Mrs. Wyatt," he said, placing a kiss on my forehead.

The doula tended to me as the midwife, and her assistant took care of the baby. Cas cut the cord before they placed him on the scale. "Wow, he's 8lbs 9oz and 21 inches long."

"That's my big boy," Cas said, tears filling his eyes.

"What's his name?" the doula asked.

"Micah Phoenix Wyatt," I replied, tears running down my cheeks as I smiled at our baby.

"Such a powerful name," she commented. I knew from the moment I met Keanna that she would be the perfect addition to my team. I always wanted to have a natural birth, and after Liz had a baby a year ago and told me that having a midwife and doula was the best thing that could have ever happened to her, it all felt right. They both were so knowledgeable and helpful. And my midwife, Margo, was terrific.

Cas and I eloped a year ago with our small group of friends and family on the white sands of Maui. Since I had won the bet with my dad all those years ago, we saved the trip and he paid for everything. We had a huge reception a few weeks after returning from our honeymoon in Morocco. Which was magical, by the way.

We'd found out we were pregnant after moving into our new house together. The internship I had gotten with Raphael turned into an actual job after graduation, and I was making six figures by the end of my first year. Cas continued to teach, and he had forgotten to tell me four years ago that he was teaching at an Ivy-League college, also making six-figures. Although we both had money, we bought a simple four-bedroom home in Mansfield. We didn't want a long commute from either of our jobs, but I decided I would take a year off to raise our son. I'd saved up a lot of money to keep me afloat in the meantime. Cas took a month off, but I told him he could go back because my mom would stay with me for a bit to help with the baby. She was so excited to have her first grandbaby, and Constantine was excited to be an uncle.

"Where is he?" Mom asked as she came through the door.

"He's over there with Cas. But be quiet; he's asleep."

Mom walked over and giggled, picking the baby up from the bassinet. "Only one of them is asleep, honey," she said as she walked back over toward me, holding the baby in her arms.

"He's so cute. How are you doing?"

"I'm okay. Tired."

"I'm proud of the woman you have become. You went from not knowing what you wanted to do with your life a few years ago to graduating with a bachelor's degree and now making big money. Your father and I couldn't be prouder. And your biggest accomplishment? Is this little boy right here." She placed Micah in my arms, and I sobbed.

He was such a beautiful sight to see, with his chubby cheeks and round face. His eyes were a light gray, and I hoped they would stay that way. His hair was dark and straight for now, but I hoped some curls would pop in as he got older.

I never thought in a million years any of this would have been obtainable for me. I had no plan, no goal. I didn't even feel love was possible for me. I had preconceived notions about the one, and now that I've met Caspian Wyatt, it changed everything. The day he gave me that promise ring was when things shifted for us, all in a positive way. And now that we have created our own little family, the only thing we could do now was live our lives to the fullest. I knew Cas wanted to try for another one soon because he wanted a big family. I agreed to three kids and told him we'd see how crazy we were after that.

"Taylin, you have made me the happiest man on the planet. I thank you for never giving up on me all those years ago," Cas said, wiping the sleep from his eyes.

"Now, let me take the little man so you can get some rest."

"Right after I feed him, he's all yours."

My brother Tine had come over with my dad, and they both stood and stared at me as I fed the baby. "It's okay, guys. It's just a boob," I joked.

After feeding the baby, I let my dad and brother hold him and get all their pictures and excitement out before giving him to Cas. I was exhausted, and it was only the second day after I'd given birth. So I knew I needed time to heal.

Caspian

Watching Taylin bring this little life into the world meant everything to me. Having her in my life meant everything to me. I never thought in a million years that I'd actually get to be a dad. And now that Phoenix was here, I was elated. I never knew how much love I could hold in my heart until I saw his precious little face. My mom and sister agreed to come by the next day to see him and get their baby fix in. I knew Tay's family would be over, and I didn't want her to get overwhelmed with all these people in our house.

Anna and Jeremiah were expecting their first child in the next few months, and I was excited to be an honorary uncle for the second time. Carlos and Emilia had their beautiful baby girl, turning four this year, and seeing Carlos as a dad inspired me because he was so good at it.

Taylin and I got lucky, surrounded by all of these wonderful people who love us. If I had stayed in my relationship with Melinda, I don't think I would have this much love and support in my corner, and although she is no longer here, she did teach me a lesson. That there is always hope as long as the sun still shines. I always said I would never sleep with a student, but in this case, I'm glad I did.

The End.

Acknowledgments

To my girls, I started publishing because of you! If there's one thing I want you to remember about me, it's that you should always go for your dreams no matter how big or how small they are. You can do this! And just like you have believed in me and my stories, mommy believes in you and your future goals too. We did it!

Beta Nymphs, without you, the plot to this story would have sucked. I appreciate all of your feedback!
Special shoutout to Sydney, Taryn, Paula G., Debbie, Mercedes, Amy C., Sarah, Tati, and Andrea.

To my Wow family, thank you for holding me down and cheering me on. Ya'll are my biggest hype men and women, I love you!

To my besties, Chi, Melissa, and Esha thank you for talking me off the ledge and believing in me. Your manifesting power and support is lit! Success is upon us.

To my family, thank you! Without your support, this would still be just a simple dream and not my reality.

To my readers, and my reader group, thank you for waiting for me!

About the Author

Niquel is a self-diagnosed coffee addict, lover of rice and beans, and chocolate—preferably not
all together. She's the creator of multiple stories full of love, passion, and power. She may toss in a ghost story every once in a while.

When she's not busy taking care of her two preteen girls, she's writing or creating graphics. Or you can find her binge watching TV.

Boston born and raised, she's always been a creative soul: attending multiple colleges to develop her love of the visual arts.

Niquel loves to meet new fans and she'd love to hear feedback from you. Whether it's positive or negative, your reviews help her grow as an author!

You can contact her directly through any of the sites posted below.

Facebook~http://www.facebook.com/author.niquel
Twitter~http://www.twitter.com/authorniquel
Website~http://www.authorniquel.com/
Email~Authorniquel@aol.com

Goodreads~http://www.goodreads.com/authorniquel
Instagram~https://www.instagram.com/authorniquel
Tiktok~https://www.tiktok.com/@authorniquel
Pinterest~https://www.pinterest.com/authorniquel/
Bookbub~https://www.bookbub.com/authors/niquel
Signup for my **Newsletter!**~
(https://bit.ly/niquelnewsletter) No spam I promise.
Request to join my **Reader Group!**~
(https://www.facebook.com/groups/niquelsnymphs/)

Other Books By Niquel

A Forbidden Love

An Endless Love

The CEO

Good-bye, with Love

Jamison (Spasm Rockers #1)

Reginald (Spasm Rockers #2)

Bed of Lies Volume 1

Bed of Lies Volume 2

Bed of Lies Volume 3

A Note from the Author

If you've made it this far, thank you! Caspian and Taylin have been in my head since 2017. However, I couldn't focus long enough to give their story justice during that time.

After many shifts and changes, I finally buckled down, heard them speak loud and clear, and even got the ending of the story while getting an MRI (yes, everything is fine!)

I hope you loved them as much as I did, along with their crazy friends and family. If so, please leave a review!

If you'd like to receive bonus content, make sure you signup for my **Newsletter!** (https://bit.ly/niquelnewsletter)

www.ingramcontent.com/pod-product-compliance
Lightning Source LLC
Chambersburg PA
CBHW031057260626
47172CB00001B/109